A Riot MC Biloxi Novel

KAREN RENEE

CONTENTS

AUTHOR'S NOTE

This book is intended for mature readers 18+. There are scenes focused on the aftermath of sexual violence and situations which may trigger or upset some readers. Please do not read if you are uncomfortable with those types of scenes. Thank you.

Playlist

VOLARE by Dean Martin
GLORIA by Laura Brannigan
BLOCK ROCKIN' BEATS by The Chemical Brothers
BIG GIRLS DON'T CRY by Fergie
2AM by Slightly Stoopid
FIRE IN THE MIDDLE by Nightmares on Wax
GANJA BABY by Michael Franti & Spearhead
AMBER by 311
IT SERVES YOU RIGHT TO SUFFER by J. Geils Band
FEELS LIKE RAIN by Buddy Guy
SOFA ROCKERS by Sofa Surfers
ANYWHERE I GO by Slightly Stoopid
SHE WALKS THIS EARTH by Sting
THE GAMBLER by Kenny Rogers
PEACE ON THE STREET by DJ Swingset

CHAPTER 1

HERE TO THANK YOU

VICTORIA

As I approached the courthouse security checkpoint, Officer Remy greeted me with his signature grin. "Miss Victoria, how are you doing this fine morning?"

I smiled. "Pretty good, for a Monday."

He nodded. "I hear that. Looking forward to watching New Orleans basketball tonight. That's the only good thing about Mondays this time of the year."

I put my large attaché case on the conveyor belt along with my purse and nodded before I walked through the metal detector.

"Don't stay up too late for the game, it's a school night," I chided.

He chuckled, but it died as he turned to the person behind me. I glanced that way and my smile fell.

Behind me stood one of the best-looking men I'd seen in all of Biloxi. His brown hair was cropped short. He had mesmerizing blue eyes. With a friendly look, those eyes probably made panties melt. Since he was looking at me, they weren't the least bit friendly.

Best of all, he was tall. Taller than me, which was a rare thing since I stood at five-foot-ten, and my love of high heels meant I was a towering six feet right now. Unlike most other tall men I encountered, who were gangly and lanky, this man had bulk that made him burly.

But he was a biker, and he didn't like me. I knew he was a biker because of the leather he wore. I knew he didn't like me because of our first meeting a few weeks ago, which had left a lasting impression on me.

As a woman, I'd endured my fair share of mansplaining and condescension. But the way this man had spoken to me, it went way beyond anything I'd experienced.

Since it had been the end of the day, I hadn't kept my cool. I'd told him he had things all wrong. I wasn't representing his friend. He didn't listen until his friend confirmed what I'd said. After a long day and his inability to listen to me, I'd huffed out a breath and stalked away from them. It wasn't my best moment by a long shot.

So, yeah. Definitely a bad first impression.

Such was my life.

The moment that thought vanished, a staggeringly more cynical thought struck me. He'd probably be in the same courtroom as me.

Nope, I needed to be positive and not entertain such defeatist thoughts.

I worked as a public defender. As in, 'if you can't afford an attorney one will be provided.' Problem was, I loved the law, but this side of the law didn't love me. So I desperately needed a firm to schedule an interview... a job offer would be better, because my student loans had to be paid. I had more resumes out now than when I graduated from law school.

As Dad said, "Any port in a storm, pumpkin."

Mom never said anything. Probably because I never told her anything. But Dad could read me like a book, and he'd given me his stellar piece of advice. I knew that was mainly so I wouldn't quit my job and waste my education.

But, until an interview led to an offer, I was stuck.

The elevator doors opened. Three people stepped out before the five people waiting before me stepped on.

A court reporter I knew by face, but not by name, preceded me. "Going to the third floor, Vic?"

"Yes, thank you," I murmured, surprised she knew my name.

When I turned around, I watched her punch the three button and then the four. The doors were sliding shut when a large masculine hand waved between the doors.

The biker, whose name was Gamble, if his vest was to be believed, stepped inside the crowded car. The only space left for him to stand happened to be right next to me. I tried to move back, but realized there was nowhere to go.

No matter how much effort I put into it, I couldn't ignore his scent. It was soapy with only a trace of cologne and leather. Even though there was only a trace of the cologne, it was strong enough it didn't just fill my nostrils, it filled my head. Like, I could think about this potent scent for an hour, it was that delicious and that mysterious. It wasn't woodsy, but it made me think of Christmas. It wasn't musky, but it had sticking power.

I shook my head because I didn't need to be examining or dwelling on his cologne-soap scent.

I saw his eyes slide toward me for a moment, then they went to the panel of buttons. He didn't push any of them, so he was headed to either the third, fourth, or fifth floor. For the next two minutes, I prayed he wouldn't get off on three.

The doors slid open, and he didn't move. Relief swept through me.

"Excuse me," I murmured and stepped past him. I heard other high heels following me on the linoleum floor and didn't bother to look back.

Twenty minutes later, he sat five rows behind the Assistant District Attorney. That surprised me. It was an assumption on my part, but a man like him, I totally expected him to be seated on the defendant side of the courtroom. Since the room wasn't crowded, I knew he'd sat there on purpose.

The judge entered, and I forced myself to ignore Gamble's presence. I needed to do the best job I possibly could.

Four hours later, I wove around cars in the parking garage toward mine. The temperature had to be approaching ninety degrees, and with the high humidity I lamented parking at the farthest end of the aisle. It was noon, I was starving, and I *wished* I could go home to forget all about this horrible morning.

Aruba would be better. Though hurricane season was starting in a few days, so maybe the coast of Brazil.

My client could have argued his case better than I did, such was my epic fail. Then again, he *was* guilty.

I heard footsteps behind me. That wasn't unusual, since numerous court sessions had let out, but these steps were gaining on me. With female precision, I shifted my keys so my car key fit between my index and middle finger before I turned around.

Gamble stood behind me. He stopped, spied the key in my hand, and held his hands up low in front of his abdomen. "You can retract the claw, lady."

"Why are you following me? To tell me I *better* do my job, again?"

At my reference to the first time he spoke to me, one side of his plump lips tipped up. "No. I'm here to thank you."

"Thank me?" Then I shook my head. I didn't care about his nonsensical statement.

He grinned. I blinked against the power of it. Since when did I lose my self-control because some tall, bad boy grinned at me?

"Yeah. Never thought I'd see the day, but thank you for failing to get that scum-bag asshole a shot at freedom."

I should have been insulted, but I didn't have time for that.

"Whatever. I shouldn't be seen with you."

"Why?"

My eyes widened. "You can't be that thick. Because someone catches you talking to me, it raises questions. I could face an ethics committee. That's a pain in the ass I don't need these days."

A look of disgust flashed through his eyes before he hid it. "You *want* to defend assholes like him?"

I rolled my eyes. "Like most people, I want a lot of things, but I don't need to face an ethics board because you wanted to thank me for being such a failure."

Like the disgust that had flashed through his eyes, a look of amusement flitted across his handsome face. Then he frowned. "Word of advice, Ms. Carlton. Learn to take a compliment."

On that note, he turned and walked away. Watching him walk away was torturous because it gave me plenty of time to study his picture-perfect ass as he left. It also gave me time to take in the fullness of his Riot MC patch.

Being a public defender, I had a certain familiarity with gangs and other routine offenders. Yet the Riot MC members' cases never came through our office. Not because they didn't get arrested or arraigned.

No, they had a lawyer on retainer, and no need for public defenders like me.

I memorized the shape of his ass so I could imagine my fingers sinking into it when I got busy with my vibrator later tonight. To my shame and chagrin, he looked over his shoulder and arched a brow. I felt heat in my cheeks and whirled to my car.

When would I learn? If things could go bad for me, they damn sure did. Every single time.

"Vic...Tor...Eee-ah! Oh, oh, oooh!" Mick bellowed from behind the extensive counter.

I smiled even as I debated what was more mangled, the melody of "Volare" or my name as he sang it when I entered Bayou Moon Pizza. I'd stopped telling him my four-syllable name wasn't made to fit the tune for a three-syllable word. Not only would he not hear it, but my reminder also served as a special challenge to him. Such was his stubbornness.

Besides, it was far and away better than when he tried to fit my name into Laura Brannigan's "Gloria." *That* was atrocious all around.

Not that he'd hear me say it, but the singing was a brilliant idea on his part. When he did that to his servers, (who only worked the dinner rush, lunch customers had to grab their food from the counter) it got every patron's attention. Back when I had worked here, it was rare my tables didn't know my name. It might have been why my tips were better, but he always said it was my work ethic.

I put my elbows on the counter and leaned toward Uncle Mick for a cheek-kiss. He wasn't really my uncle, but my godfather, and Dad's best friend, who I'd known all my life.

"What'll it be, gorgeous?"

"I'm so hungry, I want to say a large Dean-o, but I know better. I'll have my usual, a slice with artichoke, shrimp, and green olives."

He shouted my order over his shoulder, then shook his head with his eyes closed. "You are the only reason I keep green olives on hand. Not even working here anymore and you cost me money, girlie."

I chuckled. "You lie. I know better *because* I used to work here."

A college-aged guy behind Uncle Mick put a pizza on the counter and bellowed out the order number. I glanced at the pie and saw it was a chicken, spinach, and mushroom pizza. Then I focused on Mick, who was watching the customer approach from behind me.

"Jesus. Are you following me or something?" a vaguely-familiar voice asked.

"Watch the tone, bub. Nobody talks to my Vickie that way," Mick grumbled.

I turned to the side.

Gamble stared down at me, those blue irises dancing over my stunned expression. I glanced past him at the three tables pulled together near the far wall. Six bikers and four women sat around the table watching Gamble.

I pulled myself together and focused. "I'm *not* following you." I shook my head and turned back to Mick. "Make my order to-go."

"Anybody's got to *go*, Vic, it's this bozo."

I fought laughter mainly because Gamble was anything but a bozo, not to mention every time Mick used the term it made me giggle.

I leaned over the counter to pat Mick's bicep. "It's all right. I got a busy afternoon anyway. You need all the large groups you can get, Uncle Mick."

He gave me a chin lift, but his eyes were on Gamble. "Stop starin' at her ass. Biker or not, regular or not, I'll fuck you up for starin' at her like that."

I made big eyes and opened my mouth to tell Uncle Mick it was okay, but Gamble spoke.

"My apologies, sir. You're right. I shouldn't stare at her like that. Thanks for the pizza."

I came down from my tiptoes and watched as Gamble took the pizza to his table.

"What's the story?" Uncle Mick asked.

I shook my head. "No story. Won't be a story. We don't like each other. He was at a hearing of mine today. He took the time to approach me and 'thank' me for not doing my job very well."

Mick balled up the rag in his hand. "I oughta kick his—"

I held up a hand. "No. It's fine."

I liked to run. And not the way some people claim they 'run' to the liquor store. No. I had long legs and sitting behind a desk for ten or twelve hours every day made me feel cramped and squished like I'd taken a five-day car-trip. That meant every weekday, except Fridays, I ran after work.

Today being Monday, I had pavement to pound. Unfortunately, I was running late. But it was late May, and the sun was setting later and later. I threw on my running gear. Then, I put in my ear buds, cued up some music on my phone, which was attached to my armband, and headed out.

Midway through my run "Block Rockin' Beats" by The Chemical Brothers began and I really hit my stride. My mind cleared and I felt nothing but the beat of the music and the air rushing past my face.

I ran on the sidewalk as much as I could, but certain parts of my route forced me to run street-side. As I jogged my way to the side of the street, I looked over my shoulder. No cars appeared to be around, and I faced forward. A low-riding car was approaching from the opposite direction, but I paid it little mind since I was on the other side of the road.

Just before the spot I would veer back onto the sidewalk, the car accelerated. Then I realized it was barreling toward me. I darted to the side, around a telephone pole, and onto the sidewalk. A man got out of the car and came after me.

Here's the thing about being a runner. People who run for exercise, don't necessarily run fast. Or at least, *I* didn't run fast. Which boggled the mind of my best friend, Heidi, since she pointed out I had the long-lost legs of a gazelle. Nevertheless, I knew I wasn't fast.

This meant that as I ran, I threw over every garbage can or recycling bin I came across.

It didn't work, though.

The man gained on me.

I yanked my phone out of the arm band, and fumbled to get the numeric keypad up to dial 911.

Except it was too late.

A heavy weight hit me, and I went down to the ground.

Face-first.

The last thing I remembered was the vision of concrete rushing toward my face before my head hit.

Then it was lights out.

Gamble

The brothers were gearing up for a party. It promised to be a blow-out since Cynic had put a cut on his woman Fiona. From inside the clubhouse, Gamble had heard his name being called and the urgency in the prospect's voice had him on edge.

Har, Cynic, Blood, and Brute were huddled around something. As he came closer, he saw Stephanie, Abby, and Fiona were hunched over a... woman's body.

Fiona looked at Cynic. "She needs an ambulance. I know that's not y'all's style, but—"

Dread filled him.

"I'm with her," Abby said. "Way she's bound up, there's no way they didn't sexually assault her. She needs care the two of us aren't equipped to provide."

At Abby's words, anger quickly replaced the dread. He forced himself to get a grip on his temper. While his brothers stared at Fiona and Abby, Gamble trudged forward, his eyes not leaving the woman on the ground. Tightness invaded his chest. It couldn't be who he thought it was.

Absently, he heard Abby speaking. "Or your private doc either."

"Why'd you call for Gamble?" Sandy asked.

The prospect sighed. "There's a note on her."

Fiona leaned over, but he saw the ugly handwriting on notebook paper.

For Gamble. Stop fucking with Juan.

He leaned down grabbing the note, but Fiona called out, "Wait! There's more on the back."

Gamble made brief eye contact with her before looking at the back-side of the paper.

Your sister is next.

He let go of the paper and straightened. A primal roar exploded from him. In two quick strides, he threw a vicious fist at the door to the clubhouse. Pain radiated up his arm, but it did nothing to calm his rage.

9

"Is he trying to break his goddamn hand?" Abby asked.

"I think he knows her," Fiona muttered.

He heard others talking about seeing Victoria at Bayou Moon Pizza. She deserved better than to be peered at and talked about like that. He strode back to the huddle and wedged between Har and Cynic.

Har knew his intentions, and muttered to Stephanie, "Move, Miss Priss."

As soon as Stephanie got out of the way, he scooped up Victoria, taking her straight to his room. It took effort to ignore the blood caked around her swollen nose. He despised her suffering such a reprehensible crime. Overwhelming guilt ate at him, and he vowed he'd do anything he could to help her.

From behind him, Cynic said, "Dr. Silverman's on his way, Prez."

She stirred in his arms. As he sidled into his room, she whimpered.

He lowered her to his bed. "You're safe, kitten. Doctor's on the way."

Fiona and Abby bustled inside. As much as he didn't want to, he moved aside.

CHAPTER 2

HOLDING EYE CONTACT

FIONA

D r. Silverman, the club's doctor-on-retainer, had also advised getting Victoria to the hospital, but Gamble (and Roman, to my surprise) raised holy hell at the idea. During the examination, neither of us believed she had any broken bones, other than her nose.

As we cleaned up her face, I recalled the night I met her. She'd exited an interrogation room while I waited for a ride. She stopped to organize her things, and we'd been making idle chit-chat when Gamble arrived. I'd noticed how gorgeous she was that night, but now... I just hoped the spunky light in her eyes returned. And that Dr. Silverman's plastic surgeon was as good as he said he was. The surgeon, who owed Silverman a favor, had set her nose as best he could. From the tense body language and hushed voices, I suspected Har, Roman, Gamble, and Dr. Silverman had made it clear that if she needed more help, he'd provide it —at no charge, most likely.

Abby's suspicions were spot-on, unfortunately. Victoria had been raped. Her panties were missing, and traces of blood and other dried fluids were all over her exercise pants. However, I was still certified as a sexual assault forensics nurse, so I collected all the evidence I could from Victoria.

The worst had been when she woke up. She saw me and Abby first. I would never forget how terrified her eyes were or how strong her grip was on my forearm. Working in an emergency room, Abby had more experience calming patients down, so I was grateful she was there.

When she saw Dr. Silverman behind us her body went tight, and he astutely ducked out of the room.

We helped her into one of Gamble's t-shirts; even with her height, it fell to her mid-thigh. I draped a blanket over her because I could see her shaking.

She took a deep breath. Then she pulled the blanket to her nose and a strange look came over her. She whispered. "Why?"

"Why what, hon?" Abby asked.

She looked at me. "Why does it smell like him?"

I blinked, wondering if she was talking about Gamble. We were in his room. I didn't know if the blanket smelled like him or not.

Abby misunderstood. "The blanket smells like your attacker?"

Victoria's eyes shot to Abby's. "No. Smells like," she paused and glanced at me before she whispered, "Gamble."

I went down on my knees next to the bed, so I was closer to her face. "It's Gamble's blanket, Victoria. You're in his room at the clubhouse."

"Okay," she whispered.

"How bad does your nose hurt?" I asked.

"Really bad."

"Dr. Silverman... He was just in here. He can give you some medication to help."

"Okay," she said.

After she took her pills, she fell asleep fast. By midnight, Dr. Silverman had left. There wasn't much left to do for her, so Abby and I cleared out of the room.

In the hallway, I found Gamble slouched against the opposite wall. He rose and gave Abby a hug. I heard him murmur his thanks to her. When he turned to me, I expected the same treatment, but he wrapped me in a fierce bear hug.

"Thank God you were here, Princess Fiona."

12

I patted his back. "Not a problem, Gamble. But, I wouldn't plan on being in your room tonight."

He let me go and glared at me. "She can't be alone."

Abby sidled up to us. "You're right. She can't. That's why I'm gonna be in there. She's out cold right now. Gonna have Blood drag a recliner in there. I'll hear her if she wakes up."

"I want to be there," he said.

I caught Gamble's gaze. "She was terrified when she saw Dr. Silverman in there. I'm not exaggerating when I say that."

He tore a hand through his short hair. "You think I don't know that? It's my goddamn fault. I'm gonna be there."

Abby started, "I don't think—"

I cut her off. "I told her she was in Gamble's room. It might be okay." I looked for Cynic's room and realized it was next to Gamble's. "I'll be with Cynic in the next room. There's a problem, he can get me, assuming I don't hear it first."

Abby pinned me with her gaze. "That is not how your man wants to spend tonight."

I tilted my head. "Tonight ended like twenty minutes ago. It's the wee hours of the morning, Abs."

"Fine. Blood and I'll be in a room upstairs."

Gamble

Gamble learned the hard way that a recliner wouldn't fit through his doorway. He sent a prospect out to Wal-Mart to get him a sleeping bag and an air mattress. While he'd heard what Fiona had to say about Victoria freaking out about Dr. Silverman being in the room. that wouldn't keep him from being there for Victoria.

Laying on the air mattress, he dwelled on things he shouldn't. Har not calling an immediate session of church ranked very high. No matter what the others had to say, they needed to know why Victoria had been followed.

He couldn't believe it was his fault.

Even if the note addressed her to him, why would they attack her?

Part of him thought it was her being in the wrong place at the wrong time, but that was wishful thinking.

And that was the *very* reason he needed church.

Hashing that shit out with his brothers would help him in a way he couldn't explain. And no matter how irrelevant it felt to his brothers who weren't involved, church helped in ways he couldn't express no matter how much he tried.

He'd interacted with her... four times, if his memory served. The night he'd picked up Fiona from the police station and he'd mistaken Victoria for Fi's legal representative. That morning in the courtroom; then, the parking lot; and later at Bayou Moon Pizza.

That didn't signal that the two of them had a connection.

Yet, their confrontation in the parking lot hadn't been as brief as he'd intended. As he replayed it in his mind, someone looking at them from afar might have taken it for flirtation. They had chemistry —even if it was sour rather than sweet.

Calling her kitten had felt better than it should have.

Christ. This was why he needed church.

He wouldn't be dwelling or overthinking a damn thing like he was right now.

He wanted to turn off the desk lamp, but Victoria had fallen asleep with it on, and he figured it would be better to leave it. His room didn't have windows. The small nightlight in the bathroom wouldn't cast any light on him lying on the floor if she awoke.

As though his thoughts caused it to happen, the sheets rustled, and Victoria sat up.

He curled forward, but then she repositioned herself and settled back into bed.

Once he laid his head down again, he heard her shifting.

"Do you need me to leave?" she asked in a small voice.

Something in her tone made him question if she was fully with it, though she had obviously seen him on the floor.

"No, kitten. I don't want you to be alone."

He wished he could be in the bed with her, but he damn sure knew better. When his sister Brittney had been raped, she couldn't handle any physical touch for a while. It took weeks before he was able to hug her again.

His anger rose and he forced himself to take a deep breath. Those bastards were going to pay for what they did to Victoria. Even if the vote didn't swing that way, he knew. He was going to find every one of those assholes and fuck them up.

"You shouldn't be on the floor," she said.

"You freaked out at Doc Silverman being here. No way I'd be in that bed with you."

"I don't know him. But I know who you are."

He almost nodded. Instead, he said, "Go to sleep, Victoria."

"You can sleep on the other side of the bed," she argued.

"I'm fine, kitten."

"You're stubborn is more like it," she whispered.

"Did you mean for me to hear that?"

"Don't know, but it's true. Good night."

He smiled and that surprised him. There wasn't a damn thing to smile about in this sitch, but she made him do it. He was stubborn. Yet something told him, so was she.

He closed his eyes on that thought. He hadn't expected to fall asleep, but he did.

When he woke up, he saw Victoria's foot disappear under the covers and he heard the toilet running. He grabbed his phone. Quarter to six in the morning. He wanted to sleep another hour, but that wasn't happening.

Quietly, he used the bathroom and left the room. In the kitchen, he brewed an extra strong pot of coffee.

Roman trudged out while Gamble doctored his brew.

"Why aren't you with your woman?"

Roman's lips twisted and he focused on his coffee. After a moment, he glanced at Gamble. "I sent her home before Victoria was dropped off. And I stuck around because I know what you're going through."

Gamble inhaled through his nose. He wanted to argue that, but of all the brothers he and Roman had sisters who'd been raped. To top it off, Roman had found out later that Trinity, his woman, had also been sexually assaulted. Gamble and Cynic had helped him mete out retribution.

He didn't think it was enough, though.

He never did, and probably never would.

"It kills biding your time, but you can't go after them right now."

"Why? Why not tonight?"

"They're going to be ready for that."

He shook his head. "They're going to be ready no matter what. Why do this shit otherwise?" Another thought hit him before Roman responded. "Hell, you didn't wait before going after Ink."

A malicious chuckle rumbled out of Roman. "Difference is, Ink and his crew weren't good enough to get in with any gang. They were fuck-ups. You know that and so did everyone else in town."

Gamble sighed and sipped his coffee.

"The Abeyeta brothers aren't a bunch of idiotic asshats. They followed you, they're goading you, and your brothers aren't gonna let you fall into their fuckin' trap."

"What I want to know is why you went to that trial yesterday," Cynic grumbled, pulling down a mug from the cabinet.

Gamble kept eye contact with Roman. Then he sighed and looked at Cynic. "I can't explain it, man."

"Try," Cynic muttered around his coffee cup.

Gamble recalled a favor he did for Cynic a few months back. Cynic's sister Lisa had come to town and was partying like it was 'her birthday' with every man inside Twisted Talons – the bar run by the Riot MC. Rather than have his sister picked up by some random guy, Gamble,

Tiny, and two prospects showed up without their cuts —which killed— and acted as though they were interested in Lisa.

He caught Cynic's eyes. "God forbid, something as awful as what happened to my sister happened to Lisa. Wouldn't you hold a grudge?"

"I thought just one guy attacked her," Roman said.

His anger built and his tone hardened. "Yeah. But his *three* brothers kept me out of my house while he did it. And they knew there was fuck-all I could do about it without my goddamn parents around. Had no cell, no decent neighbors in that shitty complex. I fought all those bastards as hard as I could, but I was fifteen and —"

"Sorry. Forget I asked," Cynic said.

Gamble shook his head. "No. Don't be sorry. But you gotta under-stand. They're *all* fuckin' responsible. Every last one, even if they didn't touch Brit."

Cynic frowned and nodded while his head turned to the side. "Yeah," he muttered. "I can see that, absolutely."

Roman put his mug down with a thud. "There a reason you didn't tell Har or any of the others about this?"

"I told Har. But, Christ, that would've been just before I earned my patch, six or seven years ago."

Roman shook his head. "You tell him you were tracking their trials and shit?"

Gamble looked out the window.

"Right," Roman muttered.

"Your sister still in town?" Cynic asked.

He caught Cynic's dark eyes. "No. She... the attack delayed her grad-uating. Fucked up her GPA and shit, but the moment she could, Brit moved to Seattle. If a work visa weren't required, I swear she'd have moved to Canada. Anything to get as far from this place as she could."

"Why didn't you follow her?" Roman asked.

He gave Roman a small smile because he understood where that came from. Roman's sister had survived her ordeal, but then relieved her suffering by overdosing on pain meds. Gamble knew Roman would've given anything to have his sister back.

"She told me she didn't want me to, and I had *just* turned fifteen. I had no license, didn't know how to drive. After the attack the police got involved and our parents had to act like they gave a damn about both their kids. Trust me, I'd have been a dead weight for Brit. Not to mention, I wanted some fuckin' payback."

Cynic shook his head. "But you never got it."

Gamble smiled. "The Abeyetas weren't the only bastards at fault. I wanted payback from my no-good parents. They hadn't been out gambling that fuckin' day, who knows where Brittney would be. Hell, if they hadn't been gambling all our lives, we wouldn't have lived in that shitty apartment, wouldn't have gone to that fuckin' school. None of it."

Raw fury surged inside him, and he clenched his fists, barely getting his mug to the table instead of throwing it across the kitchen.

"Jesus Christ, G. You look like you're gonna pop a blood vessel. You okay?" Roman asked.

He heaved out a few breaths. "No. It's a slight stretch, but no fuckin' doubt, my goddamned sorry excuses for parents led to Victoria being attacked, too."

"That *is* a stretch, man," Cynic said.

When silence ensued, Gamble looked at Roman. He was staring into space, warring with himself.

Gamble turned to Cynic. "Pretty sure you're wrong, seeing as the one man who can relate to me, doesn't agree."

After a moment, Roman spoke. "You're right, but so is 'Nic. You can't put Victoria's attack on yourself."

His jaw clenched to the point his teeth hurt, but he felt his temper recede. "There's no other explanation, man. It's also why I'm so fuckin' pissed we haven't had church or any goddamn mention of it in nearly twelve hours."

Cynic's head lifted high with his nod. "That's exactly why we aren't meeting. Yet."

Gamble took his mug to the sink to rinse it. "What the fuck? We need to meet so we can plan."

"We will, but man you gotta bank this anger. Save it for when we execute the plan," Cynic said.

18

He felt unsettled. With a deep breath, he forced a calm expression and looked at his brothers. "Yeah. You're right. I'm gonna hit the shower."

As he walked away, he knew he hadn't hidden his impatience from Roman or Cynic.

He came out of his bathroom wearing jeans and an Imagine Dragons t-shirt. Victoria was lightly snoring. He was glad she could sleep while he showered. Sitting in his armless office chair, he pulled on his socks. His boots were across the room, but he couldn't stop staring at her in his bed.

He wanted to hold her. Hell, he'd wanted to wrap her in his arms and kiss her the first night he met her. The only reason he didn't was because of Fiona. And the fact a lawyer like her would never spend time with a man like him.

He refused to dwell on that. Maybe that made him delusional or maybe he was a glutton for punishment, but he wanted her more than he'd wanted any woman. But aside from joining the Riot MC, he rarely pursued what he wanted.

The urge to hold her snuck up on him again, but he knew —truly knew like no other brother besides Roman— that wasn't a bad idea, but the worst idea.

Her breathing changed. She rolled over and her eyes caught on him.

He thought she would freak out, but she only stared at him.

After a long silence, she whispered, "I'll never be the same."

"Of course, you won't," he spoke so fast, it almost sounded snappish.

She shook her head on the pillow. "How do you know?"

"My sister was raped. It didn't kill her, but it killed part of her. She was never the same happy-go-lucky girl."

"What do you mean?"

"They killed her... her innocence, I guess."

Her eyes widened and he added, "She wasn't a virgin, if that's what you're thinking, but that doesn't matter. Her whole fuckin' personality was changed by that goddamn shit."

"How old was she?"

"Seventeen. And yeah, I've been told her age played a bigger role in her personality changing, but I don't buy it."

Her head moved in a small nod.

They stared at each other.

He should feel awkward, but he didn't. If holding eye contact was the only way he could 'hold her,' then he'd take it. For now.

"I'm sorry you had to sleep on the floor," she whispered.

"Don't be. Don't apologize for a damn thing, Victoria. Not a chance I was going to let you sleep in here alone."

"Why?"

He paused. His instinct was to shrug her question off, but he couldn't do that either.

"I wanted to be here for you, in whatever way I could be."

An emotion flitted through her eyes, but she hid it before he could figure it out.

Someone knocked softly on his door. For another moment, he stared into her hazel eyes, which looked light brown in the desk light. Then he crossed to the door and found Fiona standing on the other side.

"Is she awake?"

He nodded.

"Her clothes are evidence. I don't know if she wants to wear something besides your t-shirt. I can loan her a shirt if she wants something more feminine."

"She can keep what I've given her," he murmured.

Fiona nodded. "Cynic's taking me to get my SUV and I'll come back to take her home."

He wanted to take her home, but having a woman take her would be better.

Fiona walked away and he closed the door.

"Should I get up?"

"No. You got some time. Try to snooze if you can."

"Are you leaving?"

"Not unless you want me to."

"Going to stare at me while I sleep?"

He fought a smirk. "Got some things to work on at my desk."

Her eyes skated to his drafting desk. He sat down, she looked at him for a moment before letting her eyes close.

A fresh sheet of sketch paper begged him to draw on it. He knew the moment he put a pencil to paper he'd only be able to sketch one thing. Those eyes staring at him. The same eyes he wanted looking at him in a different way.

His portfolio of sketch work had helped him bolster Har's business. No biker would walk into Har's shop and request a set of hazel eyes to be painted onto their bike —not that he'd put her eyes on anyone's ride. It would be a drawing just for him, something he hadn't allowed himself to do in over a year. As he picked up his favorite pencil, he prayed those eyes wouldn't haunt him.

But he knew they would.

Chapter 3

Blanket

Victoria

I wanted this tie-dyed fleece blanket with every fiber of my being even if the colors would clash with my lavender and grey bedclothes. It was warm and soft from wear. No matter how I tried, I couldn't convince myself not to steal this blanket. And it didn't make sense. Okay, that wasn't true.

It *did* make sense, because the damn thing smelled so much like Gamble. Something about him watching over me struck me deep. The blanket was a reminder of him and it made me feel better. More secure.

Good grief, had I regressed to childhood? Did I really need a blankie to feel secure?

I needed to leave. Fiona was willing to take me back to my apartment. I didn't want to hold her up.

The door opened. Fiona and the red-haired woman who'd helped last night came into the room.

"I'm not rushing you, Victoria. I just want to be sure you're okay."

My eyes went to the side. How many times were people going to ask me if I was okay? And I understood that need. That drive to help.

But I didn't think I would ever be okay again.

"Is his shirt too big? You could—"

"I want his blanket," I whispered.

Fiona's blue eyes almost lit up at my words, but she hid it.

"You take it," the other woman said.

Fiona glared at her. "Abby, I don't—"

"He won't care," Abby said to her.

"I don't have my pants," I said.

"They're evidence now in case you decide to press charges. Stephanie offered some yoga pants, I'll go get 'em," Abby said.

For some reason, Fiona followed Abby. As they left Gamble came into the room.

Since I was never good at being a sneak, I admitted, "I'm taking your blanket."

His eyes landed on me, and they looked pained. "Have at it, kitten. Anything I can give you, it's yours."

I closed my eyes and turned my head away.

Pity. He would give me the blanket because he pitied me.

Guess I'd have to get used to that too, in the days ahead.

Abby came back in with yoga pants and Gamble cleared out.

I put on the stretchy pants.

Then I folded the blanket and left it on his bed. I didn't want it anymore. No matter how much it smelled like him.

At eight-thirty, Fiona pulled up in front of my building. Before I left the vehicle, I asked to use her phone and called into work sick.

She took her phone from me. "Where were you when you were attacked?"

I shook my head. "Why do you ask?"

She gave me a patient smile. "Abby and I will look for your phone, sweetie. No way in hell are you going back to look for it."

I told her where I'd been, and I went up to my apartment.

I took a twenty-minute shower, but it did precious little to help me feel cleaner. If it weren't for my eczema, I'd have soaked in the tub all day. I put on a pair of my own yoga pants and my softest, comfiest t-shirt.

At nine-fifteen, someone was knocking the brass knocker on my condo door. Most people just used their knuckles. I suspected it was a salesperson, because there was no way Fiona had found my phone in the span of forty-five minutes. I tiptoed to the door.

"No," I whispered after I peeked through the peephole.

Gamble pressed his lips together and looked to the side.

Then he used the knocker again. Something told me he wouldn't go away.

I opened the door. "How do you even know where I live?"

He stared at me for a long moment. Then he extended a small, colorful bundle toward me.

It was his blanket.

And pity.

I shook my head.

"Take it," he said. His voice sounded strained.

"No," I said in a small voice.

"You said you were going to take it, but you didn't. Have it."

I sighed. "It's bad enough I took one of your t-shirts. I changed my mind. Keep it."

"What changed your mind?"

I closed my eyes for a moment. "It doesn't matter, Gamble. I'm sorry you came all the way out—"

"Take the blanket."

"No."

"It's the fucking least I can do to help you."

It was on the tip of my tongue to say it was the least he could do to pity me, but the steely look in his eyes made me keep quiet and brace myself.

"Because make no fuckin' mistake, kitten. I'm damn sure gonna help you get through this shit."

My eyes narrowed. "You don't need to help me."

His eyes widened. "It's my goddamn fault you were attacked."

25

"How is it your fault? I was out running and—"

With surprising gentleness, he moved me out of the doorway and came into my unit. He closed the door and leaned toward me, yet managed to keep his distance. "They dropped you at my club's doorstep with a note addressing you to *me*. It is my goddamn fault, and it's tearing me up that they did that shit to you."

He stalked over to the sofa and dropped the blanket there.

He came back to the foyer. His finger delicately traced the apple of my cheek. "Keep the blanket, kitten. I'll be back."

I stood staring at the door after he left. Then the knocker went again, but just once.

"Lock the door, Victoria," he said.

"Right," I whispered, and I locked the door.

My resolve to ignore that blanket lasted a whopping three seconds. I hustled to the couch where he'd left it. Holding it to my face, I sniffed it. Then I took it to my bedroom and spread it out on top of my bed.

Yes, it made me crazy.

I didn't care.

It made me feel safer, though not entirely safe.

I wasn't sure I'd ever feel entirely safe again.

Without my cell or a landline, I realized my boss wouldn't be able to call me back. I sent an email letting her know my cell phone was missing. If she needed to speak with me, we could Skype.

I hadn't heard back from her. Yet. Dread welled inside me as I thought about that impending conversation.

I didn't want to report the crime, but I'd gone to law school for a reason: I believed in the justice system. Or at least I thought I did; after last night I didn't believe in much of anything.

My mind ran through all the scenarios if I reported it.

I never saw my attackers. After my fall, I'd been unconscious. When I came to, a bag was over my head. They'd knocked me out before taking me to the Riot Clubhouse- or at least I had to assume they did. I couldn't identify them, and yet, if I reported my attack, I'd have to rehash every bit of this with an officer.

Just thinking about it made my stomach churn.

They'd ask why I hadn't gone to the hospital. I'd probably have to submit to a rape examination. That made me nearly gag. My memory was fuzzy. I didn't recall if the doctor who'd been at the clubhouse had done that. It would be nice to ask Fiona about that, but I didn't know her last name.

I didn't know anybody's full name associated with the Riot MC, come to think of it.

The urge to shower again came over me, but I fought it off. Instead, I opened my laptop and logged on to my social media. My best friend Heidi tended to be a text-only woman, but without my phone I had to pray she noticed my direct message.

My PC went into screensaver mode, and I saw today's date. On the off-chance Heidi missed my direct message, she was scheduled to swing by my place today, anyway.

Oh, no.

Every Sunday during the winter and summer, she and I, along with three black men, were volunteer coaches of youth basketball. The summer session was set to start in a week and a half. Tonight, Heidi and I were reviewing our plans. The other main coach, Royce, had said he might show up tonight too, but he hadn't confirmed yesterday.

If it were just Heidi that would be one thing, but Royce would lose his mind if he saw me this way.

He had a heart of gold and the motivational skills to change the world, if only he had a platform from which he could be heard. Though he certainly changed the worlds of forty or fifty basketball players every season. His enthusiasm was contagious, and the world needed more men like him in it.

But I knew he'd seen more than his fair share of hardship and struggle. He'd mentioned watching his mother hustle to make ends meet. And every so often he'd hint at violence he'd seen his mother endure when he was too young to help her. It explained why he was so protective of

27

me and Heidi, insisting we wait to open the gym until he was there with us.

One glimpse of my nose and blackened eyes and he'd be on the warpath.

I needed to encourage him not to show up tonight. Again, my missing cell phone posed a problem. He and I typically conversed via text. Sending him a direct message would raise more of a red flag than the most well-crafted excuse ever would.

My laptop made the strange noise indicating a new message and I logged back in. Heidi's message opened with a GIF of a late-night talk show host and a sub-title that read, "What nonsense is this?" Then she asked why I didn't have the ability to text her.

I stretched the truth, saying my phone had fallen while I was running and had bitten the dust.

That wasn't my best move.

The PC pinged in succession with her messages.

You're lying!

Which was followed by:

You never take your phone out of your arm holster.

I deflected by asking her to text Royce so he wouldn't come by tonight.

That prompted her to start a video call. I accepted, but had the slider engaged so my camera would show up as a dark screen.

Heidi's blonde hair fell across her forehead stylishly. She pulled off layered hair like a hair model. As she tucked a lock behind her ear, I saw she wore her silver, Tinkerbell hoop earrings, which were probably the smallest pair she owned. Her big green eyes peered at the screen, then squinted and I watched her expression turn annoyed.

"Victoria Carlton, I know your camera works. We were just on a damned Zoom meeting five days ago. What are you hiding?"

I took a deep breath. "I'm fine, but I was attacked."

Heidi had a no-bullshit attitude like no other woman I knew. Still, she stammered, "A... ah, attacked? No. My friend, that's a word that covers a multitude of sins. Women don't get attacked. They get mugged. They get...," she trailed off. "You need to tell me what happened."

"I was raped."

She was silent, but I saw her looking off to the side. When she looked back at her screen, her eyes were curious. "I'd ask if you're okay, but Vickie... you led into this with 'you're fine'? I don't think I've ever met a woman who's been even a shy away from rape and claimed to be 'fine.' Jesus Christ. What can I do to help? And who did this?"

"I don't know exactly," I said.

"Now that doesn't make sense."

"I don't want to talk about this over the internet. Do you understand?"

She nodded, but asked, "Have you reported it? Did you go to the hospital?"

I did a deep breath and switched on my camera. "I'm not talking about that on—"

"Oh, Vickie," she whispered, her eyes wide at the sight of my battered face.

I sighed.

She shook her head, the Tinkerbell earrings swinging with the movement. "I... there are no words, sweetie." She sighed. "At least now, I understand why you need Royce to stay home."

"Thanks," I whispered.

"I'd say you're welcome, but I'm ditching work and heading over there now."

"Heidi, no. You can't. Your boss has been riding your ass for months now, you could get—"

She rolled her eyes. "Yeah, yeah. I could get fired. Totally true. I'm replaceable, but so is a job. *You* aren't replaceable and this is a fucking emergency."

Tears welled in my eyes, and I pressed my lips together hard.

"Don't do that. You start, I'll start. Wait until we hang up. You want anything? I'm across town, so I can pick up whatever you need. Potato chips, cookies, a Glock."

I blew out a breath wishing I could laugh at her lame attempt at humor. "A gun isn't going to do me any good now, Heidi."

"Make me feel better if you had one."

Her words instantly brought Uncle Mick to mind. Shortly after I'd moved into my apartment, he'd cornered me and Heidi at his restaurant. He spent a good twenty minutes trying to convince me to get a gun and offered to take me to a shooting range to find one that felt right. We never made it to the gun shop, and I hadn't entertained the idea since then.

I shook my head. "Okay, Uncle Mick."

She pointed a finger at the screen. "Hey. He's got the right idea. You don't want comfort food?"

"No. Can't say I have much of an appetite. And seriously, you can wait until tonight to swing by."

She gave me a flat look. "Not happening. I'm hanging up because I gotta text Royce."

"No multi-tasking?"

"I think he's going to call me after I send this text."

"Don't tell him—"

"I'm not going to tell him, but he's..."

She was quiet for so long, I asked, "He's what?"

"I think he's sweet on you, and he's going to be concerned."

Heidi thought every man was 'sweet' on me. Royce would be concerned, but who wouldn't be? He didn't have feelings for me or anything. That was her wishful thinking.

"Do what you have to, but tell him I'll see him next week."

She barked out a laugh. "I wouldn't be so sure about that. See you soon."

Gamble

Har had told Gamble last night that the shop would be closed today. He had every intention of catching a nap at the clubhouse. Unlike other brothers, Gamble didn't have an apartment or other residence. He couldn't decide on a place he wanted to buy, and he wasn't going to throw his money away on rent, especially since he had a room at the clubhouse.

As he entered through the back door, he stopped short at seeing Abby, Blood, and Har in the kitchen.

Gamble went to the fridge and grabbed a bottle of water.

"She needs to press charges," Abby said.

"What have you done with my woman?" Blood asked. Then he added, "And it isn't our business, Abs."

Har put his travel mug on the counter. "I agree with her."

"What?" Gamble asked.

Har nodded. "This doesn't involve us."

Gamble clenched his fists. "They're threatening my sister. They attacked Victoria because *I* interacted with her. Hell, they dumped her right fucking here. That alone involves the club. But since when do we allow women to be violated and treated like punching bags?"

"If she were any other woman, I might see this differently," Har said.

Gamble shook his head. "What the hell does that mean?"

"She's a lawyer. Works for the county, and she might be able to call in sick today. But she won't be in a courtroom, for weeks most likely, because of this. She's gonna get pressure to report the crime, or if not that, then pressure about why she *won't* report such a heinous felony."

He'd pushed that to the back of his mind. She led a life a world away from Gamble's, even if they were in the same city. The whole situation was fucked and continued to get more fucked.

"Call me the devil's advocate, but I have to ask, what's she really going to be able to tell them?" Blood asked.

Gamble looked between Blood and Har.

31

KAREN RENEE

Blood spoke. "She was out cold when they dropped her here. They hadn't blindfolded her, so my guess is that she was out when they put her in the car from wherever they were." He looked at Abby, "Did you or Fi ask her what happened?"

Abby gave him a dry look. "No. Though, for what it's worth, Fiona collected evidence from her while Dr. Silverman did his examination. Fiona's certified for sexual assault forensic exams and I'm sure she could testify."

"That's just it," Gamble grumbled. "They addressed her to me. I'm the one who knows who wrote that note, but that isn't enough to say those assholes raped her."

Har blew out a long breath that wasn't quite a sigh. "Yeah, that's a problem. Still, cops have resources we don't. She knows where she was last. She was out running, then there's probably traffic cameras or some shit that can get a plate—"

"And then what?" Blood asked.

Har gave him a long look. "This ain't your chapter, man."

"No, but that doesn't make you, or," he tipped his head to Gamble, "him, any less my brother. And this has landed him in some serious shit."

Cynic came around the corner from the common room. "What the hell? Why are we hashing out Gamble's shit in the kitchen? When are we having church?"

"We aren't," Gamble muttered.

Har speared him with a look. "Watch yourself, G." He looked back at Cynic. "Call Block, Two-Times, and Roman. Find out if six tonight works for them. Pretty sure everyone can make that."

Cynic nodded. "And I'll get two of the prospects to be at the bar."

Gamble shook his head trying to bite back the words, but he couldn't. "I can't believe we're waiting on this. What the hell do we stand for if we're not—"

Har stepped closer to him. "Nobody said we're not meeting. It's just not happening as fast as *you* want it to."

"It ain't right," Gamble muttered. As soon as he could break away, he was getting his hands on some weed. He needed something to mellow him out. Since busting someone's head wasn't up anytime soon, a joint had to do the trick.

Har's eyes flashed at him. "We cleaned this club up for a reason, man. Plenty of people —a few cops included— are just waiting for us to fuck up and land our asses in jail." He sighed as quietly as he could. "We take these fuckers on, we're *all* on the line."

"Always been that way, Prez," he said.

He shook his head. "No. We've never had a woman dumped on our clubhouse doorstep. Every last one of us is pissed as fuck, G. You may not think so, but we are. That means more of you are likely to lose your shit, and there aren't enough people to get you all to pull back when needed."

He hated how damned logical Har could be, but then again, that was why the man was president.

"Fine. I'll be back at six."

"Where you goin'?" Cynic asked.

"To get some fuckin' weed, man."

After Cynic called the meeting to order, Gamble rolled his neck to work out some gathering tension.

From across the table, Har speared Gamble with his eyes. "I know you want to go after Juan's crew, but we don't know it was them."

"There was a note," Gamble bit out.

"That doesn't mean they did it. Could've outsourced it," Brute said.

He clenched his fists. "Why take credit for it then?"

Everyone kept quiet, but Gamble noticed Block contemplating it.

"We don't like women being abused in anyway. That isn't a secret on the street. They take credit, you get pissed —hell, we *all* got pissed— then we roll up on a trap. It's a stretch, maybe, but it could happen. Then your ass is taken in, and maybe Juan's got a plan for you there."

"No disrespect, Block. But, all of that's a stretch," Gamble muttered.

"Might be. Might not be," Har said. "We need to do this shit carefully. She's a lawyer. The men who attacked her end up in the hospital—"

"Dead would be better," Roman muttered.

Har gave Roman a dry look. "Or they disappear... that will come back on us since she was dropped here and addressed to you."

Finn, having earned his patch six months ago, raised his hand before speaking. "I've never heard of Juan Abeyeta, but maybe that's because he's inside. Is he part of the Latin Apostles?"

"No," Cynic said. "I've heard two different versions. One version, he and his three brothers were going to start their own gang. Then Juan got caught up in a sting. He resisted arrest, managed to run, but when a cop nearly caught him again, he shot the officer. The cop survived, but they're throwing the book at Juan. The other version I've heard is that the Abeyeta boys never measured up for the Apostles." Cynic looked at Roman. "Like that asshole you had a beef with, wasn't his name Ink?"

Roman lifted his chin with an affirmative.

"How does anyone not measure up for the Apostles?" Mensa asked. "It's my understanding they'll take anybody, the younger the better, since underage thugs only face juvie."

Cynic shook his head. "Your guess is as good as mine, man. I just know they aren't members of any of the active gangs –including the Apostles."

Roman sighed. "So, if any of Juan's brothers end up hurt or missing, blaming it on gang wars or some shit won't fly. It'll absolutely come back on us or Victoria."

Gamble didn't give a damn about whether shit blew back on him or even the club. He never thought he'd think that regarding his brothers, but he wanted vengeance for Victoria even more than he'd wanted it for his sister.

Shit. How did that happen?

Nothing should get in the way of him and his Riot brothers. Hadn't he sworn that before he earned his patch? Not only did he hardly know Victoria, but they were complete opposites.

Didn't mean he didn't care, though, because he absolutely did.

He'd been so wrapped up in his own thoughts he almost missed Brute's suggestion.

34

"We make any move, there's blowback. I say we hold tight," Brute said.

"For how long?" Gamble asked, with more force than he intended.

Cynic glared at him. "For as long as they say, G."

Har held a hand out to Cynic. "For a while. Few weeks to a month."

Gamble inhaled deeply before he spoke. "Why so long?"

With a flick of his hand, Har kept Cynic from rebuking Gamble. "We need to wait because she's going to report it. No question on that, due to her job. Agreed?"

Gamble nodded.

"She might not be a police officer, but a public defender gets attacked –and possibly by her own client's family– that's going to demand focus. If not from law enforcement, the media's definitely going to latch onto it. The accused attackers can't show up injured or missing or else we get that same focus from cops *and* the media."

From the far end of the table, Tiny asked, "So, we don't want any bad press? Is that what I'm getting out of this?"

Har closed his eyes and his chest rose and fell with his deep breath. "Not exactly. But, there's naturally more press on this once Victoria comes forward."

"Could we convince her not to come forward?" Finn asked.

Har, Brute, and even Gamble shook their heads.

"Finn, were you even listening?" Cynic demanded.

Har said, "Not happening, Finn. She upholds justice, which is most likely going to drive her to report it. Even if it doesn't, her boss will pressure her."

Gamble stared at the table for a long moment. "I'll take the fall."

"Say what?" Block demanded.

He turned his eyes to Har. "I mean it, Prez. She deserves more than what the fuckin' justice system will deliver. It's my fault. Juan's locked up. If I hadn't been at Ramone's arraignment, they wouldn't have targeted her. She was addressed to *me*. I want their fuckin' blood. I'm willing to do time if I have to."

Mensa lifted his hands as though he wanted nothing to do with the conversation. "Did I hear him right? This is fucked up. Since when do we *let* a brother take a fall? And how in the *fuck* is it Gamble's fault?"

Har wasn't one for formalities, like banging a gavel or shit like that. But flying in the face of that, he swung his gavel to get everyone's attention.

"Gamble, brother. Hear me clearly. You are *not* to go after the Abeyeta brothers. No fucking with them in any way."

The glare he sent Har's way should have singed the man's hair. "I can't agree to that. With Juan and Ramone locked up, that leaves just two brothers walking free. They fuckin' kept me from saving my sister and faced no consequences. Now they've hurt a good woman who deserves so much fuckin' better in life, and you expect me to abide that order? There's no fuckin' way, Prez."

Brute leaned forward over the table. "It's for the brotherhood, Gamble."

Gamble's hold on his anger broke. He mirrored Brute's posture leaned over the table. "If it were your woman violated, battered, and bruised you'd tell every one of us to fuck off."

Brute's dark eyes twinkled with his wry smirk. "She's not your woman, though, is she?"

Part of him wanted to say, 'Not yet,' but he knew Brute had him dead to rights. Rather than say anything, he shoved out of his seat, sending the chair flying toward the wall. Then he stomped out of the room, straight to his bike.

Once outside, he straddled his Harley. Even though he didn't know where he was headed, he knew that for the first time ever, the open road and wind in his ears would help him more than his brothers ever could. As much as he looked forward to the ride ahead of him, it was the first time he hated riding alone. His brothers had always been his rock. There wasn't any issue that couldn't be resolved during a church session.

They said there was a first time for everything.

He wished he hadn't been around for the first time church didn't cure what ailed him.

If he was lucky, wind therapy would cover what church with his Riot brothers hadn't.

CHAPTER 4

NUZZLING

VICTORIA

"Thanks for spending the day with me, Heidi. You were more help to me than you'll ever know," I murmured as she dug her keys out of her purse.

Her head whipped up. "You don't need to thank me. Watching back-to-back music documentaries all day isn't a problem for me, and you know it."

I grinned. "Nothing like Tina Turner on a bad day, right?"

Her lips twisted. "Yeah, and following it with the Bee Gee's documentary was a great decision. I still wish you would've taken a nap or something earlier, but I'm gonna get going so you can get some shut-eye."

I yawned as I stood up. "I can't believe it's after ten already."

She smiled. "Time flies, girlfriend."

After Heidi left, I turned out the lights and crawled into bed. Maybe fifteen minutes later, I heard loud pipes outside. A crazy part of me hoped Gamble had done what he said, and come back. But I knew better. My curiosity warred with my comfort because I was wrapped up snug under my covers... and Gamble's blanket.

I needed to sleep, but I couldn't.

With a sigh, I tossed my covers aside and crept to my window. I peeked out and saw Gamble on his motorcycle street-side. He was putting his helmet on the handlebar.

Did he really think my attackers would invade my home?

I defended people like my attackers, so yeah, they could be that stupid and do something that risky. It made me want to report the crime. Yet, I couldn't bring myself to do it.

He swung off his bike and walked toward my building.

A knock came at my door, not using the brass knocker.

I checked the peephole before opening the door.

His eyes searched mine for a moment while he stood in the doorway. "Someone staying with you tonight?"

I shook my head, feeling my brows lowering.

His lips pressed together, and he executed the move from this morning. He stood in my foyer, had closed the door behind him, but rather than stride to my sofa he shoved his hands in his pockets. His eyes stared into mine.

"Is someone staying with you tonight?" he repeated.

"Why?"

He exhaled long and quiet. "Victoria, you should have someone here tonight."

"They aren't going to come for me here, Gamble. I was out running. They don't know where I live."

His hands went to his hips as he cocked his head. "How do you know that? These men didn't just see a woman running down the street, they targeted you. But, we're off track. That isn't why you need someone tonight, sweetheart. Shit comes out at night. Your brain should be at rest, but you can count on your mind serving up ugly crap instead."

I was so exhausted I doubted my brain would do that to me, yet I knew his words to be true.

"Can you call your girl who just left?" he asked.

My head reared back. "How do you know Heidi just left? You pulled up five minutes ago."

His lips tipped up. I wondered why until I realized I'd given away my nosiness.

"Roman was watching you. He called when Heidi left. I wasn't far, and I told him to follow Heidi to be sure she wasn't running an errand or something for you. Since I'm here, I figured I'd ask you direct."

I wouldn't dwell on the fact Gamble had sent someone to 'watch' me. Instead, I said, "She just spent the whole day with me. I can't ask her to spend the night. I'm not some little kid—"

"I'll see if Fiona will do it," he muttered, pulling his phone out of his back pocket.

I touched his forearm and immediately retracted my hand. "No. Don't do that. I don't want to be a bother to anyone."

"You aren't a bother for anyone, Victoria."

His eyes slid to my couch where he'd laid the blanket. The way his brows went up just a touch, I knew he'd noted it wasn't there. When our eyes locked his lips twisted. "Fuck it. I'll sleep on your couch."

"You don't—"

He grabbed my hand and gave it a quick squeeze before letting it go. "Stop. I know I don't have to, but I'm going to."

I hated the idea of him being on my couch only slightly less than I had hated seeing him on the floor in the wee hours this morning. Again I wanted to suggest he sleep on the other side of my bed. Just sleep, but that would be weird.

We didn't like each other.

Sure, him calling me kitten didn't say that, but whatever. Just because he was being nice didn't mean he liked being around me.

The logical side of my brain kicked in: if he didn't like being around me he'd damn sure find someone else to stay with me.

Hmm.

"Suit yourself, Gamble. Um, what's your legal name? Do you ever let people call you something other than Gamble?"

If I wasn't mistaken, warmth filled his gaze. "My given name is Gage."

His mouth was open as though he had more to say, but I tilted my head and waved at his name patch. "Your name is Gage, and they didn't give you *that* for your biker nickname?"

39

He chuckled. "It's a road name, not a nickname. And it's rare the brothers let anyone keep their given name. The story behind mine's a long one. Tell you that some other time."

I led the way back to the couch. "Well, have a seat, Gage." I hesitated, not liking the sound of that compared to Gamble. "Since I've been nosy, I'll keep it up. What's your last name? You know mine. Fair is fair in my world."

"Garrison," he said.

That didn't help. I wasn't going to call him Garrison either. Triple G came to mind, but that wasn't right at this stage.

"Do you want anything to drink?" I asked.

"I'm good."

I nodded and grabbed the remote, moving to the other end of the couch. "Want to watch something on TV?"

"I don't watch TV."

Were there tires screeching?

No, that was in my head. I stared at him, open mouthed. "You don't watch TV? I feel the need to check your pulse."

He chuckled. "Stop it."

I shook my head. "No. You are the first man I've ever met who doesn't watch TV."

"Maybe I *will* call Fiona," he muttered.

"What? Why?"

He shrugged a shoulder. "Two of you could commiserate over my refusal to watch TV."

I nodded and looked away. Fiona seemed a little older, but maybe that was the sort of woman Gamble was into. He had picked her up from the police station. Who else would do that but a man who cared about her?

"She's with Cynic, one of my brothers."

I looked back at him. "I didn't say anything, Gamble."

"Your actions did. I was protecting her a few weeks back. Cynic couldn't be there one night, I filled in and she asked why I don't watch TV. And she gave me almost as much shit as you are."

"Almost?"

"She didn't need to check my pulse."

"She's a nurse, she knows better."

He laughed. "I'm fine. Do your thing. It's getting late and you don't strike me as a night owl. Especially after the last thirty-six hours."

"I was in bed when you roared up. But I wasn't sleeping. Not sure if I'll be able to. Bottom line, I've done my nighttime routine."

He nodded. "If that's the case, don't let me stop you from watching TV."

I woke with a jolt, fear tightening my every muscle. My living room was lit by the smart TV screen saver. I felt a hand resting on my hand which was at my belly near my hip. Seemed my muscles weren't as tight as I thought because feeling that hand, I tensed further.

Someone shushed me, then said, "It's okay, Victoria. You're okay."

Gamble.

How did this happen?

Earlier, I had put on *The Mandalorian*, thinking Gamble might like it, and I loved "the child" so bonus for me. At some point I caught myself as my head lolled to the side with my doze, but I did *not* recall leaning up against Gamble's solid bulk, or one of his legs bracketing mine. His other leg rested just under mine which made me comfier. As I took in our legs, I noticed his socked feet, so he'd taken his motorcycle boots off, too.

"Take a deep breath, kitten," he whispered.

I did as ordered and I felt myself loosen up a little.

My eyes hadn't left our legs. I liked the looks of them. His solid weight behind me felt good. No, great. He felt like security, even if it was clear I didn't need it in my living room.

His hand gave mine a squeeze. "What woke you?"

I just stopped myself from saying 'I don't know' because I suddenly did know. "I had a... I wouldn't call it a dream. It felt more like a memory inserted itself into whatever I might have been dreaming."

"Could you see who was in that memory?"

For a moment I closed my eyes. "No."

I felt his body move as he nodded his head. "That's all right. You gonna climb into bed now?"

"How did we get like this?" I blurted.

His body moved again with his chuckle. "You fell to the side and that *really* didn't look comfortable. I wasn't about to lay you out here and take your bed, so... I put that chair-pillow thing under you, but you didn't seem to like it."

"Why didn't I wake up?"

"I don't know, but that left me with few options. Once I had my boots off, I positioned you pretty much the way we are now and that was maybe half an hour ago."

"Really?"

"Yeah. Get yourself into your pajamas or whatever and go to bed."

I wasn't putting on my pajamas. The yoga pants I wore were as comfortable as anything else I owned. And if I were honest, I forced myself to wear the yoga pants because otherwise I feared I would never put on my running pants again.

I pried myself away from his warm body and stood up. He rose, turned around, and pointed down the hall toward my office. "There a bathroom down here?"

"Yes, first door on your left," I called.

I stood rooted to the spot for what felt like forever, but was probably ninety seconds. Then I went to the kitchen, grabbed two glasses, and filled both with water.

By the time I filled the second one, Gamble had come back. His leather cut was in his hand. He draped it on a stool in front of the breakfast bar.

He did a double take when he caught sight of me. "What are you doing, Vic?"

I took a deep breath and hoped he wouldn't hate me. "This will sound really freaking strange —especially since you don't like me— but, I really would prefer if you were in my bed."

That didn't sound right to me, and I added, "I mean, sleeping next to me. Just, you know, sleeping."

He kept quiet for a long moment.

In a small voice I said, "It's not that I'm scared, but it... you... I don't know how to explain it—"

"You don't need to explain it, Victoria. Go, get in your bed. I'll be there in a moment."

"You, uh... You will?"

He nodded. "Yeah. Gotta run down to my bike. Should have a toothbrush there. I'll be back up."

While he went downstairs, I snuggled under my covers (and his blanket) on the right side of the bed. I left my lamp on so he could see.

After he closed the main door, I heard him in the bathroom. He came into my room without his boots based on the sound of his footsteps. His belt was missing from his jeans, and he carried something at his side.

"You travel with your toothbrush? Your dentist must be pleased." I said in a playful tone, not expecting a response.

"I keep a spare in my saddlebag, but I also had to get my gun," he said, putting a matte black firearm on the nightstand.

I stared at it. My Uncle Mick was all about guns and gun safety. I wasn't kidding when I said Heidi was filling in for him today. But, I was rather ambivalent. I didn't own one. To my mind, I didn't have a need for it. And I knew it could be wrestled away from me if I wasn't willing to pull the trigger.

During my time in law school and doing internships, I'd seen photographic evidence of gunshot wounds. I could look at those images in a clinical and removed way for the sake of presenting a case. But my reactions said it all. I didn't have it in me to use a gun... though the pain in my nose, ribs, and more private places besides might make me change my tune.

"You got an issue with guns?" he asked. His voice was so firm it almost sounded like he was disgusted by the idea that I might say yes.

I shook my head. "Not really. I'm a little surprised that you carry a gun with you."

His blue eyes bored into me for a moment. "My club has cleaned up our act, but that doesn't mean assholes don't come after us. Or see us as open targets. I'm not anybody's target. And neither are you."

The easy way he included me in his statement struck me strange, but I nodded. His eyes darted to the foot of the bed, and I knew he'd made note of his blanket sitting on top of the comforter.

"Hit the light, Victoria."

I gave him a look since he wasn't in the bed yet, but he returned my look and added a chin dip. As I rolled toward the nightstand I halted because the outside of my right arm hurt when I put pressure there. Fiona had mentioned that when I was dumped from the car, I'd landed on that side. Going up on an elbow, I tagged the lamp.

Once the room was dark, I heard the rustle of Gamble's clothes. Then the covers moved, and the bed jostled as Gamble got in.

I rolled to my left, toward Gamble, but I kept my distance.

After a long moment, he spoke in a low voice. "Never said I don't like you, kitten."

"What?" I whispered.

"Earlier, when you tried to explain yourself, you said 'especially since you don't like me.' I don't know what's put that in your head."

I scoffed. "I'm sure you can guess."

The bed shook and I knew he was chuckling silently. "Fair enough. But, don't think that I don't like you. That isn't true."

"Duly noted... Gage."

He grunted into the dark. I didn't blame him. I wasn't used to calling him that yet. Then he said, "Goodnight, kitten."

Gamble

If Gamble thought last night was torture not being next to her, he found he was dead wrong. *This* was torture. She had curled onto her side facing him tempting him to do the same. Her blackened eyes and taped nose served to anger him and remind him how fragile she was. How fragile anyone was, but especially women.

In a bizarre and perverse way, those injuries, despite their ugliness, enhanced her beauty. She had endured, she was healing, and he knew she would overcome it. He knew she wouldn't see it that way, and being a lawyer, she'd argue it to death. Part of him wanted to engage in that argument, but he knew better.

He wasn't the man life had in store for her. She deserved a man as upstanding as she was. When the Riot cleaned up their act, Gamble did the same... to an extent. He was morally dubious. Or morally skeptical was more like it. He believed in minimal law and order. The fact rapists, child molesters, and murderers could get parole had destroyed his belief in justice over a decade ago.

As he lay there fighting an urge to drape an arm over her waist, he felt the jerk of her body through the bed.

He expected her breathing to change, but it didn't. She settled and after a moment he knew she was out.

With a sigh, he forced himself to close his eyes and mimic her breathing.

It felt like five minutes later that he woke to Victoria thrashing in the bed.

Memories assailed him of his sister battling the same thing. He recalled how he'd calmed Brittney, and he prayed the same would work with Victoria.

"Victoria," he called.

She didn't respond. He added a thread of steel to his voice and repeated her name.

He put a gentle hand to her shoulder, praying they hadn't held her down there.

The thrashing slowed, but she was still out of it.

"Victoria, it's me, Gamble. Wake up."

She gasped and her body stilled.

He stroked her shoulder. "You're okay, Vic. Guessing you had a night terror."

"Yeah," she croaked.

In the dim light, he didn't see the outline of a glass. He flung the covers off his legs and went to the kitchen. Her glass sat next to the sink, and he filled it with water from the fridge dispenser.

He trudged to her side of the bed noticing she lay staring at the ceiling. Her breathing seemed a little labored.

"Mind if I sit?" he asked.

She exhaled hard. "No. I mean, you were just lying next to me."

He sat on the edge of the bed near her hip. "Victoria, those fuckers stole all of your choices and freedom yesterday. I won't assume shit where you're concerned. If you need space or don't want a man near you, I get that. I respect that, and I'm gonna ask you rather than impose on you in any way. Got it?"

"Yeah," she said, her voice heavy with emotion.

"Sit up and have some water."

She scooted up the bed, grabbed the water from him, and took three long swallows. He took it from her and placed it on the nightstand. As much as he wanted to let her get back to sleep, he had to push at what she might know.

"Did you see anyone in this one?"

She sighed. "Not really. I know there was more than one." Her voice broke on the word 'more,' and he took a deep breath.

"All right. Not going to ask you for—"

"I swear I saw tattoos. But that doesn't help much because I know they had my head covered the whole time. It felt like I saw flashes through a gap in the bag, so it's probably my subconscious putting ink on them, right?"

Reflexively he patted her thigh, but he jerked his hand back. "It could be."

She slouched down. "I hate that I don't know who did this. And then I hate myself for that! In a way, I'm better off not knowing, aren't I? Except I can't press charges against anyone if I never saw them, can I?"

He twisted at the waist, put his hand on the opposite side of her hip, and leaned toward her. "Kitten, I can tell you who did this. Juan Abeyeta has a limited posse."

In the dimness he saw her head push back into the pillow. "Juan Abeyeta? His brother is in jail because *I* can't do my job very well. What's he got to do— They attacked me because I failed?"

He wanted to kick his ass for the shit he said to her in that parking garage.

"Victoria, you didn't fail. That asshole is guilty of that crime, and God knows at least fifty others. You must have forgotten. They addressed you to me, and they told me to stop fucking with Juan."

After a moment, she exhaled hard. "How are you fucking with Juan? He's in jail. That's ridiculous."

He wanted to smile. How she did that to him, he didn't know. Fucked up situation and he wanted to smile because of her.

"Doesn't change that note. If you're pressing charges, I'll get the note to you, but I don't know what the cops can do with it. It got touched by me, Fiona, and probably four other people before we got you into my bed."

She blew out a raspberry. "And how many other men out there are named Juan? Still, it would point the police in a direction. I don't think my boss is going to let this slide."

"You talk to your boss?"

"No, she never Skyped me back."

He shook his head. "Skyped you back?"

"I don't have my phone. Fiona and Abby were going to look for it."

He fought a groan. "You have to press charges. I'll tell the cops about Juan and his crew. And, before I leave, I'll call Fiona. Hell, I can go look now—"

She touched his forearm. "No. It's bad enough I forced you to sleep in my bed. You should rest if you can."

"Pretty sure you're the one who needs some sleep, kitten," he said standing.

Enough moonlight shone into the room that as he rounded the bed, he caught her eyes following him. Or following his ass to be precise.

That was knowledge he didn't need.

He picked up his phone and saw it was just after two in the morning. With a sigh, he went to her guest bathroom, used the facilities, and returned to her bedroom.

She had followed his lead, and came out of her master bath. In a brief flicker of light, he caught sight of her still wearing her yoga pants and tank top.

Once she settled on her side again, he asked, "Why didn't you put on pajamas, Victoria?"

"I didn't want to," she whispered.

That didn't ring true to his ears, but he let it slide.

"Why do you ask?"

"Figured you'd want to be comfortable at night."

After a moment, she said, "Wimpy as it sounds, I want to be secure."

He felt his brows furrow.

She continued, "I have scratches on my... hips, where they struggled with my pants. It didn't stop them, obviously, but I've always loved my exercise pants and I'm afraid if I don't keep myself in the habit of wearing stretchy but tight pants, I won't wear my running leggings again. Does that make sense? I'm babbling, of course it makes zero sense."

He lost his fight to stay away from her. Propping his head in his hand, he rolled to his side toward her. "Honey, you don't have to make sense to me or any-damn-body else. If that gets you through, then that's what gets you through each day."

She looked up at him and let out a breath that sounded relieved. "As much as I hate that your sister went through what I did, I'm grateful that you're here to help me because of it."

That pissed him off and left him feeling strangely grateful too. Not in a million years did he expect to ever feel that way about what happened to Brittney so long ago.

He gentled his voice. "I meant what I said yesterday. I'm gonna help you through this as much as I can. Now, let's go to sleep. I gotta get up at six, so I can maybe catch a few more hours of sleep."

"Okay, Gamble. And, if I haven't said it, thank you."

He reached out and gave her shoulder a squeeze. "Don't thank me. Sleep well."

48

After he drew his hand away, she stared at him in the dimness. Her words about wanting to be secure echoed in his mind. Before he could think better of it, he asked, "Would you like a... like me to hold you? Until you fall asleep?"

He heard her inhale hitch. Then she said, "Yes, please."

That made him fight laughing. Like she'd need to say please to any man holding her.

As gently as he could, he snaked an arm under her shoulders and drew her to him. To his surprise, she burrowed into him. Her nose was close his collar bone.

She drew back. "You always sleep shirtless?"

"Can't say I'm sleeping, Vic."

She made a small groaning noise. Then rested her head against his shoulder again.

It didn't take long for her to fall asleep. He'd meant to extricate himself from her hold. Yet, he knew a fleeting opportunity when it came along, so he let himself have just two more minutes.

Two more minutes in which he fell asleep.

He woke to sunlight and Victoria's dark hair tickling his face. From the sunlight, he knew he was late, and he wondered why his alarm didn't go off.

From the way his lips were so close to Victoria's neck, they must have shifted in the night. He inhaled her scent. She smelled like sugar cookies. Before he knew it, he was nuzzling her neck.

Then he realized the *last* thing he should be doing is nuzzling her anywhere.

He pulled away to find the skin surrounding her hazel eyes crinkled. His eyes moved down her face to her lips. A big smile on her face.

"That was sweet," she whispered.

He looked away, sighing. "It wasn't sweet. Took a fair amount of control for me to back off because what I wanted to do is completely wrong, regardless of timing."

That brought her up short. She pulled away from him and got out of bed. "I disagree, but I'll grant you the timing is bad."

Only after the bathroom door closed behind her did he grab his phone and fire off a text to Har. He wouldn't be into the shop at six-thirty like he normally was. Holding his phone, he recalled hers was still missing. He shot a text to Cynic to have Fiona call him when she was up and moving.

His phone dinged with a message from Har.

No problem, man. It's a good morning to be late.

Something about that message struck him. His guess, Har was getting busy with Stephanie. He quickly sent another message.

If Steph has the day off, think she'd mind hanging with Victoria? I need to search for Victoria's phone.

Har's response came much quicker than the last.

Not sure how you knew she's off, but she says that'd be cool.

His lips tipped up. Men could be damned predictable, but he'd never tell his president that.

Another message came through from Har. Stephanie would be there within half an hour, once Gamble provided Victoria's address.

That done, he went to the guest bathroom to brush his teeth.

He exited the bathroom to find Victoria making coffee. Her coffee maker sat next to the fridge. He leaned his ass against the opposite counter, crossed his arms, and waited for her to finish.

She flipped the switch and turned to him. "What's up?"

"Your friend swinging by today?"

"No. I don't want to be a bother."

He nodded. "You would not be a bother, Vic. Need you to get that out of your head."

"I'm not the first woman to be—"

"No," he clipped out. "It's fresh. It's raw. Don't be a martyr. Someone else should be with you today."

She looked up at him with a forlorn expression, an expression so strong he could practically hear her ask, "But why?"

Even though she didn't speak, he said, "You especially need someone if you're gonna press charges. My president's old lady is comin' by soon. Be good if you get someone else to stick close tonight."

Her expression bordered on alarm. "Why? I mean, I understand if you have plans, but, um—"

"It's gotta be someone else, kitten. In case you forgot from last night, I don't hate you. But if I come back tonight, I'll hate *myself* because I can't be trusted."

He nearly laughed at her wrinkled brows.

"You can't?"

His chin dipped. "This morning proves that, Victoria."

She had her mouth open to argue, but a knock sounded at the door.

He had to admit, Stephanie had stellar timing.

Chapter 5

Protective

Victoria

One thing I knew for certain that morning, I had to keep my stupid facial expressions to myself. Gamble could read me like a damn book. From me wanting (more like needing) to be held to me wanting (also more like needing) him to come back tonight.

Hearing that he didn't dislike me made me feel fantastic. Feeling his beard against my neck this morning, made me feel fantastic in better ways. Seeing the look on his face when he abruptly pulled away doused those feelings like a bucket of ice water.

I watched as Gamble strode to my door. He'd put on his jeans, but hadn't pulled on his t-shirt. I knew his chest was inked, bulky, and burly, though I didn't allow myself to examine his tattooed chest because that felt intrusive. But the beauty of his back demanded my attention. His muscle structure was so defined I wanted to trace it with my fingers at a minimum. In the back recess of my mind, I imagined running my tongue along those ridges instead. Unlike portions of his torso, he had no tattoos on his back. Such a stark contrast enhanced his appeal.

Gamble opened the door, interrupting my contemplation of his tattoos (or absence thereof).

A woman who appeared to be my age walked in holding one of my favorite sights in the morning –a brown paper bag from Panera. She had the most beautiful curly brown hair I'd ever seen. Gamble took the bag from her and came to the kitchen while she toed off her flip-flops at the door. She looked like she was ready to hit the beach in her khaki-colored shorts and a purple tank-top.

As she entered the apartment, she smiled at me which made her hazel eyes twinkle. "Would have done donuts, but I didn't know your preferences. Bagels just seemed easier," she paused as a thought struck her. "You aren't gluten free are you? I should have—"

I interrupted her rambling. "No. I'm anything but gluten-free. My godfather would lose his mind if I ever changed my diet like that."

She held out her hand to me. "Hi, I'm Stephanie."

I shook her hand. "I'm Victoria. Thank you for the bagels. And for coming by."

She dropped my hand only to shoot me a stern glare. "Girl... stop. You sound so formal. I'm not in a court room. Bringing you bagels is nothing."

I arched a brow at her. "But you don't know me."

She grinned and the twinkle returned to her eyes. "I know you can rock a pantsuit like nobody's business. You like great pizza. And, whether you like it or not, Monday night you gained a *bunch* of new friends."

My jaw dropped and Gamble stepped forward. "Steph, thinking you're coming on too strong."

She laughed a throaty laugh. I wished I could pull that off because it was sexy as hell. "No, G. Bringing Kenzie and Sandy with me would be coming on strong."

Gamble gave her a hard look for a while. "Kenzie would have been okay. But I can't argue with you, Sandy would have Victoria pulling her covers over her head."

Stephanie's smile turned sly. "More like you running for cover."

Gamble's eyes widened at her, but she was focused on me.

I shook my head. "Would you like a cup of coffee?"

"Absolutely!"

I poured her a cup and heard Gamble close the door to the bathroom. Since I had the creamer out for my coffee, Stephanie doctored hers.

Gamble's words from before Stephanie showed up rattled around in my head. The idea that he didn't trust himself around me raised a red flag. He'd spent the last six hours next to me and the night prior he'd slept next to me, too. It was on the floor, but it was still right next to me. No matter what he thought, Gamble could be trusted.

He came out of the bathroom, grabbed his cut from the stool and shrugged it on while nabbing a bagel. "Victoria, I need your cell number. Hoping it still has a charge and that'll help me find it. Fiona meant to ask you for that info yesterday, but didn't have a way to get back in touch with you. Short of comin' by here, and even then, she didn't know your unit number."

That was a fine point. "How did *you* know my unit number yesterday?"

He grinned. "I followed you to your vehicle. Saw a similar car in a parking spot. Spaces are assigned with unit numbers on the lot. I made an educated guess. Fiona had no way of knowing your vehicle, though, to make the same deduction."

I cocked a brow, then I gave him my phone number.

"My older sister would tell me to have some couth or something, but I just don't pussyfoot around about things. I was violated —in a different way— quite a while ago, but it was scary enough. Even though I have no idea what you're going through right now, I know what it feels like to have your power taken away from you," Stephanie said.

I swallowed. "Okay."

"My point is that if you want to talk about it, I'm more than willing to listen. And that's what Suzy would have told me to say to start with, but like Gamble mentioned, I can come on a little strong."

Something about that last statement made me smile. "Thank you. I appreciate that. Um, I need to take a shower, get on my computer, and hopefully talk to my boss."

She nodded. "Have at it, chica. I'll hold down the fort."

My eyes slid to the side and back to her. "Um, Gamble just left, and you pretty much just got here. I feel bad just—"

She tossed a hand out at me. "I've got coffee, need to fix my bagel. And I've got my phone. It has a reading app on it, so I'll be fine. Har is *not* a reader, and I never knew how much that would cramp my style. Not that I'm complaining. He's good at distracting me in the bedroom... sorry, that's insensitive of me."

I shook my head. "No, it isn't insensitive of you. What happened to me was violence that happens to be sexual in nature. It isn't the same as hearing a girlfriend has a good man in her bedroom. So, I'm happy you have that. Even if we basically just met."

She cocked a brow. "That's a good outlook. Think you're trying to convince yourself more than me, but I'll let you get to it. And it doesn't matter if we 'just met.' I wasn't joking. You got yourself five new girl-friends, whether you like it or not."

I did a long blink. She ignored my blink, tore off a paper towel, put a bagel on top of it and slathered it with cream cheese. On that note, I hustled to my bathroom to shower.

Gamble

It boggled Gamble's mind. Victoria's phone held a charge for the past day and a half, which meant he heard it ring when he called. Within twenty minutes of trekking up and down the alley, he held her phone in his hand.

Though, the phone died not five seconds later. He tucked it into a hard-sided saddle bag on his bike and left the alley. If he hung around there much longer he'd only work himself into a worse temper. He was going to have a serious conversation with her... his body went taut at the idea. As much as he wanted to ask her why she ran so far from her own home, it wasn't his place. He cared that she ran a good six miles from her home, but he had no business insisting she stop.

After he left the back alley, Gamble swung by Har's body shop. It was on the way to returning Vic's phone to her, but he needed a breather. She'd done okay thus far without her phone, she could wait until lunch for him to drop it off.

He had a bike that needed a clear-coat before the owner could pick it up. Rather than call Har about the paint work, he'd tell him face-to-face. His mind wasn't completely with it between his lack of sleep and feeling responsible for Victoria's situation. With those things in mind, he found himself grateful that his day should be relatively easy.

As he put the kickstand down on his bike, he noticed Roman's bike and Cynic's chopper were in the lot.

He forced himself to go inside to Har's office and say hey to his brothers.

Standing in the doorway to Har's inner-sanctum, the three men gave Gamble assessing stares.

"You all right, man?" Har asked.

"You look like you haven't slept in three days," Roman observed.

He nodded. "That's because I haven't, though it's only been two days."

"Why didn't you sleep last night?" Cynic asked.

His instincts told him he was setting himself up for a hard time, but he admitted to staying at Victoria's.

All three men left it alone.

"You got someone watching her place now?" Roman asked.

He shook his head. "Not yet, but I don't think they'll pull any shit during broad daylight. Stephanie came by, and I'm hoping Fiona can come by when Steph needs to leave."

"Has she reported the crime yet?" Har asked.

Gamble shook his head. "Not yet, but she'll probably do it soon. Said her boss wouldn't let it go unreported."

He saw Cynic nodding, heard Roman sigh, but Har pointing at him stole his attention. "Be better if you go down there and report it before her."

Those words were a sucker punch. Three years ago, they were neck deep in dealing marijuana and there wasn't a chance they'd go out of their way to report anything to the police.

The idea of walking into the police station to pave the way for Victoria felt wrong in many ways... and yet, it felt almost protective. It wouldn't protect her from anything outright, but it would damn sure make things easier –which was protection of its own kind.

He'd told her more than once he would help her. Making this easier for her, was the very least he could do.

"You're right. Got a Road King that just needs a last clear-coat—"

Har shook his head. "Done, man. Don't worry about it."

Roman pulled out his cell. "Trinity's best friend is dating Dennizen. Could have her ask him to take Victoria's statement."

"Thought he was homicide," Cynic muttered.

Roman shot him a devious grin. "That's why Olivia needs to ask. Who gives a shit what department they're in? Crime is crime. I'm sure when Olivia mentions it to him, Detective Dennizen will find a way to help out."

"Do that," Gamble said. "Even if his hands are tied, anything to help Victoria is appreciated."

"That sounds innocent, but why do I get the impression there's more to it?" Har asked.

He shook his head. "There isn't, Prez."

Cynic chuckled. "He's lying. Did you see him carry her to his room?"

"Shut it, 'Nic. I don't give a damn if you're the sergeant-at-arms or not. Any woman gets dumped like she was, I'm gonna get her the fuck off the ground."

"Yeah, but would you—"

Har and Roman giving Cynic looks shut him up.

"Roman, if your woman can help me out, I'd appreciate it. Then I'll head down to see Dennizen, or whoever is taking Victoria's statement."

Roman had his cell halfway to his ear. "You got it, man. Where you headed?"

"I found Victoria's phone in the alley where they nabbed her. Gonna take it back to her, then give my statement."

CHAPTER 6

SAVING THE DAY

VICTORIA

S tephanie put her phone on the coffee table. "That is some bullshit, if you don't mind my saying. Sorry, I couldn't help but eavesdrop."

I chuckled. "Yeah. Short of standing in the breezeway, you'd be hard pressed not to hear that. But, it isn't bullshit."

"Sounds like it to me. You're being pulled from a case you've been working on for weeks now because you've got a black eye."

"And a broken nose," I added. "Believe it or not, impressions matter with juries. If I look like one of my clients beat me up, while it's not a given that it won't go well for us, it's certainly not going to help us."

Two minutes ago, I'd gotten off a Skype call with my boss. She took one good look at my face and gasped. Then she launched in on how I wouldn't be defending counsel for an upcoming case next week. I had expected that. What I hadn't expected was having an audience when my boss told me as much.

Stephanie's lips pursed and she looked cute with such a pouty face. "You would know better than me about juries. But I still think it's wrong. And... well, I'll shut up."

I shook my head. "No, no. You've been so vocal thus far. Let's have the rest of it, Steph."

She grinned. "About time you called me Steph. But, I hate that you've been banished to what sounds like desk duty because of an attack that was completely out of your control."

I nodded. "You're right, but the same thing would happen if it had been a car accident."

"That shouldn't factor either," Stephanie cried.

"But it does."

She sat up from the corner of my sofa where she'd been slouched reading. I knew she had something else to say, but the brass door knocker drew our attention.

Through the peephole, I saw Gamble standing in the breezeway.

I opened the door. "Hi. Did you forget your bagel?"

His eyes did a full body scan before he frowned. Then he came inside, closing and locking my door behind him.

"Why are you dressed? You going to the office?"

I shook my head. "No. I had a Skype call with my boss."

He shook his head and held his hand out toward me. "The battery died right after I found it. Don't know if it got run over or something in that alley, but the screen is cracked, and it definitely needs a charge."

In his palm sat a phone that had to be mine. I grinned so big I couldn't stand it. When did my entire life start revolving around a rectangular gadget? It was pathetic, but the amount of relief I felt couldn't be described.

Rather than grab my phone, my hands went to his bearded cheeks, and I said, "I could kiss you!"

His eyes and his nostrils flared before he gently pulled his face out of my hold.

After an awkward moment, in a husky voice he said, "That's good, but take your phone, Vic."

I plucked my phone out of his hand and scurried off to a corner of the kitchen where I charged my devices.

"Well, aren't you the hero saving the day?" Stephanie asked.

"Goin' a little too far there, Steph," he grumbled.

I turned around. "I definitely owe you one for finding my phone, Gage. Thank you for that."

Stephanie spluttered.

Gamble glared at her. "Shut it, Steph." Then, he looked at me. "Gonna help you, Vic. You don't owe me shit. Later."

"Wait! Where are you going?" Stephanie asked.

He glanced over his shoulder at her. "Not gonna be here when she reports the crime."

Stephanie's glare said it all, and what it said was that 'here' was exactly where he should be when I reported my rape.

As though he read the same message from Steph, Gamble shook his head. "Fiona's comin' by at lunch. Between you and her, I'm sure you can help Victoria make it through."

Stephanie just stared at him for a while. Then, "Not half as well as you could...*Gage*."

His jaw clenched. He blew out a big exhale and said, "Later." His blue eyes hit me and the annoyance they contained dissipated. "Lock the door behind me, Victoria."

At the door, I made the mistake of muttering, "I haven't decided if I'm reporting this yet."

He bent toward me, so we were eye-to-eye. "Do not let them get away with this shit, kitten."

I opened my mouth to argue, but he lifted a finger.

"Doesn't seem that way now, but it will give you closure. You need that no matter how much you think you don't. If I could report it for you or press charges for you, I would, but I can't, sweetheart. You got this. I know you do. And God knows, if you don't, Steph and Fi will get you through it."

He made a convincing case, but I still wanted to argue. Problem was, I couldn't collect my thoughts quickly enough. Suddenly, he came closer, ever so gently kissed my cheek, and straightened. "Take care, Victoria."

He delivered that last so firmly I knew he wasn't coming back. Not tonight. Not tomorrow night. Probably not ever.

Shit!

I couldn't control the amount of dread I felt at not seeing him again. Why did I do such stupid shit like this? Like latching on to a man who —even if he didn't hate me— made it clear we had boundaries.

If there were boundaries, then what was with this morning's neck nuzzles? The devious part of my brain asked.

His hand cupped my cheek, pulling me from my thoughts. "Bye, kitten."

"Bye," I whispered.

The chatter between Fiona and Stephanie served as background noise. I wandered to the kitchen. While there, I checked on my phone. Aside from the large crack down the screen, now that it had a half of a charge, everything seemed all-systems go. I had a number of missed calls. Most from Heidi, a few from Royce, and two from the office. But the most recently-missed call came from a local number not in my contacts. A number I knew belonged to Gamble.

I couldn't decide if I should save his contact info or forget all about it.

"I'd save that if I were you," Fiona murmured from my other side, making me jump a foot in the air.

Her eyes widened. "Sorry. Sorry. Thought you heard me come up behind you."

I put a hand on my chest as I deep breathed. "No, I didn't realize. Sorry."

The small smile on her face said I hadn't hidden anything from her.

"Are you sure what you collected Monday night can be analyzed still? It's Wednesday now."

Her face sombered and she nodded. "Yeah. We're cutting it close at this stage, but you report the crime, it can be examined."

I nodded.

"This may seem out of the blue, but you are more than what happened to you. It's important for you to know that, Victoria."

My body stilled. "Yes. I... I know you're right."

She sighed. "Not sure if you were conscious or not for this, but when we found you, Abby and I –she's an ER nurse in another city– we both wanted to take you to a hospital. And this is just one of the many reasons why we should have done that."

I shook my head. "I'm kind of glad they kept me at the clubhouse."

Her head wobbled as she thought about that. "Yeah, but if you'd been in an ER, a victim's advocate would have been notified and very likely someone from psych would have been called in to help you."

It was on the tip of my tongue to say I was fine, but I knew better.

She continued. "When you report this, it might take a toll. That's part of why I'm here."

I nodded. "You are really cool, Fiona. Thanks."

She squeezed my bicep. "Don't thank me. Do you need a list of counselors? That's a stupid question. I'll get you a list of some people. I'm not sure if these ladies specialize in sexual assault, but they do handle PTSD and other traumas, so I think they could help."

Her blue eyes were so sincere and concerned, I couldn't keep eye contact. "Thanks. That will help."

"Hey, don't hang your head like that, Victoria."

I looked back at her. "Gamble thinks I need someone here at night."

She nodded slowly. "He might be right. Was someone here last night?"

"He was," I whispered. "But he told me to find someone else tonight."

She exhaled in such a way, I knew she had something to say about that.

"I guess I'll stay with my parents tonight, but that feels like I'm delaying the inevitable."

Stephanie came into the kitchen. "Do they know what happened to you?"

"Not yet," I muttered, dreading that conversation.

Fiona sighed. "I don't know what your relationship with them is like, but if it's the least bit loving, you can't go wrong with their support."

A skeptical look crossed Stephanie's face. "I shouldn't say this, but if your relationship is anything like mine with my mom, you might want to keep it to yourself."

Fiona shrugged. "I'm not much help here. My mom abandoned me with my dad, but only you can make that decision, Victoria. We should probably hit the police station soon."

"Let me get my purse," I said.

Dad and Mom sat frozen on my denim-blue sofa. I'd just recounted what happened Monday night. It should have made me feel... a little better, but instead I felt overwhelming guilt because Dad looked like his heart was broken. Part of me felt dirty again, but as Heidi and Stephanie had pointed out, I couldn't give my attackers that power. Though, even if I wasn't as dirty as I felt, 'powering past' this feeling was easier said than done.

Dad rested his elbows on his knees, then his hands tore through his thinning hair. When he raised his head, his eyes held a mix of anger and remorse. "I failed you, pumpkin."

I shook my head. "No, Dad. It's nobody's fault but the men who attacked me."

Mom sighed. "I knew being in criminal defense would get you in trouble."

Dad stared at Mom like she'd materialized from outer space.

Mom persisted. "Your sister hasn't been raped and dropped at a biker bar."

"It wasn't a biker bar," I blurted stupidly. Where I was dropped after the fact was completely irrelevant.

"You weren't joking," Dad whispered.

My mouth dropped open and I stared at Dad.

He said, "She plays favorites. Jesus, Erin! How could you say shit like that?"

"Now, Henry—"

Dad stood, shaking his head. "No. We're leaving."

"We just got here," Mom said.

"Yeah. And you're causing more stress for her. I'm taking you home and," he looked at me, "I'll come back so you can talk to your pop about it."

"Dad, it's..." I trailed off.

I stopped myself from saying 'all right' because it wasn't. My mother's words were far from okay. I needed my mom. But only if she was going to be supportive.

His head swiveled to me. The ravaged look on his face should have undone my mother. How could she be impervious to that?

"It's what?" he asked, standing in front of me with his arms open to me.

I stood, taking a much-needed hug. "I need you both here. Or at least until Heidi gets here."

Dad sat down in the center of the couch, with me beside him. "Did you call Miranda?"

Mom leaned forward. "She isn't calling and messing up the last of Miranda's education."

"She needs support," Dad said. Then he added, "From *all* of us."

I closed my eyes. Maybe Dad had been right before. He needed to get Mom out of here. Being stuck between them intensified my guilt. Not to mention, it didn't help me feel any better.

Mom sighed. "It isn't that she doesn't have my support."

I spoke before Dad argued. "Don't worry. I'm not going to bug Miranda with this. I'd rather her be here when I tell her."

"This is your private business. Miranda doesn't need to know at all," Mom muttered.

My chest felt like a crater had opened up within me. It was hard enough to share this with them, but that brought on more shame —the last thing I needed.

"Where's the warm, loving woman I married?" Dad demanded.

I stood up. "Dad, you were right. You and Mom should go home. I'll talk to you both later."

Dad's eyes widened. "One of the most heinous crimes has been committed, and you're going to talk to me later?"

"I can't deal with the bickering."

He hung his head and sighed.

Mom whispered, "We weren't bickering."

After a blink, I caught Dad's eyes. "I spoke to a counselor briefly this afternoon. She recommended a support group. I'm glad you're willing to listen, Dad. I'll call you later."

"I'm being supportive, too, Victoria. It's just more than your sister needs to deal with right now," Mom muttered.

My mouth ran away from me. "And what about the things I need to deal with, Mom?"

Mom shook her head. "Miranda will insist on flying home from California. We all want to support you, Victoria. Just... let her finish her residency in peace."

I blinked hard against feelings of guilt and anger from Mom's words.

"Let's go," Dad clipped out.

He gave me another hug, pressing a kiss on my forehead for a long moment. "Love you more than you'll ever know, pumpkin."

"I know, Dad," I whispered.

"Get some rest, sweetheart."

After he let me go, Mom wrapped me up in her arms. "I love you, too, Victoria."

That was the thing. She did love me, but it felt like she loved herself more. Or... she somehow didn't know how to love her children as deeply as Dad did.

It was weird, but over the years I'd come to realize that was all on her. There wasn't anything I could do about it and pointing it out to her only put her on the defensive.

I hugged her tighter. "Love you, Mom."

She pulled away. "You can stay at the house, honey. Anytime."

I nodded. "I know, but I need to fight this head-on. Or as much as I can, anyway."

Her lips twisted to the side like she had something to say to that, but Dad opened the door. "Let's go, Erin."

Heidi showed up twenty minutes after my parents left. She tossed her duffel bag on my sofa and turned to me. "Why didn't you ask me to stay last night?"

I shrugged. "I didn't think about it. Then, when Gamble found out you'd gone home, he came up. In fact, he suggested I have you come back, but I wasn't cool with that, so he stayed."

Her lips puffed out in a strange pout. "Okay. And why isn't he here tonight?"

I pressed my lips together. "He just couldn't be here tonight. I'm sorry if—"

"Vickie don't say you're sorry one more time around me. You're going through some tough-ass shit. God forbid, but I'll probably go through some tough shit at some point, and I'll need you around. It's all fair in love and war, and I love you like the sister I never had. Now. Why couldn't Gamble be here?"

"Please let it go," I whispered.

Her eyes widened. "Did he hurt you?"

"No!"

"Then what's his problem?"

My eyes slid to the side. "He doesn't trust himself. Even though I know he's more trustworthy than he realizes."

She scoffed. "That's lame. Anyone can sleep on a couch. He's a douche."

I glared at her. "I insisted he sleep in my bed. But *just* sleep."

She withstood my glare and raised her eyebrow. "Sleeping next to you isn't a hardship either, Vic."

Irrational emotions welled up inside me and I did my best to tamp them down. "It is difficult when I take him up on his offer to hold me, and he wakes up nuzzling my neck. I enjoyed it, but he beat himself up over being so damned weak. Satisfied, now? You got the whole story."

Her face fell and I felt like a jackass.

"Sorry," I said.

"Don't say that! I shouldn't have pushed. You got any vodka? We should get good and sloshed."

"No. Besides, I'm going to—"

"You aren't going to work tomorrow."

I opened my mouth to argue, but Heidi held up a finger.

"Nope. Forget it. You get sick days for a reason, Vickie. So, you can take care of yourself... but you seem to have forgotten that 'self-care' is a form of taking care. You might not have a fever, but you're hurt and injured. You need to take time for some self-care."

"Right," I whispered.

"And, I don't know about this biker. On the one hand he's stupid to give up the chance to take care of you, but on the other hand, he might be incredibly smart because giving you space is the most sensitive thing he could do."

A wan smile curled my lips. "His sister was—"

Heidi held up a hand. "Yeah, but you aren't his sister. Hell, that's all the more reason for him to stick around, but it's nearly a stroke of genius to play it this way."

"He's not playing," I said, more of an edge to my voice than I'd intended.

She shook her head. "I know, but I'm trying to keep our eyes open here."

It didn't feel that way, but I was in no mood to bicker with anyone. My parents had done enough of that already.

Heidi grinned at me. "Do you need me to snuggle with you tonight?"

I rolled my eyes. "Lovely as that sounds, I'll pass."

"Then I'm going to bed. It's been a long week and it's only Wednesday."

CHAPTER 7

STEP BACK

VICTORIA

Royce's eyes darted to a spot behind me. We were in the third week of the basketball summer session, so it wasn't unusual for him to look at parents or players who might be against the wall.

"Who the fuck is that guy?" he asked. Even over the squeak of sneakers and thud of basketballs, I heard the malice in his voice. I wouldn't have believed it was Royce, if I hadn't seen him speak.

I looked over my shoulder. Four feet from the gym entrance, Gamble leaned against the wall. Right behind our portable scoreboard-slash-game clock. He had a booted foot to the wall and his head bowed to his phone. His bicep bulged as he held the device. He wore his club cut along with a maroon t-shirt and a pair of well-worn jeans. His spiky hair looked shiny, like he'd just showered or put fresh gel in it.

I hadn't seen him since he gave me my phone, three and a half weeks ago. Seeing him here thrilled me and for some stupid reason it had me blushing.

"He the asshole who fucked you up?" Royce demanded.

I whipped my head back around to him. "No! He isn't. Don't curse around the kids. Why would you think—"

"You're suddenly pink as can be. Noticed that happens when you're angry. Plus, he's a thug," he said, his voice rising.

I shook my head. "Stop. He isn't the person who did this to me. He and his... people are helping me. Or helped me, I guess."

This was true. The day I reported the rape, I found out Gamble had already submitted a statement. Because he did that, when Fiona and I showed, I didn't have to go through the awkwardness of announcing why I was there. They were expecting me. Another way he helped me without me even knowing about it.

Royce stared at me for a long moment. "What do you mean, 'his people'?"

The less Royce knew about Fiona helping me out, the better. I shook my head at him. "It doesn't matter. I don't know why he's here, but let's keep this practice moving."

With the exception of the first practice, I acted as more of a master of ceremonies for each session. While Royce went back to his group of eleven-year-olds, I jogged over to Gamble.

He looked up as I approached, a small smile on his face.

"What are you doing here?" I asked.

"I like the ponytail."

My eyes slid to the side as I frowned. When I looked back at him, he was smiling full-out.

"Gamble, I'm serious. Why are you here? Is something wrong?"

He shook his head. "No. Mensa mentioned he'd followed you here and what you were doing. I wanted to come check it out."

"Why?" I blurted.

The fact was, it didn't matter. Part of me thought I should ask him to leave. He didn't have a child at the practice, and it was just weird that he was here.

"You know why," he said.

"It's been weeks. I'm not going to get attacked here. I appreciate you keeping me safe, but nobody needs to follow me or watch my apartment. It's overkill."

70

"I'm not here to keep you safe, kitten." His eyes gazed past me. "You better get back out there. But thanks for telling your muscle that I'm not a thug."

My mouth dropped open as I blinked in surprise. "How do you know that?"

He grinned. "I read his lips. You shook your head while speaking. His expression changed just enough I knew you were making a case for me."

"You should go," I said.

Rather than listen to his response, I turned around and helped Heidi with her group.

She blew her whistle and told her group to get water. "That Gamble?" she asked.

"Yeah."

"Why's he back?" she asked.

Heidi had been cagey about her thoughts on Gamble. From her tone of voice now though, I suspected she didn't approve.

"I don't know. I told him to leave. Not like he has a kid here."

Heidi chuckled. "It's not like you can check every schmoe who walks in that door for whether they're related to a kid on the court. I like how he looks at you, though."

I gave her a dry look. "Gonna say he's sweet on me?"

She shook her head. "He's not sweet. He's hot for you, but he's holding it back. It's part of why I like it. Takes a lot for a man to hold that back."

I shook my head. "He's not hot for me, and you can't read that from how a man looks at a woman. You are too much, Heidi."

I turned toward Royce's team, but Heidi caught my arm before I could run off.

I looked into her green eyes.

"I'm serious, Vic. He wants you. And I'll tell you right now, there's something about him I don't like. I just can't put my finger on it."

I sighed. "Thanks. But it's not like that."

She let go of my arm and I jogged to the other end of the gym.

As I locked the door to the equipment room in the gymnasium, Royce sidled up to me.

"We need to call the cops on that motherfucker?"

I shook my head. Though, I wondered why Gamble had stuck around for the past three hours. "No, Royce. It's fine."

"Heidi said you told him to go, and he stayed. That does not say fine to me."

Why did Heidi have to run her mouth?

I faced Royce. The concern in his eyes overwhelmed me. Maybe Heidi was right about him.

"I appreciate you worrying about it, Royce. But, seriously, he's all right."

He pressed his lips together, but eventually he nodded.

We turned around to find Gamble sauntering our way. "Victoria. It might help if you introduce me. Put his mind at ease."

"Would have put my mind at ease if you'd just left when she asked you to."

Gamble shot me a confused look. "To be fair she said I *should* go, she didn't ask me to leave. It was more of a suggestion."

Royce turned toward me, outrage in his eyes. "And you think he's *all right*? He's over here splittin' hairs and shit."

I fought laughter.

"Don't you laugh, Vickie Victoria. This is serious bullshit," Royce said, stepping closer to me.

I took a deep breath. "Royce, this is Gamble. Gamble, this is Royce, one of my co-coaches."

Gamble held his hand out, and after a long moment, Royce shook it. "It's nice to meet you, man."

Royce nodded, but didn't say anything.

The three of us stood awkwardly, but I didn't have the heart to ask Royce to go.

Heidi spied us from across the gym. "Yo, Royce, come get your bag out of the way so I can lock the locker rooms."

Royce gave me an irritated look, then pinned Gamble with his gaze. "I'll be watching you. Your leather doesn't faze me."

Gamble gave him a chin lift. Then Royce took off at a sprint.

"He likes you," Gamble muttered.

"I'd ask if you've been talking to Heidi, but you haven't."

He chuckled. "If she sees it, then you know it's true."

I shook my head. "No. She sees it with *everybody* who meets me, which is her seeing what she wants to see or just plain craziness. Maybe both."

He pressed his lips together like my words bothered him. "No, Victoria. It's definitely not craziness. What's crazy is you not seeing it yourself."

"Whatever. Why are you here? And seriously... you don't watch TV, but you stood for three hours watching kids practice and then play basketball. What's up with that?"

He grinned. "I like watching live sports, not highlights. Even better when I can do it in person. This was even better than watching pros. You can see the kids with raw talent, and also the kids who may not have the talent but definitely have the drive. It was fascinating."

It was like he was in my head listing all the reasons I liked volunteer coaching.

"I'm glad you enjoyed it. Now, answer my question."

"The Fourth of July is coming up. I figure you got the day off, right?"

I nodded. "Yes."

"My club has a big blow-out party every year. One of my brothers is a pyrotechnician, so you might enjoy it more than hanging beach-side or whatever for the city's show."

"Okay. Are you picking me up? You'll have to text me the address otherwise. I remember the building and your room, but I don't remember how I got there. And my mind was on other things when Fiona drove me home."

His chin lifted slowly as he whispered, "Yeah." He rubbed the back of his neck. "This isn't a date. I just thought you'd like to hang with Fiona, Stephanie, and some of the other ladies. So, I'll text you the address."

Part of me hurt that it wasn't a date, and another part of me couldn't wait to tell Heidi she read Gamble wrong.

"You do that, Gamble. Mind if I bring Heidi with me?"

He smiled. "Sure. The more the merrier."

I tilted my head, considering him. "You could have texted or called with that information."

He nodded. "Yeah, but then I wouldn't know how you're really doing."

I focused on a spot over his shoulder. He was sending such mixed signals, I struggled with whether to call him on it or let it go. Finally, I looked him in the eye. "As you can see, I'm doing fine. I'll see if Heidi wants to come with me to your club's party."

"Victoria..."

I shook my head. "No. No. Don't worry about it, Gamble. If you don't mind, we have to close the gym before one in the afternoon. Thanks for coming out, I'm glad you found it fascinating."

He ran a hand through his hair. "I don't want to waste your time, Vic. You deserve a man who's worthy of you. Who can give you—"

I couldn't bear to hear his excuses. "Gamble, I mean it. We have to shut this place down, and lock up soon. There are no problems between us, but there will be if you don't get moving."

His bearded jaw shifted, and hell if it wasn't supremely sexy. "All right. Later."

Ten minutes later, Royce stood next to Heidi watching as I locked up the gym.

I grinned at him. "There's nobody here, Royce, but thanks for looking out for me."

"That thug's still out here, along with one of his friends. So, you're wrong. There are people here."

Heidi turned around. "Why's he still here? And did you ever find out what he wanted?"

I shook my head. "I don't know why he's still around, but he invited me —and I'm inviting you as my plus one— to a Fourth of July party."

"He doesn't want me tagging along."

I chuckled. "He said outright, it isn't a date. So, he's not interested in me."

Royce glowered and shook his head. "I'm goin' to my car. I won't drive off until either he leaves, or you do. So, do a brother a solid and don't stand out here gossiping for long."

As Heidi and I walked toward our cars, I took in Gamble on his bike. In the daylight, I could better appreciate the sleek lines of the Harley. The hard-sided saddlebags hung so low, I couldn't see the rear wheel. His bike had a red and orange color scheme that made me think of phoenix feathers. There were streaks of gray coming up from the underside of the saddlebags. Rather than shiny chrome, the bike had matte black pipes. I didn't have to be an aficionado to know his bike was seriously hot.

A man on a less-flashy Harley glanced our way and Gamble looked over his shoulder. His bike roared to life, and he rode up to the driver's side of my car.

Heidi scoffed. "Yeah, right. That does not say he's not interested in you. At the risk of sounding like Royce, you better be careful. He's dangerous."

"He really isn't. Are we still on for lunch next week, since there are no practices?"

"Yes, we definitely are." She turned and gave me a hug. "Take care of yourself, Vickie."

I opened the passenger side of my car to drop off my gym bag. With my keys in hand, I rounded the hood.

Gamble shut down his bike, put down the kick stand, and swung off. He walked up, but unlike in the gym, this time he got toe-to-toe with me, my breasts grazing his leather.

"Know we got an audience, but I don't give a fuck. You need to understand, kitten. I've wanted you since we butted heads that night back in May."

"When you mansplained to me. I recall."

He lowered his chin, his blue eyes glaring. "I didn't mansplain. Hell, I don't even know what that is."

I shook my head. "You did, but continue."

"Thing is, you're too good for a biker like me."

I huffed out a chuckle. "How do you figure? And for that matter, you hardly know me, who are you to say I'm too good?"

"You're a lawyer. Not so sure it'd go over well, you have an outlaw as your man."

75

"Unless you're directly involved in a case I'm representing, it shouldn't matter."

"Things don't operate they way they *should*. That day in the garage, you mentioned an ethics committee. Wouldn't that come up again? I may not work with you, but I know it will matter."

One of my hands went to my hip. "I know that it won't. How would anyone even find out?"

He arched a brow. "Do you argue about everything?"

I grinned. "As my dad says, I was born arguing."

"I should stay away from you, but I fuckin' can't."

My gut said he shouldn't stay away, but I sensed he was holding on by a thread. "Do I get a say in any of this? It hasn't sounded that way so far."

He tore a hand through his hair. "What do you want to say?"

I tilted my head. "It's the part about me being too good. Turn that around, you're saying *you* aren't good enough for me. And *I* say you're wrong."

"You don't know what you're talking about, kitten."

I tossed my arms out to the side, then settled my hands on my hips, pushing toward him. "The hell I don't. I know you're loyal –possibly to a fault. You've got five women who are falling all over themselves to help me because *that* is them helping *you*. On top of that, there are men on my street every night because *you* asked them to be. And as crazy as I find it, you think what happened to me is your fault, when it bloody well isn't!"

We were nose-to-nose by the time I finished.

"Step back," he growled.

"Why?"

His eyes flared. "Because if you don't I'm gonna kiss the fuck out of you in front of your girl and a man who is more than sweet on you."

The thought of him kissing me made me inhale, which pressed my boobs into his chest. A curl of warmth flooded my body, but I didn't want him kissing me in front of Royce. If Heidi was right, I didn't want to rub anything in his face. I stepped back, my butt grazing my car door.

My mother had told my sister and me that women never, *ever,* went after men. If it was meant to be, the right man would come after us. It happened to be one of the few pieces of advice I had always followed.

I knew he was going to retreat from me like a wave washing back out to the gulf. Standing in front of this man who checked nearly all of my boxes, I couldn't leave it to him. I had to ignore that old piece of advice.

"Have you had lunch?"

"Not a lunch kind of man."

I crossed my arms. "Is this like you and TV? You don't eat lunch? Or you're not willing to eat lunch with me?"

He looked to the side. Even though he was forty yards away, the other biker threw his head back and laughed.

"Fuck," Gamble muttered before he turned his face to me. "I'll be by your place tonight."

His hand wrapped around my neck pulling me toward him, and he kissed my forehead. He let me go and slung his leg over his bike.

"Is there a *time* tonight?"

He paused with his helmet in his hand. "I'll text you."

As soon as his bike roared away, Heidi rolled by in her Mazda Miata braking near me. From her open window, she said, "I can't believe he didn't lay one on you!"

"Shut it, Heidi."

She cackled. "Not a chance! I told you. That man isn't sweet, he is hot for you. Though that forehead kiss made me say 'aww.'"

I gave her a closed-lip smile. "Goodbye, my friend!"

Royce drove by right after her. His windows were rolled up, but I still caught him shaking his head at me.

Gamble

If the way Victoria argued with him today was any sign, she held back in the courtroom. The sight of her riled up and listing all the ways she thought he was good enough. No matter what happened between them, he'd never forget that.

Her lean body pushing up against his and the fire in her gorgeous eyes threatened to undo him. She pushed at all his restraint. He hadn't wanted to kiss someone that bad since his teens. But he knew she didn't want to hurt Royce. And he didn't want to hear it from her friend, or Mensa for that matter.

He didn't know if he loved or hated how quick she was to call him out about not going to lunch, though that was the best example of how she could do better.

When one of her colleagues saw her with him, it would raise questions. No matter how much she argued. And going to lunch with him would prove that to her.

Maybe he should have said yes.

As though on autopilot, he'd pulled his bike into the forecourt of the compound and stopped next to Cynic's bike. He recalled that the only thing in life he wanted *and* went after was his membership in the Riot. Was it time for him to give himself something else he wanted? A woman who would stand by his side and ride at his back... Victoria said all the right things to make it seem like she was that woman, but he didn't believe it.

For a fleeting moment, he thought about standing her up. That was wrong in so many ways. Not only was it uncool, but it was a wuss move and he was better than that.

He was also selfish. If she wanted him to spend time with her, it would be in a time and place where he could kiss her like he'd wanted to for so many weeks.

But he knew he had to leave it at kissing. A month may have gone by, but it was unlikely she was anywhere near taking it farther than that.

Remembering her tits pressing against him, though, he would struggle to stop himself. Yet, he would never hurt her. Definitely not like that.

But he wanted her. Bad.

Stretched out on his bed in his room, he focused on his book, but his mind wasn't comprehending anything. It rankled that he and his brothers hadn't delivered a beatdown to the Abeyetas. He knew that was due to Victoria reporting the crime and the police rounding them up quickly. That didn't change the fact Gamble wanted their blood.

His phone chimed with a text. As he picked it up, a tingle went up his spine because it was from a corrections officer he hadn't heard from in months. Not since Ramone had been arrested back in early May.

FYI - Ernesto and Luis bonded out Thursday afternoon. Meant to tell you sooner. My bad, man.

He sat up and fired off a quick text letting his buddy off the hook. Then he called Mensa.

"Yo, you comin' over here any time soon. Thinking we don't need to watch her day and—"

"Luis and Ernesto got out on Thursday. Just found out. Have you seen anything strange?"

"No. I'll keep my eyes peeled, but I don't think they'll come here this soon."

"You might be right, but I'm not taking any chances. Be there soon."

He ended the call and hit Victoria's number. When he'd dropped of her phone weeks ago, he should have insisted she save his number. If she'd deleted it —and he wouldn't blame her if she had, because he'd given her so much space— she might not recognize the number. Plenty of people didn't answer calls they didn't recognize.

"Hello," she answered.

"Hey, it's Gamble. You busy right now?"

"No. I just got out of the shower."

He fought against that visual. "Great. I'm swinging by in fifteen."

"And you still don't do lunch, I presume?"

"What?"

"I'm about to eat. If you haven't eaten, I can—"

He shook his head. "I ate already. Don't worry about me. Just keep your door locked."

It sounded like she started to speak, but he'd already hit the icon to end the call. He knifed off the bed, grabbed his gun, shrugged on his cut, and headed out. Sunday afternoon, most of the brothers were riding.

He rolled up next to Mensa ten minutes later.

"You're overreacting, G.," Mensa said.

He shook his head and put his helmet on a handlebar. "Better that than she's violated again."

Mensa's lips straightened to a flat line, and he nodded.

"Thanks for watching her, man."

"Shut it, brother," he muttered.

While he jogged across the street, he heard Mensa fire up his bike.

The apartment door opened right after his knock. Victoria stood barefoot in a pair of black shorts and a pale pink sleeveless shirt that hugged her breasts. He closed his eyes for a beat before he gave Victoria a glare. "You gotta be sure who's out here, Vic."

She returned his glare while gesturing him inside. "And your bike announces your presence. Pathetic as it may be, I watched you come across the street."

That pleased him as much as it unsettled him. He couldn't remember the last time a woman gave a damn about his coming or going.

"So be it. You still need to be careful."

"All right, boss."

He resisted rolling his eyes. "Did anyone tell you Luis and Ernesto posted bail?"

"Of course."

He did a double take. "'Of course'?"

She shrugged as shoulder. "It's procedure."

He took a deep breath. "You should have—"

Her eyes widened. "I should have what? Called you? I haven't heard from you in weeks. That tells me everything I need—"

"It doesn't tell you anything."

She inched forward and demanded, "Doesn't it though?"

He had moved toward her, so he lowered his voice. "It doesn't."

80

"It does, but how was I to know you wanted me to call you?"

She had him there, so he deflected by changing the subject.

"What are you doing to keep safe?"

Her head gave a tiny shake. "I'm not running outside for one damn thing."

He put his hands on his hips. "Do you have a gun?"

"No."

"Mace?"

"No. Besides, a strong wind and I'm rubbing my eyes in pain, too."

"Holding your car key between your fingers isn't enough."

She leaned toward him. "They aren't coming for me again."

He couldn't stop himself. His hands cupped her face, his thumbs gently rubbing along the apple of her cheeks. "Your nose looks good."

Her lips pursed at his subject change. "It's fully healed according to the plastic surgeon your guy sent me to."

"Good. It doesn't hurt?"

"No," she whispered.

"You drive me crazy, you know."

She made a weird choking sound before her laughter bubbled out. "That's mutual."

His thumbs continued to graze the soft skin along the high ridge of her cheekbone. "Normally I don't ask this, but is it all right if I kiss you?"

Her eyes went so wide he expected her to say no.

"It's high time you did."

He burst with laughter at her unexpected response. When he had his laughter under control he brought his face closer to hers, but that was when he saw her smiling at him. Somehow, he'd forgotten the sucker punch she landed every time she smiled.

His tongue darted out to moisten his lips and her smile faded. Those hazel irises sparkled green, and he saw the anticipation in her eyes.

He brushed her lips with his. The moment he did, she snaked her hands between them to wrap her arms around his neck. The tip of her tongue traced his lower lip. It was all the invitation he needed. His tongue met hers and her mouth opened further.

She tasted faintly of lime. His left hand slid into her hair, and he kept her still while deepening their kiss. He wanted more of her citrusy flavor, but it was like chasing a cloud. Elusive and impossible to attain.

She broke their connection and he feared he'd come on too strong.

Her lips closed around his lower lip for half a second then she pulled back fully.

"That was something," she whispered.

"Something good, I hope," he said before he could think better of it.

She kissed his lower lip again. "Definitely good."

He stared into her eyes willing his blood to stop rushing south. It wasn't working.

Her eyes slid to the side and back to him. "So, now what?"

"You ever been on a bike?"

"Like yours? No," she said, shaking her head.

He grinned. "Then grab your keys, and let's go."

Chapter 8

Weight

Victoria

It was official. I had a new passion: riding behind Gamble on his motorcycle. It would beat out running if only I could burn calories while we rode. As it was, he'd taken us to a Dunkin' Donuts that also had a Baskin Robins inside. We had milkshakes and then rode along Beach Boulevard before coming back to my place.

I took off his helmet and handed it back to him. His lips were pressed together like he was fighting a grin.

"What's funny?" I asked.

He shook his head, as he put the helmet on the seat of his bike. "Nothin'. Glad I could put that huge smile on your face."

"Thanks for the ride. And the milkshake."

He grabbed my hand and led me up the stairs to my apartment.

We came to the top of the stairs and even though we weren't near my door, I knew something was wrong. Gamble must have sensed it too because he pulled his gun from his hip.

"What are—"

I stopped when he put a finger to his lips.

As we came even with my door, I saw it was ajar.

Gamble turned to me, putting his lips right by my ear. "Stay out here. Get your phone out and call 911 if I don't come out in two minutes."

He started to pull away, but with a hand on his bearded cheek I pulled him so I could whisper in his ear. "Be careful."

His blue eyes flared at me, and he nodded.

Did nobody ever tell him to be careful?

While I pulled my phone from my back pocket, Gamble carefully nudged the door open enough for him to move inside the apartment.

On my phone, I dialed 911 and had my finger poised over the green call icon.

As I stood out there, I realized I should have started a timer. I had no idea if two minutes had gone by or twenty seconds.

Then Gamble swung the door open. His lips were pressed into a hard line. He folded his arms across his chest, reminding me of just how thick his forearms were.

"Eyes on me, Vic," he said in a low voice.

I looked into his eyes, trying to hide my annoyance.

"Go ahead and call 911. We're gonna be here a while, but you aren't staying here tonight. Or anytime for the foreseeable future."

My breath left me in a whoosh. "I get not staying here tonight. It's obvious that the door's going to have to be repaired. But, why wouldn't I stay here once that's done and they're arrested again?"

He turned his head to the side like he didn't want to talk about this. Then he leveled serious eyes on me. "Tryin' to protect you here, kitten. Bad enough what they did to you, this is just salt on the wound. Come on, you'll see why you won't be here for a while."

I stepped inside and felt an instant headache from the fumes. My apartment had a very open floor plan. The dining area and living area were essentially one big space that was only delineated by the hanging light fixture over my small dinette set. For some bizarre reason, there were black shoe prints all over the tan carpet. My sofa sat against a huge wall, and I could only thank my past self that I hadn't decided what to hang there. That wall had the word 'cunt' spray painted in black above my couch. Or what used to be my couch. The cushions had been pulled off and ripped apart. The back of the couch was also shredded. Bits of stuffing littered the carpet.

My fingers pinched the bridge of my nose.

"Let's go outside, Victoria."

"No, I need to see the rest."

He shook his head. "You don't. Other than the master bedroom, they left the rest alone. I almost think they were interrupted or something." He mulled that over. "Shit. I wonder if *we* interrupted them."

"It doesn't matter now. How about you step aside so I can see my bedroom."

"No."

I tilted my head. "What do you mean no? It can't be any worse than that," I gestured to the spray-painted word.

His hands gripped my shoulders. "It is, kitten. And honestly, you're gonna fuck up the scene. Let's get the cops out here, and handle the rest as it comes."

"At least tell me what they did, Gage."

He cocked a brow at me using his given name.

"They doused your closet with a can of red paint. Your clothes are shot to shit."

That made my stomach sink, but my wardrobe could be replaced.

"Okay, that's... repairable. The landlord won't like it, but—"

"They also hit the bed with a can of black paint."

My first stupid thought was whether his blanket was okay, but I remembered I'd tucked it in my nightstand two weeks ago.

He continued. "They also busted up your dresser. Guessing they took your jewelry if you had any around."

"Did they ransack my nightstand?"

He shook his head. "It's strange, but no. Which is another reason I think they were interrupted."

I nodded. "Then they didn't get my jewelry. I don't have much, but what I have is in my nightstand."

"Make the call, Vic."

I gave him a look. "I still don't understand why I can't go see the room."

He shook his head. "It won't help you, sweetheart. Just make the call."

Three hours later, I had a grocery bag of toiletries packed along with a small box containing the most important things from my nightstand: my jewelry, my insurance documents, a photo album, and Gamble's blanket.

I also had the knowledge that Gamble had been protecting me. Again.

On top of the paint on my bed, they'd dumped all my underwear. The walls had been tagged with what looked like a gang symbol –though the investigating officers said it wasn't a gang yet, but a known graffiti artist in the area.

The *piece de resistance*, though, was in the bathroom. They'd painted the word 'again' on the mirror and had printed a picture of me with the bag over my head and my naked body while they had attacked me.

It was insanely stupid to do that, and I could attest that most criminals weren't that smart. But this took it a shade too far.

Why make it clear they'd been the people to do this? Unless they planned to say they were framed?

My landlord rubbed the back of his head. "Gonna do what I can to get your unit back in shape, Victoria."

I nodded. "I'm sorry, Mr. Beck."

"Hush. You have nothing to be sorry about. Especially... that word. I catch them around here, won't be any need for—"

"Mr. Beck," Gamble said, and tipped his head toward an officer as a warning.

"Right, right." He looked at me. "I have your number. Let you know when things are livable again."

As we left, another biker came up the walk. He held a slender auburn-haired woman close to his side. She was a little shorter than me. Her rich brown eyes twinkled when she smiled at me and Gamble.

"Hey Trinity, I didn't expect Roman to bring you with him," Gamble said.

She chuckled. "Yeah, well, I don't think her box will fit in anyone's saddlebags. Besides, I haven't met her and thought she could use some of my clothes. Kenzie was going to offer a few things since she wears business suits and stuff, but she's so short, we weren't sure if that would work." She held a hand out to me. "I'm Trinity, by the way."

I shook her hand and introduced myself.

"Thank you, it's very thoughtful of you to offer me some clothes."

She shook her head. "It's nothing. I can't believe they would do something like this in broad daylight."

Roman pulled her to his side again. "Sugar, one of the brothers has been out here every night. Gamble taking her for a ride was probably the first time they knew her place wasn't guarded."

I shook my head. "I was gone all morning since seven. They had plenty of time then."

Roman dipped his chin at me. "Those bastards are like rats, they don't come out until mid-day at the earliest."

Trinity held her hands out for my box. "You want us to take that? We brought my car. You can see some of my clothes at the clubhouse."

I grinned. "That sounds good."

"Are you really going to work tomorrow?" Gamble grumbled.

I turned to him. "Why wouldn't I? I've already missed a few days while recovering... from my broken nose. I'm not going to let those assholes force me out of work."

"Better to be out of work than out of—"

I squeezed his hand. "They aren't going to come after me at work. Hell, they only did this because they knew we were gone."

Gamble sighed. "Fine."

Rather than let Trinity take it, Roman grabbed my box. They turned around and walked toward a Lexus sedan.

Gamble grabbed my hand, leading me to his bike. I had to scurry to keep up with him.

"What is your hurry? And what about my car?" I asked when we arrived at his Harley.

He stared at me for a moment. "Not letting you out of my sight. We'll get your car in the morning. The sooner this is done, the sooner we can hang."

My brows furrowed. "Isn't that what we've been doing? Until the cops arrived, obviously."

His fingers stroked my hair near the top of my head, his eyes watched their progress. "We haven't gotten to hang the way I want to, kitten. But, the day isn't over yet."

Warmth curled through my torso at his words. Suddenly, I found I was in a hurry, too.

No matter how big a hurry Gamble was in (or me for that matter), we didn't get to 'hang' until after six. As soon as we walked inside the clubhouse, Stephanie and Fiona dragged me to Roman's room where Trinity had some clothes. Seemed Fiona, Stephanie, and a woman named Sandy –who I'd yet to meet– had added to the pile. Their kindness was so overwhelming I found myself in tears.

Fiona stroked my back. "It's all right. Let it out."

I looked at her through watery eyes. "I can't believe y'all did this so fast!"

Stephanie spoke from my other side. "Sweetie, this is nothing. And Kenzie wished she could have been here, but Brute feared she'd bring her whole closet."

I chuckled.

Fiona shook her head. "Men. Brute should've known Kenzie couldn't unload her whole wardrobe. She's like four inches shorter than Victoria."

"Yeah, but men are crazy like that," Stephanie muttered. She pulled a sage green pantsuit from the pile and held it out to me. "Try that one. I bet it will make your eyes pop."

With a shrug and thinking I would try on one or two outfits, I went to the bathroom. Next thing I knew, I'd put on at least ten different dresses or suit combos. Fiona, Trinity, and Stephanie all had opinions and I didn't get out of the room until dinner time.

I started to gather the hangers in my hands, but Trinity stopped me with a gentle touch to my wrist. "Don't worry about it. I'll have Roman get these into Gamble's room or wherever you're going to be."

I shook my head. "I can handle it—"

She gave me a look. "No, really. Roman is quite determined to help you. It's the least he can do, and I can't take that opportunity from him."

"Okay," I whispered. "Thank you again. This is so kind."

"Forget about it, Victoria. Go find Gamble."

I twisted the handle to Gamble's room, but it was locked. With a frown on my face, I turned to go back to Roman's room, but then the door opened.

Gamble stood there shirtless and barefoot wearing just a pair of gray sweats —even though it was the end of June, the clubhouse had air conditioning that could chill Lucifer.

"It's about fuckin' time," he growled. Then he grabbed my hand and yanked me into his room.

Someone had dropped off my box, but my bag of toiletries wasn't sitting on top anymore. Which meant at the top of the box sat his fleece blanket.

"I put your bathroom shit in my bathroom," he muttered.

Staring at the box, I gave a stiff nod. "I see that."

He moved in front of me. "You gonna tell me why my blanket was in your nightstand, instead of on your bed?"

I looked up into his probing blue eyes. "No."

His chuckle sounded ominous, but his smile said it was anything but. "All right. I'll let you play it that way."

"I'm not playing at all."

He cocked a brow. "You are. You just don't know it."

After a moment, he said, "Take your shoes off."

I looked at him. "Why? We haven't eaten yet."

"We're gonna relax before we eat. And you don't strike me as a woman who wears shoes in bed."

He let go of my hand. I watched him cross to a dresser where a classic iPod was docked to a speaker. Then some very mellow music started, but there was enough heavy-hitting percussion that you paid close attention. It sounded like reggae, but not quite.

"What are we listening to?"

He stalked back toward me, and I struggled to maintain eye contact because his tattooed chest was on display. Spanning from one side to the other in scrolling script were the words, "Live & Learn." Beneath that in the center of his chest was the Riot MC patch without the rockers. A fist upholding a skull with wings jutting out from behind, it was impressive. Yet, I wondered why he didn't have it right over his heart, an area that didn't feature any ink.

"Tell you what's playing, when you take off your shoes."

I shook my head and toed out of my sneakers.

He looked down at my socked feet. Then his eyes lazily roved up my body. He locked eyes with me for a moment before his hand darted out wrapping around my waist. Then I found my hands resting on his bare shoulders and our bodies side by side on his bed.

He nuzzled my neck like he did weeks ago in my bed. His lips kissed a path upward. He paused by my ear. "We're listening to Slightly Stoopid."

I chuckled. "That's the band name? Really?"

"Yeah."

I pulled my head back a touch. "It almost sounds like reggae. Are they called that because they get high?"

"Yep. That a problem?"

I shook my head. "Why would it be?"

"When I get edgy, I'm not opposed to using the devil's lettuce to take the edge off."

I did a big nod. "Ah. And you think I'm going to go all law-abiding citizen on you, is that it?"

His body jolted and I knew he'd laughed silently. "Didn't say that, kitten. Just want you to have the full picture of the kind of man I am."

I leaned down and put my lips to the juncture of his neck and shoulder. For a brief moment I sucked at his skin there.

He made a growly noise and I pulled away. His blue eyes blazed at me.

I grinned. "It's more like you want to scare me off with all your bad boy behavior."

I'd been wrong before. *Now*, his eyes were blazing. Rather than give me a verbal response, he rolled toward me and kissed me hard and long.

One of my hands hooked under his arm to hang onto his shoulder while the other one went up behind his neck. The kiss he gave me earlier had been great, but from this one I knew he had been holding back, because this was a kiss I never knew I needed.

His tongue flicked at mine and unbidden the idea of him doing that to another part of my body made me moan. My hand behind his neck traveled down along his chest. I wanted to watch my fingers trace the ridges between his pecs and abdominals, but Gamble growled into my mouth and intensified our kiss.

I hiked a leg up and around his legs. He stilled and pulled away.

I opened my eyes, praying they conveyed my sincere intensity. "I'm fine, Gamble. As much as I love that you treat me like I'm made of porcelain, we're good. Better than good, honey."

Our faces were inches apart, but he just stared at me.

I'd already ignored Mom's advice once today, what was another time?

I angled my head, planted my lips on his and did my damnedest to kiss him while pushing him to his back.

He growled into my mouth again, but this time was louder. His hands slid down my body to my backside. He squeezed the globes of my ass, and I couldn't help but move my hips. Through his sweatpants I felt his erection. I widened my legs. His stiff cock would have been perfectly lined up... if it weren't for us being clothed. Still, he hummed with approval. To further demonstrate this, his hands slid down only to slide back up underneath my shorts and panties. He squeezed my ass skin-to-skin and *I* growled.

He broke the kiss so he could chuckle.

"Nothing's funny here," I whispered.

His eyes glittered with desire. Then he leaned up and kissed me harder than before. It was so good my hips rocked against him. I sighed into his mouth thinking how great it could be. Then he rolled so I was on bottom. His weight pressed into me.

Pure fear shot through my veins, turning my body rigid.

He pulled his head away while his hands came out of my shorts, but his eyes were intent on me. As they roamed my face, he hissed, "Fuck."

Then he flung his body to the other side of the bed.

The moment I had caught his eyes the fear had left me, but the damage was done. Only, I had to mitigate that damage. If I didn't, Gamble would blame himself for that, too.

Slowly, gently, I rolled toward him. Six inches still separated us after my maneuver. Being subtle on a bed like his wasn't easy. I got within three inches, and he heaved a huge sigh.

"Stop, Victoria."

Since being subtle wasn't working, I pushed up to an elbow and scooched close enough that barely an inch separated us.

"Don't tell me to stop, Gamble." I pushed my luck and put a hand on his torso. "I'm sorry I had—"

His hand covered mine on his abdomen. "What'd I tell you? Don't you dare apologize for anything where this shit's concerned."

"It was a moment, Gage. I recognize that you aren't those assholes. I know that I'm reacting out of fear. I'm not—"

He turned his head to glare at me. "And *I* told myself this wouldn't go any farther than kissing. You hiked your leg along my hips, and I should have stopped, but I gave in."

I took a deep breath. "Stop, honey. Don't blame yourself for this."

"Kitten, there's no way around that."

I leaned forward and kissed his cheek. "You're not to blame."

His eyes slid toward me, but they were skeptical.

I kissed another spot on his cheek, closer to his lips. He exhaled and his hand loosened on mine. Even though I was pushing my luck, I inched it toward the waistband of his sweats. Of course, I did that while I kissed his lips.

He'd allowed the lip touches, but his hand wrapped around mine before I could slip it inside his pants.

"What are you doing?"

I stared into his eyes. "I want to make you feel good. There's no reason you should be in pain because—"

"If I'm in pain, that's on me, Vic."

I pushed enough to get under the thick waistband. "But I could make you feel better."

He stopped my progress. "That is *not* how this is gonna go, kitten."

Part of me knew I should let it go, but I couldn't. "How *is* it gonna go, then? Because my guess is you're gonna give yourself a handjob. Why not let me do that for you?"

He glowered at me, but didn't speak.

I continued. "The counselor I've been seeing has helped me process the attack. What they did wasn't about sex whatsoever. I've realized, they violated me, but they didn't steal my sex drive, Gage."

He arched up onto his side facing me. "No, they probably didn't, but they took something else. Something you haven't identified until now. A man who gives a damn about you puts his weight on you and your whole body goes tight as a bow. No. That ain't right. I shift my weight into you it should give you security and tell you just what I mean to do *with* you. And what I'm going to do with you is not even close to what those assholes did *to* you."

The sincerity in his voice struck something deep inside me. "I know," I whispered.

Tenderly, he dragged my hand away from his pants and up his torso. His skin felt warm and smooth. Smoother than I expected. Since we weren't kissing, I got to watch my fingers travel over the ridges and dips of his muscles.

"Kitten," he said in a warning tone.

I looked at him, his blue eyes were twinkling.

"Like you lookin' at me that way, but I'm not going to rush us. The first time you make me come is not going to be with your hand or your mouth. That's gonna happen inside you."

His words made perfect sense, but I felt my lips pout.

Chuckling, he wrapped an arm around my shoulders and laid back down, pulling me half-way onto his chest.

"I appreciate you giving me space and time. And, I like how protective you are—"

"That's great, and I can hear the 'but' coming, so how about you stop right there?"

"But what if I want to rip the band-aid off?" I finished.

His body tensed. "That sounds good, but ripping anything off hurts. And, sometimes it reopens a wound. This isn't a wound I'm willing to reopen for you."

I wanted to argue that point, but in a strange twist, both of our stomachs growled. My eyes slid the side in embarrassment, but Gamble laughed.

"Sounds like the milkshakes wore off. Let's go see what's for dinner."

My head tilted. "Someone brings in dinner every night here?"

He grinned. "No, honey. It's Sunday and a few of the brothers always grill something on Sunday afternoons."

Gamble moved in such a graceful way for a man his size, even getting himself (and me) out of bed. I found myself on my feet and he grabbed a shirt that had been draped over the back of his drafting chair. He put it on, and my lips twisted.

He chuckled. "Wipe that cute pout off your face, kitten. I'll take my shirt off when we get back."

Gamble

Gamble didn't see any platters of meat in the kitchen, so he guided Victoria out to the common room. Blues music blared from the overhead speakers they'd installed nine months ago. Tiny and Joules were at the far end of the bar having a heated discussion.

Two stools from them, Trinity sat next to Fiona. Before he could encourage Victoria to sit a few seats over, she perched on the stool next to Fiona.

The prospect held up a pint glass and Gamble raised two fingers.

Tiny slammed a fist on the bar. "That's not what I said, Joules!"

Victoria tensed and he leaned over to whisper in her ear. "They bicker like old ladies. But if it freaks you, we'll go back to my room."

She relaxed a little.

Joules shook his head and his gravelly voice carried down the bar. "There is no better version of 'It Serves You Right to Suffer' than John Lee Hooker's version. The J. Geils Band doesn't hold a candle to the original."

"You need your hearing tested because I agree with you. I *said* this version is the best *for a cover*."

Joules shook his head and put his beer bottle down with a thud. "Now you're just changing your story."

Tiny glared at Joules. "I'm goin' to check on the brisket."

With his focus on the music argument, Gamble wasn't paying attention to the women's conversation until Victoria tipped her head his way.

"Would you believe he doesn't know what 'mansplaining' is?"

He leaned toward her. "I didn't mansplain."

She stared at him with wide eyes. Her mouth opened to talk, but she hesitated.

Then Fiona leaned forward to catch his eyes. "You did."

"I didn't, Fi."

Victoria shook her head. "You told me how to do my job without the first law school lecture under your belt."

The prospect put beers in front of him and Victoria. Then he asked, "So a man can't explain anything?"

Victoria looked to Fiona. Fiona's lips twisted to the side like she wanted to chime in, but she didn't.

Without Fiona coming to her rescue, Victoria said, "It isn't that you can't explain something. It's..."

"The condescending tone," Trinity said.

Victoria nodded. "And an assumption that I don't know what I'm doing."

He put his hand over hers on the bar. "I didn't assume anything about you."

Fiona laughed. "You said she better do her job right, which presumes she does it wrong. Not to mention, you assumed she was there to represent me when I hadn't asked for representation at all."

Victoria gave a short nod, then looked at Fiona. "Yeah, you shouldn't have done that, by the way. Always have a lawyer present for questioning."

"Gah! You sound just like Cynic," Fiona said.

"Who sounds just like me? And who's hungry?" Cynic asked, walking in with a platter of food, Tiny right behind him.

"Grab your beer, Victoria. That's brisket, so we gotta move fast."

While the rest of the brothers and their women ate at the bar, Gamble insisted they eat at a picnic table outside. It might make them seem anti-social, but he wanted Victoria to himself.

Though considering he'd just shared with her more details about his sister's attack, maybe they should have hung with the group.

Victoria put her pint glass down. "Wait, you mean your parents didn't get their act together after your sister's ordeal?"

He shook his head. "Not really, they put on a good show for social services after Brit's attack. But hell, it took until I was hospitalized after a gunshot wound for them to —"

"A gunshot wound!" she yelled.

His lips tipped up. "Yeah. I was seventeen."

"Seven— no. Seventeen?"

He nodded.

"My God, where?"

He pulled his shirt to the side and pointed to the scar between his neck and shoulder. "Upper chest. I was lucky, according to the nurses. With my sister's case on record, and me getting shot, it forced my parents into Gambler's Anonymous because it became clear to family services my family wasn't functioning."

She nodded.

Then she asked, "Where do your parents live now?"

He tried to keep the venom out of his tone, but he failed. "Don't fuckin' know and don't fuckin' care."

She gave him a long blink. "No Thanksgivings with them, I take it."

"Haven't seen them since just before I earned my patch."

"Really?"

He nodded. "Yeah. Of all the fuckin' things, they wanted to talk me out of joining... right after they asked me for money."

She stayed silent, and from the gentle look in her eyes, he suspected she sympathized with his parents.

He traced the delicate line of her jaw. "Other than Brittney, I have more family here than I ever knew with my parents."

A small smile crossed her face. "I'm glad you have that."

"So am I."

Her face twisted with reluctance. "I shouldn't ask this, but I—"

"You can ask me anything, kitten."

"Why do you look so clean-cut? I would think—"

His eyes widened. "If you saw my father, you'd get it. Knew from a young age I wanted to be anything but him when I became a man."

Her head tilted. "Why did you stay in town? I mean, gambling is practically everywhere here."

"You remember sleeping in my bed that awful night?"

She nodded.

"You accused me of being stubborn."

Her lips tipped up as she nodded again.

"You were right. I wanted to be sure those assholes who hurt Brit get theirs. By the time I thought I should leave, I'd met Block and Cynic."

"I see."

"One of the best damn days of my life."

"You think very highly of them."

He nodded. That statement didn't even come close, but he didn't have words to make her understand what his brothers gave him.

Her phone rang. She glanced at the screen and with a small smile she took the call. "Hi, Dad."

Her face fell as she listened.

"Right. There is crime scene tape on my door, Dad. I didn't—"

She sighed as she listened.

Then she said, "I wasn't attacked there. Someone broke into—"

Her eyes widened at being interrupted again.

"To be fair, I didn't expect either of you to drop by unannounced." She paused.

"No, I'm not going to stay with you."

Then, "It isn't that I don't want to, Dad. I'm staying with a friend and I'll... let you know if I need to crash at your place."

Her eyes roved the table as she became uncomfortable. "Not Heidi. We can talk about that later. I'm sorry you and Mom went all the way out to—"

Her free hand went to the back of her neck. "Well, it's great that Miranda will be coming to town. But I don't know why you had to tell me that in person."

Her lips pressed together in a frown. "Sorry, Dad, but I just finished eating. Okay, I love you guys, too."

She put the phone down and shot him huge eyes. "Sorry about that. My parents can be... well, a pain."

He squeezed her hand. "Embrace the pain, kitten. They love you, and it's damn sure more than I could ever say for my folks."

She shook her head, a conflicted expression on her face. "And see, I don't know if I'm mad or sad that they did that shit to you and your sister."

He shook his head. "Don't be either. It's life, and without their actions it's unlikely I would've found myself here. And this is one of the best places to be."

They sat in silence. She seemed okay with that, and he never felt a need to fill the silence. He liked just being with someone, and he definitely liked being with Victoria.

"They want to meet you," she muttered.

He nodded. "Okay."

She looked at him with surprise. "You're okay with that?"

He shrugged a shoulder. "Sounds more like you aren't."

She shook her head. "No, I just figured that would scare you off."

"You told them about your situation, right? Including the fact you were dropped here?"

She nodded.

"Then I understand why they want to meet me. They'd probably want to meet any man you're with, even if they never say so."

Victoria's attention shifted over his shoulder. Mensa rode by them and parked his bike fifty yards away. As he lumbered to the clubhouse a sly grin spread on his face.

He paused at their table. "We need to pick up a basketball hoop, G? I'd love to see her whip your ass one-on-one."

"Get the fuck out of here, Mensa," he muttered.

He didn't leave, instead he turned to Victoria. "Yo. I'm Mensa. Figure we should officially meet."

She grinned. "Hi, Mensa. It's nice to meet you."

He lifted his chin. "Likewise. Tell your friend she's got a front headlight out. My guess is she doesn't know."

Victoria looked at Gamble. "Well, that was nice of him to notice."

His brows shot up and down. "He notices everything. It's great in a fight or other situation, but on the day-to-day shit, it makes him a pain in the ass."

"I doubt that," she muttered, and finished her beer.

He grabbed their plates. "Get my glass, Victoria. We're going back inside."

CHAPTER 9

SMILE A LOT

VICTORIA

I followed Gamble into the kitchen.

As he piled the plates into the sink and turned to me, I couldn't help but give him a look. "Shouldn't we like, rinse those off and put them in the dishwasher?"

His lips tipped up and he shook his head. "Nope. First, we don't have a dishwasher. Second, a prospect will get the age-old honor of washing that shit."

He grabbed the glasses from my hands. "Think quick. You want another beer or something else? I'm switching to rum and Coke, but you want wine, we'll take that back to my room."

"We're not going to commune with the others?" I asked.

He stopped halfway out of the kitchen. "Not a chance. You had plenty of time with the women earlier. You're all mine tonight."

I shrugged. "I'm a big believer in that old cliche about 'when in Rome,' so I'll go with rum and diet, if that's on offer."

With a smile on his face, he dug a key out of his pocket. "Damn sure is, kitten. Here, go unlock my door. I'll be right behind you."

Halfway to Gamble's room, Stephanie stopped me in the hallway. "I never got to say this earlier, but I'm so sorry about your place, Victoria."

I shook my head. "It's not your fault."

She grinned. "No, but it sucks having your shit trashed in any way." My head tilted a fraction and she shot me a wry smile. "Trust me, it's a long story, but vandalism is a coward's way out."

I pointed a finger at her. "You're right about that."

I'd just opened the door by the time Gamble came down the hallway.

His expression turned questioning. "You have problems with the lock, Victoria?"

I shook my head. "No, I ran into Stephanie."

He nodded as he drew even with me to hand me a six-pack of diet cola. I moved into the room and put the soda on his dresser.

He set a bottle of rum on the dresser along with a bucket of ice and two glasses.

I looked up at him with concern. "There's only two of us, you know."

The deep rumble of his chuckle made me smile. "I know that, kitten. The rum will keep, but I like lots of ice in my drinks."

"Apparently," I muttered.

"Get comfortable. You got something you can sleep in?"

Of all the clothes the other women had brought for me, they didn't bring pajamas.

When the silence stretched out, I said, "Um..."

His chin dipped. "Right in front of you, second drawer, grab a t-shirt. I'm gonna take a quick shower. You change and get comfortable."

"Okay," I whispered.

Before he left, he leaned down and kissed my cheek.

Opening the drawer, I saw three stacks of white t-shirts. I tugged off my shirt, took off my bra, picked out one from the center and put it on. It felt a wee bit snug at the neck, but with a little adjustment, it was fine.

I found a hand towel and put it under the bucket of ice so his dresser wouldn't be marked. Then I put ice in both glasses –though less in mine; I wasn't a big ice fan– and I was about to open the rum when I heard Gamble snickering behind me.

"What?"

"Did you read that shirt—"

I shook my head. "What are you talking about? It's a white t-shirt."

He chuckled again. "No, Victoria, it isn't. You're wearing it backwards."

I tried to look over my shoulder, but he rushed to my side. "No, honey. Don't do that. I'll tell you what it says, but we should leave it at this: it's bad for your legal-eagle image."

My eyes narrowed, but he kept going.

"Smoke Pot. Eat Twat," he paused and was either biting back laughter or hiding a grin. "Smile A Lot."

I scoffed. "Are you shitting me?"

"No," he said.

My response tumbled out my mouth. "I'm stealing this shirt."

His expression went straight to outrage. "Why? You don't smoke—"

I raised a finger in the air. "No, but I love the idea."

Actually, I loved the idea of having another garment that smelled like him, but I especially loved the idea of him eating *my* twat, even if that wasn't happening any time soon.

When I noticed the predatory glimmer in his eyes I also saw he only had a towel wrapped around his waist. His tattooed chest and chiseled muscles could distract a nun.

"Kitten, I don't think you know what you're talking about."

"What do you mean, I don't know what I'm talking about?"

He stalked toward me. "I'm making an educated guess that you've never been high in your life, and in your position that would be a bad idea."

My eyes slid to the side as I suppressed a smile.

He traced my jaw with his finger. "What are you hiding?"

"That wasn't the idea I loved."

Realization dawned and his blue eyes glimmered with heat. "Victoria."

His tone of voice was so mixed —part reprimanding and part tortured. The tortured I commiserated with, but the reprimand had to go.

My hands went to my hips. "Don't 'Victoria' me. It's so sweet it hurts my teeth how much you bend over backwards to protect me, but... I seriously liked what we were doing earlier. More than you know. The fact you think I'm a delicate piece of glass means I *know* that you'll take the utmost care with me no matter how far things go."

I paused, expecting him to say something, but he kept silent.

Stepping into his space, I said, "I know you want to take things slow, but I'm not as delicate as you think."

When I stopped speaking I saw the heat hadn't left his eyes. His hands came up to my cheeks holding me steady. Next thing I knew, his lush lips were locked on mine and his tongue teased me. My hands went to his sides and I was reminded of his half-nakedness. His skin felt heavenly under my fingers. I let one hand skim the edge of the towel, but he reached down and stopped my progress.

"Gamble," I whispered against his lips.

An ominous chuckle rumbled from him. "I ought to say, 'don't Gamble me,' but no joke, kitten. You yank this towel off me, I'm liable to lose control and I won't fuckin' do that."

I slid my hands lazily up his torso and stopped at his neck, then I pulled back enough to look him in the eyes. "Honey, I need you to make me come. I've been working solo for months—a lot of months—and the thought of you between my legs... with the way you treat me already? How could that possibly be wrong?"

With an animalistic growl, he kissed me hard and open-mouthed as he backed me toward his bed. My legs hit the edge of the mattress and his hands whipped down to my thighs. He lifted, and reflexively my legs went around his waist. Then he lowered me onto the bed, kissing me in the most delicious way the whole time. One of his hands came up behind my neck and he maneuvered me so my head was on a pillow.

As he backed away, a wry grin cut across his face. "I should yank that shirt off you, but seein' as how it got us into this, hell if I'm gonna do that."

He gently pulled my legs from his hips, spread me wide, and with reverent fingers he stroked me outside my underwear. Then he pulled my panties down my legs and tossed them aside.

Through a gap in the towel, I spied his straining erection and I licked my lips. "I could... we could both get relief here Gamble."

With a groan, he shook his head. "Not right now, kitten. I gotta taste you, and that has to be distraction-free."

He lifted my legs while he lowered his torso. His beard tickled the inside of my thighs just before his tongue played a devious game with my clit. My hips jerked. He pulled back just enough to shush me. His tongue traced me up, down and up again, only to whirl around my clit. Then he sucked on me. I writhed and his eyes met mine, full of concern.

In a husky voice, I said, "Don't stop, I'm good... so damn good... so far."

A wicked grin made his eyes glitter. "You taste 'so damn good,' that's for certain, kitten."

He put his mouth back on me and my pleasure built, quick and harsh. His hands released my legs. One hand reached inside the shirt to massage my breast, flicking my nipple. He used his other hand to glide two fingers inside me.

"Oh, God," I breathed.

I glanced down my body, saw his eyes staring up at me. He hummed against me. The sight of him, the sensation of his beard against me, his fingers working inside me and around my nipple, added with that pleased sound of his, it was all so beautifully erotic. I couldn't hold back. My orgasm rushed over me.

I threw my head back against the pillow while tossing an arm over my mouth to stifle my moan.

He yanked his arm away from my breast so he could tug my arm free. "Give me those moans, baby. I want to hear what I do to you. Fuck if I care who else hears it, and you shouldn't, either."

His fingers kept at my spasming pussy, then he replaced them with his tongue. His thumb rubbed at my sensitive clit. Another satisfied sound came from him. I'd never had a double orgasm, and if I wasn't mistaken he gave me another. I cried out, reveling in so much pleasure, and so much tension being released.

"Yes! God," I moaned, riding his face in earnest.

Suddenly, Gamble hovered over me. He took my mouth in a brutal kiss but didn't put any weight on me. I arched my back and felt the barest sensation of his cock near my pussy.

I broke the kiss. "Give me your weight, Gage. I want it. No, I *need* it. I need you, inside me."

"Kitten," he whispered, peppering kisses along my neck.

I hooked a leg over his hips. It opened me wider, and I ground myself on his cock. He let half his weight settle on me while a hand darted out to his nightstand.

"Are you sure?" he asked.

I wrapped an arm around him. "Yes, hurry up."

He tore a condom open with his teeth, and rolled it on. I sat up and whipped the towel off his waist.

His eyes flared. "Dyin' to do that, weren't you?"

I smiled. "I want to see you naked."

His brows arched. Quick as lightning, he whipped his t-shirt over my head. "Fair's fair, kitten."

"Yes, it is," I murmured, cupping his cheek.

He read my intention to kiss him and kissed me instead. As he gave me more of his weight, I lowered to the bed. We kissed for so long, I wondered if he would ever give me his cock. I adjusted my hips to line him up. Then he rolled, taking me with him, and our kiss ended.

"Ride me, Victoria."

My eyes widened. "You did it again," I muttered.

"Did what?" he asked, his hands splayed wide across my hips, guiding me onto his thick cock.

I hovered over him. "You protected me... again," I whispered.

"Always," he whispered back.

He had girth, and I was a woman who liked girth. To savor the moment, I sank down as slow as I could.

"You're killing me, kitten." His voice sounded raw and gravelly.

I smirked. "It's worth taking my time, Gamble."

His head tilted. He groaned. "Yeah... it fuckin' is, but it's still fuckin' torture."

I had him to the hilt. He filled me in the best way. I looked down at him to see fire in his eyes. My hips raised and I sank again slowly, but his hands on my hips put on the pressure and he guided me to a faster tempo.

"Oh, yeah," I breathed.

After I kept the tempo for a few thrusts, he let a hand travel to my breasts. Then the other joined in and he pinched and rolled my nipples.

I lowered my body to his. He kissed me to distraction. I couldn't maintain the rhythm, so he rolled us and finally, I had his weight on me.

"Gamble."

He stilled instantly. "What's wrong?"

"Nothing. Fuck me. Like you mean it, baby."

On a groan he kissed me while his hips pistoned into me. My back arched, my legs wrapped around him so I could take him deep.

He trailed his lips to my ear. "Can you come a third time, baby?"

"I don't know. Never came twice in a row before."

His self-satisfied smile lit up his entire face. "Let's aim for a hat-trick, kitten."

He intensified his thrusts, grinding up on each one, then his fingers found my clit and he worked me.

His rhythm faltered as his breathing became labored. "Not much longer, Vic."

I matched his thrusts, grinding against him, and I got a hat-trick.

Gamble

Returning to the bed from the bathroom, a strange sensation filled Gamble. As much as he wanted to say he didn't know what it was, instinctively he knew. It wasn't love, but the knowledge he was with a woman who could be *it* for him. That could be the hormones, but he knew better. The moment he'd laid eyes on Victoria he'd felt the attraction, so it stood to reason sex for them would be phenomenal. And that the attraction between them would only strengthen. Yeah, this wasn't love. Not this soon.

Gramps had been the only decent father figure in his life. But he passed away before talking to him about love.

It was too damn early for him to be thinking about love.

Yet, much like he couldn't stay away from her, his thoughts kept straying back to love.

His protective urges were on high alert too. He didn't want her going into the office tomorrow. Had the other women not brought her so many clothes to choose from, she probably would have been forced to take a day off to get better clothes for the rest of the week.

But she'd said she had two decent outfits, thanks to Trinity and Stephanie. That surprised the hell out of him, because Stephanie was shorter. Victoria could nearly match his six feet two inches when she wore her high heels. Hell, if she wore stripper heels, she probably would be as tall as him.

His dick twitched at the idea.

Victoria widened her eyes at him. She stood at the dresser mixing rum with soda. She wore his t-shirt again, this time she had it on right.

"You are sexy as fuck in that shirt, kitten. Who knew?"

He snagged a pair of boxer briefs from a drawer next to her and stepped into them.

"Is that why your sizable cock moved a moment ago?"

He grinned. "You could say that."

She shook her head. "Are you making your own drink, or should I do it?"

"I'll do it."

She stepped aside, but didn't go back to the bed.

He didn't want to broach the subject, but he had to ask. "You sure you can't take the day off tomorrow?"

"I'm sure. Besides, I don't have any court dates for a while. I'll be fine."

He sighed as he poured rum into his glass. "I'm still following you to work after we pick up your car."

With her saucy smile, he fought the need to kiss her. "Gonna follow me to the door, too?"

He tilted his head. "Wasn't, but I am now."

"You're crazy."

"You've got to take this serious, Vic."

"I am, but the idea that they'll come around at seven-thirty in the morning is a bit much. Based on what Roman said, they probably don't wake up until eleven at the earliest."

He splashed some soda into his glass, put the cap on it, and turned to her. "Never assume about assholes like this. Now, you want some tunes? We can watch TV if you prefer."

She laughed. "Not a chance. I want to hear more of your music."

He smiled. "Good."

Monday afternoon, he had just finished his last set of bicep curls with twenty-pound dumbbells, when he caught sight of Victoria. She walked in, scanned her member card, and stopped when she saw him. He stood at the edge of the free-weight area, dragging a towel down his face.

The way her eyes trailed over him, there was no question she liked him wearing the old t-shirt he'd cut into a tank-top with thin straps. He recalled Stephanie had said they were really spaghetti straps. Victoria licked her lips as she stared at his biceps, then her eyes traced his chest. That didn't surprise him, since the shirt barely covered his nipples.

In return, his eyes traveled down her body, a gentle smile forming on his face.

He watched her throat bob as she swallowed. "What are you doing here?"

"I'd ask you the same question, but I don't think you're here to lift."

Her hazel eyes skittered to the side. "No."

"Here to run?" he asked.

She took a deep breath. He sensed she wanted to bolt. If they hadn't gotten physical last night, he'd think *he* made her nervous, but he realized she'd been accosted *while running*. He didn't want her being scared of something she used to do because of Luis and Ernesto.

"Vickie," he said in a gentle voice.

She looked at him.

"You want company? While you run?"

Her brow furrowed. "Don't most people do their cardio first and then weights?"

He grinned. "I didn't do any cardio. And I don't give into other people's opinions about how to fuckin' work out. Do the work, see the benefits. Not seein' the benefits, figure out why you're not."

After a short nod, she kept quiet.

He gently flung his towel at her bicep. "Come on. We'll snag the two best elliptical machines since they're open."

As they climbed onto the machines, she asked, "I didn't know you were a member here."

He set his machine for a slow pace to start. "Yeah. Today got a little crazy, which is why I'm here late. Normally, if I come in, I do it at lunch. Good way to break the monotony of the day. But most of the time I lift at the clubhouse. It depends on who's around or how I'm feeling that day."

She nodded. "That makes sense. Thanks for coming over here with me."

He gave her a sideways glance. "Don't know what you're talking about. Gotta burn calories after all that brisket yesterday."

She had her machine at a level similar to his. From the corner of his eye, he saw her look at him. He made eye contact with her, and she tilted her head at her phone. "You mind if I put in my ear buds? I don't normally talk and run."

His lips tipped up. "Have at it, Vic. But, find me before you're ready to leave."

He put in two and a half miles on the elliptical at a steady pace. Next to him, Victoria's legs moved at a rapid clip. With a glance at her machine, he saw she'd gone three point one miles. The look on her face told him she was in the zone.

Since he didn't want to interrupt that, he got off his machine and hit the locker room. He took a quick shower, and tugged on fresh clothes. As he tied his boots, an idea struck him.

He sauntered out to the main floor, and saw Victoria was still on her machine, but at a much slower pace. By the time he came even with her, she turned the machine off. He waited for her to climb down. She looked even more beautiful with flushed cheeks and a sheen of sweat on her face.

With a grin, she stopped in front of him. "Thanks for that."

He shook his head. "Pleasure was all mine, kitten. Wanna go to the Bayou Moon?"

She did a short head shake. "You mean, Uncle Mick's pizza place?"

He smirked. "I do."

"Okay, but I'll need to shower at the clubhouse because my landlord told me at lunch today that I couldn't get back in my unit yet, and I didn't bring my stuff to shower."

His eyebrow cocked. "I got a feeling your Uncle Mick wouldn't care how you show up to his place."

Her head tilted back with her laughter. "Your feeling is wrong, Gage. If you've never been there at night, it's a whole other vibe. Even after working there, I'm not sure how Uncle Mick manages to pull it off, but he does. He shows no favoritism toward me, and he would kick me out in a heartbeat for showing up like this."

An hour later, they sat at a table tucked into the back corner of Bayou Moon Pizza. Being in a corner was good because the sight of Victoria in the skin-tight forest green dress had him fighting his cock getting hard. Nobody needed to see that, least of all her godfather, who'd glared at Gamble the moment they walked through the door.

After a headshake, Mick had muttered, "I'll make an exception on his attire because it's you, Vickie."

Victoria told no lies. It was like the entire place did a one-eighty between lunch and dinner. At lunch there were no tablecloths, but now every table was draped in black, and a small tea light candle sat in the center.

Their server said her name was Skylar. They weren't likely to forget it since every so often Mick's loud baritone voice would bellow out her name to a strange tune Gamble had never heard. He'd have felt bad except it made Victoria groan and put her head in her hand, which he found amusing.

Her head snapped up. "Don't you laugh. You ought to have heard—"

"Your name sung out? I did, kitten."

"Oh, that's right," she whispered.

Mick sidled up to their table. "Don't let me catch you staring at her tush again, biker."

He smiled. "Won't happen again, sir."

Victoria's giggle had both men staring at her. "Sorry, sorry. Don't mind me."

"Right, like that's gonna happen," Mick said. "Now, I've decided Skylar needs to wait a different table, and you two get me instead. Have you decided on your orders?"

Anyone else, Gamble would be irritated at the blatant overprotectiveness, but after everything Victoria had been through, he loved that she had that from him. They placed their orders and Mick gave him a long look. Gamble nodded at the man, and after a moment he nodded back.

As soon as he was gone, Victoria said, "You staring at my ass isn't the only thing he has to worry about anymore."

He chuckled as he shook his head.

"Good day at work?" he asked.

Her head wobbled. "Long day, definitely. How about you?"

"I finished a bike today, just gotta put a clear-coat on it tomorrow."

"That's cool. A standard paint job?"

He shook his head. "No. This one, the owner picked out one of my sketches. I put a tiger on his bike."

Her eyes widened. "Wow. So, that drafting desk isn't for show."

"Nope," he said, sipping his iced tea.

"It's cool that you're artistic."

He shook his head. "It's cool that Har gave me the opportunity to put it to good use."

She nodded.

After a while, he said, "I sense something's up."

Her eyes softened. "Sorry, it's just... I don't want to unload on you."

He leaned toward her. "Don't do that. There are some things I can't help you with, but if it's listening to you, I'll do that all day long, Vic."

She sighed. "My sister's coming to town on the sixth."

"Okay," he drawled. "That's a good thing, isn't it?"

"My mom's a little strange –parenting wise. They say parents shouldn't play favorites, and Dad never did. But Mom favors Miranda in a big way."

He nodded.

She continued. "You'd think that shit would be done by now, but no."

"That blows. Your pop doesn't wade in?"

"Only when it gets too dramatic. Mom's good at slowly laying down the guilt and building up the drama."

"Fuck that shit, kitten. You got enough on your plate."

"That's easier said than done—"

"Bullshit. They know about the rape, your mom needs to lay off."

"Miranda doesn't know," she whispered.

"You didn't tell her?"

She smiled ruefully. "Mom doesn't want me and my 'private business' interfering with Miranda's medical residency."

"The fuck?" he breathed. "She's your sister. I'm guessing y'all are close."

"Somewhat. But Miranda's going to be pissed when she finds out."

Mick brought over their food. Chicken Parmesan for Victoria and Chicken Marsala for him. Fifteen minutes later, Mick returned.

"Your dad made the mistake of calling me tonight," he announced.

Victoria semi-glowered at Mick. "No. You made the mistake of running your mouth."

He dipped his chin. "Watch your tone, missy. You messed up by not introducing this guy to them."

"It's on the agenda," she muttered.

Mick grabbed a chair from a nearby table and sat down. "Well, your agenda just got rearranged. They're on their way."

Victoria spluttered. "Wait. What?"

Mick turned, giving Gamble a scrutinizing look. "You serious about her?"

"Uncle Mick, it's too soon for either of us to know that." Victoria said.

Gamble didn't like hearing her say that, but he kept focused on Mick.

Without breaking their stare, Mick responded to Victoria. "Baloney. I knew with Estelle the moment I laid eyes on her."

Victoria scoffed. "Well, the first time we met, we argued, so it's a little too soon to say, Uncle Mick."

Mick cocked a brow at him, then turned to her. "That ain't sayin' much, Vickie. You'd argue with a fork if only it could talk back."

That bordered on disrespect and Gamble could see Victoria digging her heels in for a squabble.

"That isn't true."

His face softened. "You're right." Then he looked at Gamble. "Estelle and I argued the first time I met her."

Victoria laughed. "I forgot about that. To hear Auntie Stell tell it, you still argue with her tooth and nail."

Mick shrugged. "She exaggerates."

Victoria laughed.

"You really her uncle?" he asked.

"What's it to you?" Mick asked, spearing him with a hard look.

"He's my godfather. I thought you knew that," Victoria said.

He looked at her and grinned. "I didn't."

"I'm still family, and I haven't decided if I like you."

From the front of the restaurant, a man bellowed, "Yo! Mickey!"

With a triumphant smile, he stood and looked at Victoria. "Well, I'll send Skylar over with some drinks for your parents."

As Mick walked away, Victoria leaned forward. "I'm so sorry. If you want, we can run out the back door."

He grinned. "It's fine, kitten. I'd rather they meet me now than if shit hits the fan again later."

She nodded. "That's good thinking."

CHAPTER 10

TRIPLE G

VICTORIA

I watched as Uncle Mick and Dad exchanged man-hugs. Then Dad moseyed back to our table with his hands in the pockets of his khakis. Once it became clear Mom wasn't with him, I got a bad feeling.

I pushed away from the table to stand, but Dad shook his head. "No, pumpkin, stay seated."

"Hi, Dad."

"Hi, yourself," he said, his eyes moving meaningfully to Gamble, who stood.

"Dad, this is Gage Garrison, or Gamble. Gamble, this is my dad, Henry Carlton."

As they shook hands, Gamble said, "You can call me Gamble, sir."

Dad nodded. "Gamble. Nice to meet you."

To assuage my curiosity and thwart Dad's efforts to grill Gamble, I asked, "Where's Mom? I thought you were both coming?"

Gamble sat down, and Dad settled into the chair Uncle Mick left at our table. "I should have corrected you on the phone yesterday, sweetheart. You assumed I was at your place *with* your mother, but I wasn't."

I shook my head. "Okay."

He took a deep breath. "Your mother is separating from me."

I stared at Dad. Even though I didn't live with them anymore, the idea of my parents divorcing hurt. My nose tingled, and I swallowed. There was no reason to cry. I willed myself not to cry. That had never worked for me before, and it didn't work now, so tears pooled in my eyes.

Then I heard Gamble mutter, "Are you shitting me?"

Dad shot Gamble a confused look, but then looked at me. "I'm sorry, Vickie. I know this isn't the best way to find out."

"You can say that again," Gamble ground out.

For once, the tears subsided. I focused on Gamble and saw how angry he was. My brows furrowed. "Why are you angry?"

He blew out a breath. "Why am I angry? Kitten, this is the last damn thing you need right now. You've been assaulted, had your apartment vandalized in a cruel and vicious way. Add to that, you told me just now your mother didn't want you telling your sister about your situation because it might interfere with your sister's studies... I'm guessing here, but that's not why she didn't want you confiding your troubles. She wanted all the drama and attention for herself and this shit."

Dad sat back, staring at Gamble. "You don't mince words."

Gamble turned his irritated gaze to Dad. "No, I don't, and I don't give a fuck who I offend because of it. Especially when it comes to lightening her load."

To my surprise, Dad's easy-going smile spread across his lips. "I like you for her. Never thought I'd see the day, but you are exactly the kind of man she needs."

"Dad, it's a little soon for that."

Like neither one of them heard me, Gamble and Dad kept eye contact for a long while. Then Gamble lifted his chin and turned to me.

I shot him wide eyes. "We should've run out the back door like I suggested."

Dad laughed, long and loud. Then he said, "What have I told you, pumpkin? You can run but you can't hide from what life intends to throw your way."

Gamble nodded, then looked at Dad. "Out of curiosity, did I guess right? She's looking for attention and Victoria might steal that?"

Dad sighed as his expression morphed into a scowl. "We'd have to ask Erin to know for sure. I hate saying it, but I think you're right."

Gamble's lips pressed together hard for a moment before he asked, "Does she give a damn about what happened to Victoria?"

Dad leaned forward. "Yes. She was torn up about it."

"They are two separate things, Gamble," I said.

His head tilted back and forth as he deliberated. "They would be, but in this case, I think they're tied pretty close together. Has she reached out to try and help you with this shit? Gone with you to a counseling session?"

I looked to the side and sighed. "If there's a counseling session to attend, I would think she should go to one with Dad."

Dad shook his head. "Honey, the issues in our marriage have been going on for a long time."

I nodded. "All the more reason to see a professional."

Gamble wasn't swayed by what I had to say if his eyes were any indicator. Dad noticed the expression, and I felt a little awkward.

Then Gamble said, "No offense, but I don't think I should meet her."

Uncle Mick sauntered up. "Who's he talking about? Erin?"

Dad shot him a small grin. "Yep. He's got my blessing."

Uncle Mick gave Gamble his side eye. "You always were too damn soft, Henry. I'm reserving judgment. He could still be a bozo."

I tilted my head back. "Someone shoot me."

Gamble grabbed my hand. "Not a chance. They love you."

I righted my head.

It almost felt like he left something unsaid.

From the tender look in Gamble's eyes, I had to bite my tongue. Those expressive blue eyes made me wonder if he could love me. But that was a foolish thought.

Uncle Mick grunted. "He just scored some points. Don't know if that makes him smart or a suck-up."

The idea of Gamble as a suck-up made me burst with laughter, which made all three men smile at me.

We walked into the clubhouse through the back door. I couldn't believe how loud the bluesy-rock music was.

Mensa was on his way out of the kitchen with a bag of Chex Mix. "Hey, G. Victoria. You're just in time. We're startin' a pool tournament. You want in?"

Gamble looked down at me. I kept my expression neutral, but he could still read me.

"Nah, man. Is Tiny tryin' to make everybody deaf?"

Mensa chuckled darkly. "No, but I'll tell him you asked."

"Shut up, motherfucker."

"Goodnight, Victoria," Mensa called and ambled away.

Inside Gamble's room, I nearly cringed. It was like we were at the bar. I turned to him. "Any chance I can drive to a hotel right now?"

He grinned. "It's not that bad."

"I could crash with Heidi."

"I'm keeping you safe."

"She's got a gun," I semi-lied. I wasn't certain she had one, but heaven knew she talked a good game.

He stalked toward me, shaking his head. "Just got your dad's seal of approval and 'points' from your godfather. Not gonna fuck that up by fallin' down on the job now."

He wrapped his arms around me and kissed my neck.

"Thought you didn't care about their opinions."

He sucked at the juncture of my neck and shoulder. Against my skin there, he murmured, "You aren't just any woman, kitten."

That gave me pause. Whether Gamble noticed my reaction, I didn't know because he nipped at my skin then soothed it with his tongue. It served as an excellent distraction.

The sound of glass breaking drew me up short. I pulled away gently. "You still say it isn't that bad?"

He smiled. "Some of us get rowdy no matter what day of the week it is. I have earplugs for when we sleep. Look at the upside, though: nobody will hear you when I make you come, because the music's so loud."

My lips tipped up. "You're right, but then *your* music will be harder to hear."

He chuckled. "The hell it will. I'll crank it up."

I grinned. "More of your group, Slightly Stoopid?"

He chucked me under the chin. "Not with that racket out there. I was thinking we fight fire with fire and play some Buddy Guy."

"I take it he plays the blues."

He grinned. "He is a fucking blues legend, woman. Let's get naked. You were relaxed after your work out, but dinner got you wound up again."

While slipping out of my shoes, I pressed my lips together and shook my head. "How can you tell?"

He tore his shirt over his head. "Kitten, anybody would be wound up after that bombshell."

The same urge I'd had at the gym came over me, but this time I gave into it. In a flash, I stepped into his space and put a hand behind his back to hold him still. Then I darted my tongue out and licked his nipple.

"What are you doing, Vic?"

I loved hearing his gravelly voice, especially since I knew *I* did that to him. My fingers traced their way down to the button of his jeans while I dragged my lips to his other pec. "I'm going to taste you," I said against his nipple.

As I began to sink, he caught me at my underarms. "You can do that in the bed, Victoria."

I shot him a dose of side eye. "You're not faking me out, are you?"

He laughed. "No. I want to be reclined, pillows propped behind me, legs cocked and watching everything you do to me. Can't do that standing here."

I straightened, pressed my weight against him and tried to guide him toward the bed. "Then we should get moving."

His hands went to the zipper at the back of my dress. Then it slipped down to my feet. "We'd be moving in the right direction, if you were naked."

My hands went into my panties and then I shoved them down to my ankles. In a swift motion, I stepped out of them while whipping off my bra. "Done and done. Let's go, Triple G."

His laughter forced him to pause with his pants at his knees. "What did you call me?"

I climbed on to his bed. "You heard me." He smacked my upturned tush, and I yelled, "Hey!"

He mounted me from behind, but put one arm alongside mine while the other wrapped around my belly. Then with a wrestling move, he had me on my back. "What'd you call me?"

"Triple G," I whispered.

He chuckled. "That's cute."

I shook my head. "It's not cute, it's true. Gage Gamble Garrison."

His blue eyes danced over my face. I could get used to watching him like this.

Finally, he said, "I like it."

Then he kissed me, slow and sweet. Something told me we were skipping the blow job.

Even though I didn't want to, I broke our kiss. "I can taste you while lying on my back, Gamble."

He nuzzled my neck, his beard tickling me. "We could do that later."

"I have to get up in the morning, honey."

"So do I. Trust me, you'll get your taste."

My brows lowered.

He chuckled. "Don't pout at me, kitten."

"I'm not pouting."

His brows arched as he rolled to his side and moved up the bed. "You *are* pouting, but fine. Let's see what you can do with those pouty lips, baby."

He snagged all the pillows and piled them behind his back. Then I crawled between his cocked and bent legs. I couldn't help myself. My hands rested on his knees, and I stroked his legs, loving the feel of his coarse hair on his powerful thighs beneath my hands. I moved forward, my hands sliding up his torso to his shoulders. He made a low groaning sound I almost missed.

Leaning forward, I kissed him on the lips. He took it deeper and longer than I'd intended, but I enjoyed it all the same.

I kissed my way down his built torso, letting my tongue trace those washboard abdominal muscles, and then took his hard cock in my hand.

Gamble hissed in a breath when I dragged the tip of my tongue from the base to the tip. I glanced up at him. His hand darted out and shoved my hair to one side of my head.

His blue eyes looked brighter for some reason as he stared at me. "You are too fuckin' beautiful, Victoria."

I laved the head of his dick with a flat tongue. "Could say the same to you, Gage."

Then, I lowered my mouth and took him deep, working him with my hand. He tasted good. I lowered myself to pay attention to his balls.

"Oh, shit," he sighed.

I chuckled and moved back up. With his cock back in my mouth, I used more suction, and his hips began to buck.

Then his hands were under my arms again, lifting me up. "God damn, kitten. You give world-class head, but I don't want to come in your mouth tonight."

He had a condom in hand, tore it open and rolled it on. "You want to ride me, or can you take my weight?"

I fit my mouth to his and kissed him hard. He took that as an invitation and rolled me to my back. His hands hitched my legs up and he slid inside me to the hilt.

I turned my head, hissing, "Yes. I love the feeling of you inside me, honey."

"Love the feeling of being inside you, kitten."

There was that tone again. Like at the restaurant, like he'd wanted to say something else...or not exactly else, but in addition to, what he'd said.

I had to remind myself this wasn't a courtroom. I couldn't dwell on his tone, and what was being said without words. Then he picked up the pace and I could hardly think. Instead, I savored every stroke and sensation he wrought from my body.

I watched as he thrust into me. Committed to memory, the sight of his straining biceps as he hovered over me.

God, he was simply beautiful.

He lifted a hand and tipped my chin up, making eye contact. "Look at me, baby."

I smirked. "Believe me, I was."

He swiveled his hips on an upward thrust, making me cry out. "Gamble."

A satisfied glimmer hit his eyes. "Yeah. I feel that too. Gonna make you yell my name when you come."

When he'd made me come before, my ability to say much of anything fell by the wayside. I didn't have the chance to tell him that. He lowered his weight to me and kissed me.

I threaded my fingers into his hair and gave a slight tug. He growled into my mouth, so I did it again. His hips bucked faster and harder.

He interrupted the kiss. "You're being naughty, kitten."

"I'm not," I breathed. My orgasm built and threatened to hit me like a hurricane-force storm surge, and I couldn't wait for it to fall and rush over me.

"You are. Making me want to come before you do," he grunted.

Then, neither of us said much at all. His hand snaked between us, and he homed in on my clit. With a few strategic swirls, my orgasm came on strong and fast. I bucked my hips, only for Gamble to stop on an inward thrust.

On a deep sigh, he breathed my name.

After we both cleaned up, we were curled together in his bed. He'd brought a portable speaker to his nightstand, and we continued to listen to Buddy Guy. We were listening to a blues ballad. Even with the sound so close by, the party in the common room made it hard to make out all of the lyrics.

Gamble's fingers traced soothing patterns on my back. His eyes were fixed on the ceiling. I wanted to ask what he was thinking about, but that was a bad question to ask any man.

His eyes slid toward me. "I told you a little about my parents yesterday."

I nodded. "Yeah."

"When I said they were neglectful, I wasn't joking."

I leaned up to look him in the eyes. "Believe me, I didn't think you were."

His hand came up and guided my head back to his shoulder. "That's good, Victoria." After a moment, he continued. "I mention it because there was no man in my life to talk to me about women, and damn sure not about love."

"Okay," I drawled.

"Don't know if it's the extreme nature of the shit swirling around us, or if it's a little like what your Uncle Mick said, but there's something... more between us than what I'm used to, Victoria."

I nodded against his shoulder. "I think I get what you're saying, but what did you mean by 'what Uncle Mick said'?"

I felt and heard his chuckle. "Said he argued with your aunt the first time he saw her, didn't he?"

I smiled. "Yeah."

"Well... I don't think it's the conventional way to win a woman's heart, but then again, I've never been very conventional."

I laughed and tried to roll away, but he held me close. From under my lashes, I gazed up at him. "I didn't think you wanted to win my heart."

He gave me a squeeze. "Can't win you if I don't win your heart too. Can I?"

That took my breath away. "I don't know," I whispered.

His eyes softened. "Yeah, you do know." He leaned down and gave me a lazy, sweet kiss. "Let's get some sleep."

He handed me some earplugs, then he turned out the lights.

With everything he'd said now, and the various things he'd said at dinner, I never thought I'd fall asleep. After the music in the common room finally died down, I did, but it was the most fitful sleep I'd had in weeks.

In the morning, I felt like something two cats dragged in. For a moment, I debated taking the day off.

Gamble rolled into me. "You sleep well?"

"How honest do you want it?"

"All the honesty, Vic. Always."

I nodded. With his background, honesty would be a no-brainer.

"Not well, Gage. Not even a little bit. But, I'm hungry. Let's go eat something."

He pecked my lips, rolled the other way, and turned on the light. "You're bossy in the morning, babe."

As we trudged to the kitchen, I said, "I dig sleeping with you at night, and I understand you're keeping me safe. But, I need to stay somewhere a little quieter."

He put his arm around my shoulders. "Should be quieter tonight."

We walked into the kitchen to find Cynic sitting at a small table. A bald, stocky man sat across from him. Both of them were sipping coffee.

Cynic caught Gamble's eyes. "Fiona's place is furnished and she's staying with me, so it's empty."

A look passed between the men.

I waded into the silence. "What aren't you saying?"

Gamble leveled his eyes on me. "Fiona killed a man in her living room. Lots of people don't like staying—"

"I don't care," I said.

Something I hadn't told Gamble: the lack of windows in his room weirded me out. And after last night, it was clear quite a few of the brothers partied until the wee hours. I didn't want to be a killjoy. Yet, with Gamble's room butting up to the common room bar, I couldn't deal with that noise at night. Which meant I couldn't stay at the clubhouse all week long.

"You don't believe in bad juju?" the bald man asked. As he turned toward me, I caught sight of his name patch, which read Block.

I tilted my head, but aimed my eyes at Gamble and Cynic. "I believe Fiona's an awesome woman. It wouldn't hurt for me to soak up some of her vibes."

"She's not around to hear you right now, you know," Gamble muttered.

I grinned. "Yeah, which is how you know I mean it."

"It's not likely the Abeyetas will find her there," Cynic said.

"They might if they're following her," Block muttered.

124

Cynic frowned at Block. "Which one of us is supposed to be cynical here? They won't follow her."

Gamble looked at me. "We can tour it at lunch...you take a lunch, right?"

I gave him a wry grin. "Yes. They let me away from my desk for that long."

CHAPTER 11

TWERP

GAMBLE

"**D**on't let them get under your skin, Gage," Brittney said.
He tossed a rag onto a workbench, shook his head, and kept
the phone to his ear. "You know they've been under my skin like a bad
splinter for years. They should all be in jail, Brit."

"Gage, for the last time, you need to let it go."

He ran his free hand through his hair. "How the hell can you let it go?"

Her smile came through in her voice. "Because I found a good man.
And that's the other reason I'm not worried about their threat. He's
a damn good cop, who's headed to the FBI. I should have called you
sooner, but we're moving to Virginia."

His lungs froze. "You are?"

"Yeah."

The upside was that the move brought her closer to Biloxi, but she
would still be over nine hundred miles away.

He walked out to the parking lot in front of the garage bay. "Are you
marrying this guy?"

"His name is Taylor, you know."

"Yeah. Are you marrying him?"

She paused. "I'm a pretty liberal, forward-thinking woman, but for marriage, I would need to be asked first. I'm a little old-fashioned that way."

He huffed out a laugh. "Okay, has *Taylor* mentioned marriage or any of that shit?"

"We've been living together for six years now, baby brother. We've looked at rings in the past. It hasn't been discussed much, but I'm sure he'll ask when he's ready."

"He drags you across the country and dumps you, I'm comin' up there to kick his ass. I don't give a damn if he's in the FBI or not."

Brittney laughed for a long time, which made him smile. He loved making her laugh. "It isn't the stone age anymore, Gage. He's not 'dragging' me anywhere. I went with him to find a place to live. Hell, I have to change jobs too, you know. I'm cool with this. We love each other, the legalities will work themselves out when the time's right."

"Okay," he muttered.

Part of him wondered if their parents knew about Taylor, but he shoved that aside.

As though she were on the same wavelength, his sister said, "Mom and Dad are coming up to meet him when we settle in Virginia."

He bit his lip. She'd been with him for over six years. Their parents should have met him already. Then again, his parents were procrastinators of the first order... unless a betting window was closing. They knew how to haul ass and get money on the line for that.

"Don't be angry, Gage," she murmured.

"Never gonna happen, Brit."

"You gotta let that go. It isn't healthy to hang onto your ill-will. Especially against our parents."

He tipped his head back and stared at the blue sky. "How you can be so forgiving, I'll never know."

"What happened to me was awful, but it happen*ed*. Past tense. I can't dwell on that and live in the past. If I did, I'd never know the love of a good man."

He sighed. "You're right. But you need to keep your guard up. If you want me to talk to Taylor, I'll do that."

Unlike his parents, he'd made it a point to visit Brittney in Seattle every chance he got. When she'd moved in with Taylor, Gamble flew out to meet him. It didn't go well since he'd shared who he was and who his brothers were. Taylor, being a straight arrow with ambitions to get into the FBI, frowned upon all of that. They didn't exactly have words, but the tension made Brittney uncomfortable –the last thing either man wanted to do to her– which ultimately led them to striking a truce. Gamble living over two thousand miles away helped with that.

Brittney pulled him from his thoughts when she chuckled. "I'll let you know if you should call him. He was pleased as punch to hear your club cleaned up its act. But, when I said don't let them get under your skin, I meant, don't let them manipulate you. It sounds like you care about Victoria. Juan and his brothers were always good at figuring out what matters to people... and then using it against them. I hate the idea of you possibly playing into their hands in any way."

A small smile pulled at his lips as he looked down at his boots. He'd always loved it when Brittney got protective of him. "Don't worry, sis. My brothers have all warned me to keep my head together, but I *am* getting impatient. Luis and Ernesto are out there roaming free, and it bugs the fuck out of me. But, I'll be smart. Don't worry."

"When do I get to meet Victoria?"

He chuckled. "It's been two days, Brit."

Her tone became reprimanding. "No, you said she was hurt over a month ago. Which means it's been over a month, even if you weren't going after her then."

"Whatever. Let's not split hairs. I'll introduce you to her when you have your engagement party."

"Shut up, twerp."

He laughed. If anyone else called him a 'twerp,' he'd punch them. Hearing it from her after so long, it made him feel normal... and loved. "Keep me posted on your move. Love you, Brit."

"Love you too, Gage."

The door to the shop opened and Cynic came out. "You done jackin' your jaw?"

"Yeah. You ready to ride?"

"Only if you gave Victoria the address to Fiona's."

He nodded. "I did. She said she'd meet us there."

"Then mount up, Gamble."

"Is she going to sell this place?" Victoria asked as she walked away from the guest bedroom inside Fiona's bungalow.

Cynic turned his hands up. "She hasn't decided."

Victoria shook her head. "If it weren't for my student loans... well, that's not true, either."

"What are you talking about, Vic?" Gamble asked her.

She hesitated. When she spoke, she sounded reluctant. "I have student loans to repay, as you can imagine. But, like you pointed out to me last month, I'm not that great at my job—"

Between his clenched teeth, he growled, "Kitten."

She waved a hand at him. "No, no. I don't have a great record, which says it all. And that bugs me because I'm really pretty damned competitive. But at the same time, I don't care because my heart isn't in this. It's draining me on so many levels to be the appointed lawyer to people who can't afford one."

She wandered into the kitchen. He and Cynic followed her.

As she stared out the window, she continued. "Sometimes, like with Ramone, there's no getting around the fact he should've pled guilty and taken a lesser charge. He wouldn't do that. It tied my hands, and I couldn't make the case for him. But then there are the people who don't have the money for better representation, and the deck is stacked against them. They might be innocent, but they can't post bail. Their families don't have smartphones. They can't get witnesses or anything to prove they weren't where someone else says they were, the whole thing. Losing those cases are the worst because I know that not only the legal system failed them, but many other systems over the years failed them, too."

Cynic leaned against the kitchen counter. "I don't know you that well, lady, but you need to get a new job."

She turned to Cynic and pointed at him for a moment. "Exactly! I've got so many resumes out there, it's not funny. I want to find a new job, but that's easier said than done in my field. Something they *don't* tell you in college."

Gamble hated hearing the defeat in her voice. He looked at Cynic. "What about the club's firm?"

Cynic's lips twisted into a half-frown. "What about them, G?"

"They handle all sorts of law, don't they? That's who Brute—"

Victoria shook her head. "I'll land where I'm supposed to when the time is right."

Cynic shot her a disgusted look. "Fuck that good karma bullshit. You spouted off about how innocent people have the deck stacked against them. That goes for you, too. If you got a chance at an 'in' with a firm, you need to take it. Do you want to practice criminal law? Or do you want to do something else, like family law?"

She stared off into space for a long moment. "Up until last night, when Dad unloaded about him and Mom separating, family law intrigued me. But at this point, I'm thinking wills and real estate law would be more my jam, but that's—"

"Zip it," Cynic muttered. "If that's what it is, then that's what it is. We'll see if Gower and Gower has connections. Odds are damn good they do. As much money as we've given that firm, it's high time we put it to positive use."

"You mean good use," she said, smiling.

He shook his head. "No, Victoria. Meant what I said. It was good use when it got a brother out of jail. It will be positive use if it helps you land a job that suits you."

Her grateful smile nearly undid Gamble. "Well, thank you."

"Don't thank me —or us— yet. And if it falls through, definitely don't come to blame me. Blame Gamble."

She chuckled. "Are you sure Fiona doesn't mind us staying here?"

Cynic shook his head. "Hell, you're doin' her a favor by staying here. Once a week one of us has to stop by and flush the toilets and shit. Make sure everything's still cool."

Victoria nodded, and Cynic handed her a key and a clicker for the garage. "I gotta split. Need to meet a distributor at the bar. Later."

"Later, 'Nic," Gamble said.

After he left, Victoria frowned. "He didn't give you a key."

He grinned. "Gave one to me before you got here."

"Convenient."

"It is," he said, sauntering closer to her. "I gotta get back to the shop."

Her head tilted a fraction. "So, you're not following me back to work?"

He shook his head. "Oh, I am. Not gonna let my guard down yet."

"I'll be happy when this is all done. Not that I'm not grateful for everything you and your club is doing for me, but I hate how upside-down my life feels right now."

He slid his hands around her hips, pulling her close. "I understand, kitten. But better to feel upside-down and be safe, than feel normal and get hurt again. Gonna have someone else follow you back here this evening. I'll be at the shop late, catching up on some work."

She sighed. "See, I hate that this is causing you problems too."

He shook his head. "Don't worry about it. Just don't lose whoever's tailing you, and pull your car into the garage when you get here. Fiona's got a top-notch security system, with cameras all around. We'll know if they follow you or come around on foot."

Her hands moved up to his neck and she gave him a chaste kiss. "I have to drop by my place after work. There weren't any sheets on the bed, and I have some clean linens I can grab. Plus, I'm guessing you won't be eating with me, so I'll bring some of my food that's still good."

He didn't like that idea, but he liked the idea of her getting a food delivery even less. "All right. Do my best to get back here before ten, but I'll eat at the shop."

Victoria

I rolled out of bed at ten-thirty on Sunday morning. Gamble had left around seven for a half day of work, though not until after he'd relieved his morning hard-on by getting us both off.

All week he'd been catching up on work or been out doing "club business." I didn't pry into that because it only highlighted the differences between us. I'd decided to overlook our differences and had encouraged Gamble to do the same, but asking what he was up to felt like pushing my luck.

Due to the holiday weekend, we had no basketball practice. I had just over an hour before I needed to meet Heidi for lunch. Fiona's bungalow had a great set-up. I loved her walk-in shower stall. With so much time to get ready, I did a deep conditioning of my hair and gave my legs a close shave.

Earlier this morning, Gamble mentioned Mensa would be swinging by before I left to meet Heidi. As the garage door lifted, I saw Mensa sitting astride his bike. I waved as I opened my car door. He waved two fingers at me.

I arrived early at the restaurant. My bladder was killing me, so I hit the restroom. A six-year-old girl bounded to the sink next to me while I washed my hands at the basin. She seemed vaguely familiar, but coaching basketball did that to me. I thought every kiddo looked like one from basketball.

The little girl looked at me fully and gasped. "You're in charge of basketball!"

I wasn't exactly in charge, but many of the players thought that about me.

With a big grin, I said, "I kind of am. How you doing? It's not Abby..."

"I'm Aubrey!"

I snapped my fingers and smiled. "Yes! Aubrey."

She did a little hop as she turned off the water. "You have to meet Brute."

"That's Mr. Brute, Aubrey," her mother said coming up behind her.

I usually recognized the children on the teams, but the parents were trickier. Aubrey's mom had beautiful blonde hair and bright blue eyes.

Aubrey pulled my attention away from her mom.

"Is Coach Heidi here?"

I grinned. "Not yet, but she should be soon."

Aubrey smiled. "She'll love Mr. Brute."

I wondered why the name Brute seemed so familiar to me as Aubrey led me out of the bathroom. Then we rounded the corner and I saw the patches.

A hulk of a man with dark hair looked over his shoulder, beaming at Aubrey.

I glanced at the man sitting across from him, surprised to see Gamble. He stood. "Victoria."

As the other four men at the table stood, I noticed Stephanie and Fiona.

I smiled at everyone. "Hi. Sorry to intrude. Aubrey wants me to meet Mr. Brute."

The hulk of a man held his hand out. "That's me. You doin' okay?"

I liked that he switched it up from 'how are you?'

"I'm doing all right," I said, giving him a quick handshake.

A chair scraped behind me. Cynic had grabbed a chair and passed it over the table to Gamble.

I realized what they were doing. "No, no, really. I'm meeting Heidi here."

"There's room for her, too," Gamble said.

Cynic handed Gamble another chair while Brute dragged a small table next to theirs.

After I hung my purse on the chair, I sat down. "You know, Mensa's out there. You should have him join us too."

"He needs to stay focused," Gamble said.

Across the room, I saw Heidi scanning the tables. I waved at her, and she strode to our group.

It occurred to me that the Riot brothers must be regulars here because our server didn't bat an eye at two new customers at the table. Further

134

proof they were used to the impromptu guests showing up came when the food Heidi and I ordered came out with everyone else's.

"Do you need more clothes? Sorry I couldn't make it that day," Kenzie said, her eyes sliding toward Brute.

"Zee, she's got at least four inches on you. Any of your skirts would be too short, and most of your dresses would be like shirts on her."

I shook my head while grinning. "I'm not that tall."

Heidi glanced at me sideways. "You aren't that short either."

"You're right," I said to her. Then I turned to Kenzie. "But thank you, everyone was so generous already."

Aubrey swallowed a french fry. "Why does Mommy want to give you clothes?"

Heidi leaned toward Aubrey. "Miss Vickie had a leak in her closet and her dresses got all yucky. Can you believe it?"

Aubrey's face scrunched up while Kenzie and I shared a look.

"Now, have you been practicing your dribble?" Heidi asked Aubrey.

Aubrey nodded enthusiastically. "Yeah! Mr. Brute helped me hold my hand right. So I don't slap the ball so much."

I grinned at Kenzie, but her eyes were filled with admiration, aimed at Brute.

Heidi and I didn't speak much because Aubrey was busy telling us about her summer plans. As we ate, though, I caught Heidi's eyes traveling to the far end of the table. Block sat down there, a glower on his face. Any time Block glanced our way, she made it a point to concentrate on her plate or turn to Aubrey. That was odd. Heidi wasn't a shy woman, and I'd never known her to play coy with a man.

Kenzie snagged her purse from behind her chair. "Sorry I can't stick around. It's time to get Aubrey to her dad's house. He has her the rest of the week."

Brute frowned but stood up. "I'll walk you to the car, baby."

Aubrey gave Heidi a hug. "Bye, Coach Heidi."

We watched them leave.

"You coach, too?" Cynic asked Heidi, sounding like his road name. She looked up at him. "I do. Why do you ask?"

He shrugged a shoulder. "No reason really. A little surprised is all."

She bristled. "Height never makes up for *hustle!*"

"These guys don't mean anything by it," I said, in a low voice.

Turning to me, she matched my low voice. "Oh yeah? Then why's the bald guy at the other end of the table staring at me so hard?"

Apparently, she wasn't that quiet.

Gamble said, "Because Block's our treasurer and he fuckin' hates drama."

Rather than be obvious, I let my eyes slide to the other end of the table. Block's blue eyes glared at Heidi; it made me shiver, so I could only imagine how Heidi felt.

I turned back to my friend when she scoffed. Her green eyes flared at Gamble. "That wasn't drama. I'm just opinionated."

I wobbled my head. "To men it sounds just like drama."

"Tough," she huffed. "Are we going shopping after this?"

"No," Gamble muttered.

My head turned to him. "I'm sorry, what was that?"

"Mensa doesn't do 'shops' and you need to stay safe. Buy what you need online."

From the corner of my eye, I saw Heidi lean into the table to catch Gamble's eyes. Glancing past Gamble, I saw Block tracking Heidi's every move.

"She's not going shopping for her. She's going shopping with me, so I have something to wear to the party tomorrow. Or am I uninvited because you two are done dancing around one another?"

Laughter overtook me at Heidi's words, and I threw my head back with it. The vision of Gamble dancing around *any* woman was so ludicrous it was comical.

"What is so funny?" Heidi demanded.

I widened my eyes at her while tossing a hand toward Gamble. "I can't imagine him dancing, period. We never 'danced around' each other. And seriously, you don't need me to go shopping with you. Actually, strike that. You *do* need me to go with you, but only so you buy something sensible for tomorrow. Without me, God only knows what you'll be wearing for a Fourth of July party."

Heidi gave me a pointed look. "Listen to you. Are you twenty-eight or sixty-eight? Talking about 'sensible' to a biker bash."

Fiona laughed. Then she stood and sat in Brute's empty chair. "It's not a bash."

Heidi tossed her hands out. "Whatever. I've never been to a party with bikers in the summertime."

"Or any time," I deadpanned.

Heidi looked toward the other tables and back to me. "Fair point, well made." Then she glanced at Gamble. "Still, I'd like to have some time with my girlfriend."

Gamble put his arm around my shoulders. "You'll get that time once we know she's safe. How's that for a 'fair point, well made?'"

Heidi's eyes went from Gamble's to mine. "I'm back to thinking I don't like him."

Gamble laughed and so did I.

"Give me your keys," Gamble said, as we stood in the restaurant parking lot watching Heidi drive away.

"Why?"

With his hands at my hips, he guided my body to face his. I looked up into his sparkling blue eyes. "Because I need to take a ride, and that's a thousand times better with you on the back of my bike. You give me your keys, I'll have a prospect bring your car to the clubhouse."

My head tilted. "Why do you need to take a ride, honey?"

His lips tipped up. "Partly because I just do whenever you're around. But, also because I'm antsy. I don't like feelin' that way. Two things cure it. One of them is a good long ride."

I felt my eyebrow arch. "And what's the other?"

"A joint, but I'm not in the mood to get high right now."

I shook my head. "I'm surprised sex isn't the second one."

He grinned. "Correction, three things cure it. A long ride. A joint. Or sex."

I laughed. "You are too much."

His face came closer. "Maybe, but you can handle it."

"Later, Gamble," Block muttered and strode to his bike.

My lips twisted. "I don't think he likes me... or Heidi."

Gamble's fingers tipped my chin up. "He likes you fine. And my guess is that he likes Heidi too, but he could do without the drama. Besides, it doesn't matter if he likes you or not. I like you and that's good enough for any of my brothers."

I nodded. "Where are we riding?"

His lips tipped up before he kissed me. It was lazy and sweet, but best of all it lasted for a long while. When he broke away, he whispered, "Wherever the wind takes us, kitten."

I handed him my keys. We walked over to Mensa who was leaned up against a tree near his bike.

"I feel really bad that we didn't even bring you some food," I said when we were within earshot.

Mensa smiled. "That's all right, Victoria. I got food allergies. Hard to find food in most restaurants that don't have milk products in them."

"Oh, wow. That really *is* difficult. I'm sorry."

He looked at Gamble for a moment and back to me. "Not your fault, but thanks."

Gamble handed him the keys. "Give these to a prospect. They need to drive her gray Sentra back to the clubhouse. We're going for a ride."

Mensa gave him a chin lift. "Ride safe, man."

I followed Gamble to his bike. He handed me his helmet. "What about a helmet for you? I should have asked that the last time, but figured it was a one-time thing."

A lopsided grin made him look boyish. "Don't worry about me, kitten. Your noggin is more precious anyway."

I shook my head. "That's sweet, but your *cabeza* is just as important, Triple G."

When I had the helmet in place, he swung a leg over his bike. "Climb on, baby."

Once I had my arms wrapped around his trim waist, he powered up the bike and we were off. I had expected him to take Beach Boulevard, which would give us views of the beach. Instead, he took us to the interstate, and we headed west on I-10.

The last time we went for a ride, we hadn't gone so fast. This was something else. I loved feeling the wind rushing by at seventy miles per hour. Yes, this would definitely keep a guy like Gamble from feeling antsy.

We rode for almost an hour and a half before I realized we were in Covington, Louisiana. Gamble pulled into a parking lot, and I saw the familiar logo for Abita beer.

On their own accord, my arms squeezed his middle. "You brought us to a brewery!"

He patted my arms and I climbed off the bike. As I took off the helmet, he swung off and faced me with a grin.

"Yeah. You ever been here before?"

I shook my head. "No, but I've heard it's pretty damned cool."

"It fuckin' is, kitten."

By the time we rolled through the gates to the Riot MC compound four hours later, the brothers were pulling meat off a barrel smoker. While at the brewery, Gamble and I had ordered a flight of beers. He drank one and then foisted the other three on me. To say I was loose would be a huge understatement, even after a ninety-minute ride back. The scent of barbeque hit me, and I recalled last Sunday's brisket. Yet, just looking at the crowd now, I knew this was a slightly different party. Then it hit me. Tomorrow was a holiday. My hunch was most of the brothers didn't have to work tomorrow.

No doubt, that would change the vibe tonight.

That excited me since I didn't have anything on for tomorrow, other than picking up Heidi for the party.

I handed Gamble his helmet.

He hung it on the handlebar, turned to me, and wrapped me in his arms. "You cool with sleeping here tonight? I can tell you're feelin' good.

Neither of us has work in the morning... and I'd rather not get back on the bike tonight."

I nodded. "That's cool, honey."

He dipped his chin. "There are groupies here tonight. It'll be wilder than last weekend."

I nodded. Then I saw Block headed our way. He had his head down and strode with a purpose.

Gamble followed my gaze and called out, "Yo, Block! Where you headed?"

Block glanced up at us and shook his head. "Not up for this shit. I'll be back when the groupies are gone. Later."

Gamble watched Block straddle his bike. With his head turned, he said, "That's strange. He's always up for a party. What the hell?"

I shrugged, though Gamble missed it. He looked at me, took my hand, and led me to the kitchen for some food.

Chapter 12

It's a Tradition

Victoria

In the morning, I followed Gamble out to the kitchen. I noticed three prospects cleaning up the common room. Each of them carried a half-full black garbage bag as they collected empty bottles and cans. Suffice to say, last night's party was *definitely* a different vibe. I suspected Gamble had secluded us in his room before things got too rowdy.

My contemplation of last night was interrupted when I saw Block standing at the counter manning a deep fryer.

"Morning, Block," Gamble muttered.

"Morning," Block said, but didn't look up.

"Orange juice or coffee, kitten?" Gamble asked.

"Both?" I asked. "I'm pretty sure we only got four hours of sleep."

Gamble aimed his boyish grin at me as he filled two mugs with coffee. "You grab the juice from the fridge." He turned toward Block. "Are you making beignets, man?"

"Yeah," Block grumbled.

I turned from the fridge. Block stared at Gamble. Then his eyes caught mine. "I think I love you," I said.

Gamble turned wide eyes to me. "Are you shittin' me?"

"If they're any good, no, I am not. I *love* beignets... then again, who doesn't?"

"Not anybody I know," Gamble admitted with a grin that said he found me funny.

I found a glass and filled it with juice. "You want any O.J.?"

Gamble shook his head. Block glanced at me, and I raised the jug toward him; he shook his head.

After putting the juice back in the fridge, I grabbed my glass and joined Gamble at the table.

"Got four of these ready, G," Block said.

As Gamble sauntered back to the table, Block looked over his shoulder at me. "Your friend the same age as you?"

I shook my head. "No, she's two years younger than me. Twenty-six."

Block made a noise and nodded. I didn't know what it meant, but it didn't sound good.

"What's Heidi do?" Gamble asked in a low voice.

"She's a project manager at an engineering firm."

Gamble nodded.

I popped a bite of my beignet in my mouth. It was better than I'd had in New Orleans, and if I wasn't mistaken it tasted like there might be a hint of almond extract in the batter.

Before I could compliment Block, Gamble asked, "She good at her job?"

I grinned. "Very, though she doesn't get along with her boss. But really, she's so good at planning, she should be running the basketball program."

"Why isn't she?"

I shook my head. "She says she's not a good leader, and I yell louder."

"That girl has no problems yelling," Block muttered.

My eyes widened. Then I felt Gamble's breath on my neck. "Told you he didn't like drama."

I turned and his eyes were right there. "I guess not," I whispered.

Warmth invaded my chest as his eyebrow arched. "But I think he's a liar." Then he winked at me and leaned back in his chair.

I smiled to myself. As I recalled how Block watched Heidi's every move at the restaurant yesterday, I suspected Gamble was right. Block didn't mind Heidi's form of drama.

"Speaking of Heidi," I said, "I have to pick her up for the party tonight."

Gamble frowned as he seemed to deliberate something.

I shook my head. "What? There's no way Luis or Ernesto knows where Heidi lives."

He cocked a brow at me. "That isn't what I'm thinking about, though I wouldn't put it past them to find that out. Why can't she drive herself here?"

I shrugged. "I guess she could, though that seems rude since she's my plus-one. But I'll need the exact address for this Batcave."

I noticed Block was shaking his head.

Gamble chuckled. "I'll get you that info when we're done, kitten."

"Great. I forgot to check last night, but is my car here? I need to grab some stuff from my trunk. There are some motions and things I need to work on for this coming week."

He rested his hand on the back of my chair and leaned toward me. Then he whispered, "Your car is here. How long is your work gonna take? I got other plans for us today."

My brows furrowed. "You do?"

"I do," he whispered.

I shrugged a shoulder. "It shouldn't take more than a couple hours," I said, staring into his eyes. Then I added, "*If* I can concentrate, that is."

He chuckled. "I'll let you concentrate. But you better finish your breakfast. This place will get loud sooner than you think. Especially since it's the Fourth of July."

As I closed the trunk of my car, Brute and Kenzie rolled up on his bike. He parked it nearby.

Kenzie climbed off the bike before him and while she undid her helmet she smiled at me. "Something tells me that isn't your overnight bag."

I grinned. "No, I need to get a head start on things for work. Short weeks are never easy, if you know what I mean."

She nodded. "Do I ever. But I thought you were looking for a new job?"

The fact she knew about that almost surprised me. Then I remembered that these people shared and shared alike. "Yeah, but that hasn't happened yet... so I gotta—"

"Could you move into family law?" Brute asked, putting his helmet on the seat of the motorcycle.

"Probably, but it would be better if I had more experience with those cases."

Brute pointed a finger at me. "Don't you sweat it. Pretty sure we're renewing our retainer with our firm this week. Block set up a meeting, though I don't remember when it's happening. I'll make sure he mentions you."

I gave him a small smile. "That's nice and I appreciate it, but it really isn't necessary."

Brute dipped his chin and tugged off his sunglasses. "Sure it is. Life's too short to be miserable."

"He's right," Kenzie said.

"Now give me that suitcase. You aren't lugging it inside."

"It's just an over-sized attaché, Brute," I said, holding it out for him anyway.

"Don't matter, lady. Let's go."

Following Kenzie through the back door of the clubhouse, I nearly ran her over when she stopped short. Tension filled the air. Over Kenzie's shoulder I saw Block and Gamble facing off with a lithe blonde. She stood so close to Gamble I felt a surge of jealousy. I tamped it down because she was standing that close to Block, too.

Brute pushed inside behind me, putting my case on the floor. His hands gently gripped my shoulders and he guided me to the right. Then he stepped around me and Kenzie.

"Riley. You got a problem?"

She glanced from Gamble, to Block, and then to Brute. "No."

Block's body jerked like he laughed, but I didn't hear anything.

Brute crossed his arms. "Funny. My brothers are wound up tight and you're the only other person around. You sure there isn't a problem?"

She looked past Brute to Kenzie, and then her green eyes met mine. "Who's she?"

Her snotty tone couldn't be missed. But as a younger sister, I was an old hand at playing that game. Still, I didn't sink to her level with the tone. "I'm with Gamble. Who are you?"

"She's a pain in the ass as far as you're concerned, lady," Brute said.

I bit back a grin and Kenzie hung her head.

Riley looked at Gamble. "Seriously? You, too? I'm wasting my time hanging around here."

"Door's wide open," Block said.

That seemed harsh, but it got Riley's attention, since she flinched. She stepped back while flinging her hair over her shoulder. "Whatever. I'll stick around for the party tonight."

"No," Block said.

Brute sighed. "You can come back at dusk when all the other groupies come back."

Riley's lip curled, she opened her mouth, but then she thought better of saying anything to the men. With a huff, she turned and left through the front door.

After the door closed, Kenzie said, "I'm glad you all could leave the fireworks for later tonight."

Three sets of eyes glared at her, but I laughed. "You got that right!"

I stooped over to grab my case, but Gamble beat me to it.

As he straightened, he murmured, "Sorry you had to see that, kitten."

With a short shake of my head, I turned my hands up. "See what? You didn't ask for her to approach you, right?"

"No," he said, and led the way to his room.

Once we were inside and he set my things by his desk, he wrapped an arm around my hips and the other arm around my shoulders. "You got two hours, tops, to get your shit done."

"Two hours?"

His forehead lowered to mine. "Yes. Then we're hitting the beach. It's a tradition."

"All of your buddies—"

"Brothers."

145

"Fine, *brothers*. All of them go—"

"No. It's one of my family's traditions. Didn't include my parents, but Brittney and I always did it. So, you need to get to work so we can go to the beach. Got it?"

"Okay. But I'm likely to fall asleep in the sun. Just saying. Short of sleep and all that."

He grinned. "Nope. Won't let you do that, either. Best part of today is the nap you get after the sun drains your energy. Then you wake up ready to watch the best fuckin' fireworks you'll ever see."

I dipped my chin at him. "We are right up against that wall, mister. No matter how noisy it is here, I better get my nap."

He grinned. Seeing it up close, I loved it even more. "Didn't say we'd be napping here, babe."

Gamble hunched over me as I sat on the blanket on our patch of beach, and he shook his head, dripping water all over me.

I laughed and leaned back. "Get out of here, you crazy man!"

"Nope. Come back in the water, you sexy woman."

I sighed and gave him a look. "I'm tired. It's time to go."

His hands went under my arms, and he hauled me up to standing while pulling me close. "Just come in the water one last time. No horseplay, no swimming."

"That sounds boring."

He chuckled. "Are you calling me boring? But, I'm serious. We'll just bob in the water."

Something told me we'd do more than 'bob in the water,' but I nodded anyway.

A devious smirk curled his lips just before he grabbed my hand and took off running. Which meant I had to run to keep up.

"You liar!"

He laughed and I realized I didn't hear him laugh like that very often. It was a beautiful sound and I decided to make him laugh every chance I had.

Even if Gamble made me run, he stayed true to his word about bobbing in the water. He wrapped me up in his arms and laid a hot and heavy kiss on me when the water came up to my breasts. My legs itched to wrap around his waist, but I didn't feel like having sex in broad daylight.

Gamble broke the kiss and stroked my hair away from my face.

After a beat he asked, "You ever see that movie with the cartoon characters inside a young girl's head? And they lose an important memory?"

I nodded.

"Sometimes I wish I could send those cartoons into my head so they could smash the shit out of my memories."

My head reared back. "That seems extreme, Gamble."

His chin lowered in a minuscule nod. "My most vivid memory is being evicted."

I gasped. "No."

His lips pressed together as he nodded. "Yeah. I was seven, almost eight, so Brittney would have been almost eleven years old. A cop came to the house with the landlord, who had the eviction papers."

"Honey, you don't have to tell me this—"

He put his finger to my lips as he shook his head. Somehow, I suspected being out in the deep water gave him a sense of safety and maybe even peace.

He continued. "Dad and Mom argued until it became clear they couldn't budge the landlord. I overheard the cop say, 'He even looks like a degenerate.' At the time, I didn't know what that meant, but I knew I never wanted anyone to say that about me."

I nodded. "I can see how that would stick with you."

His exhale sounded like more of a grunt. "Dad never got haircuts. Only shaved twice a week because he couldn't stand the itch. And maybe because razors lasted a while, I don't know. I had to pay for my own haircuts once I turned thirteen. Brit helped when she thought she might want to go to beauty school, but I still preferred the barber."

Something told me he liked the barber for the male influences as well, but I didn't want to ask about that yet.

"After that eviction, we rarely stayed in one place for more than six months, and they were worse and worse places to live."

I stroked his neck and down along his wide shoulder. "I'm so sorry that happened to you."

"Yeah, me too, kitten. If my mom would have had her shit together maybe she'd have left him, but they were both addicted to gambling."

He paused as a wave jostled us. Then he added, "I guess I'm just grateful they never took money from a loan shark."

"Did they work?"

He grimaced. "Mom worked temp jobs and Dad was a custodian at an elementary school until he got fired. Then he took odd jobs. It's a miracle Brit and I stayed healthy. That would've bankrupted them for sure."

I shook my head. "How did you guys not end up in trouble? It sounds like you were totally unsupervised."

He took a deep breath. "My grandparents stepped in... *a lot*. They're why this is the only summertime family tradition I have."

We were quiet for a while. The sound of the Gulf kept us company.

Then I couldn't keep myself from saying, "You are a wonder."

"What are you talking about?"

"It's a wonder you're such a good man."

He sighed. "I have Gramps to thank for that."

"Is he still around?"

He shook his head. "He passed a year before Brit was raped. Gram passed about six months after Gramps."

My thumb rubbed circles on his shoulder, but his words made me still. "I'm sorry."

His eyes focused on a point over my shoulder, and he sounded as though he were speaking to himself. "Don't be sorry. They were proof there was real love in the world." His eyes met mine. "Though I didn't believe most people found love like that."

I cocked a brow at him. "The way you trailed off, it sounds like you left something unsaid."

148

His eyes darted to the left before coming back to me. "I didn't believe it existed, not until... I met Joules and Sandy."

I had prepped enough defendants for cross-examination that I suspected he was lying before he spoke. He might believe Joules and Sandy had the same kind of love as his grandparents did, but he was hiding something. As heavy as the subject was, I wasn't going to press him on it.

"You ready for lunch?" he asked.

He held me so close, I felt his erection between us. My head turned a touch as I slid my hand down his torso and inside his trunks. "I could eat, but unless I'm mistaken, you're not ready to get out."

His hand went to my wrist. "Victoria. What are you doing?"

I smiled. "Exactly what you think I'm doing."

He shook his head and whispered, "Don't."

"You can't be serious? The water's already salty."

On a chuckle, both his hands grabbed my ass, and he pulled my body upward forcing me to let go of his cock. "Love the offer, but we aren't doing that out here. Not today, anyway. You go dry off, and I'll be right behind you. We'll grab lunch, go back to the house, eat, fuck, and then nap."

"I suppose I can't argue with that."

"I'm guessing that's a first for you."

I gently swatted his shoulder. "Very funny, smart guy. Now kiss me before I dry off."

"That's a first for me. Never thought I'd enjoy being bossed by a gorgeous woman."

My eyes widened. He smiled, lowered his head, and kissed me to stop my response.

Gamble

He couldn't believe how much he'd confided in Victoria. Har was the only one who knew about Gramps, but standing in the water with Victoria, all his family secrets had spilled out of him.

More than that, he'd nearly told her he didn't believe in the kind of love his grandparents had until he met her. As he watched her long legs carry her back to their blanket, he felt it. A falling sensation he'd never had before. He loved her.

"Didn't see that coming," he whispered.

From the look she'd given him earlier after he mentioned Joules and Sandy, he suspected she knew he'd lied. Yet she'd left him alone about it.

It had been less than two weeks. He wasn't going to trot out the 'l-word' anytime soon. But he wasn't letting her go after Luis and Ernesto were dealt with either.

Thoughts of the Abeyetas made his cock soften.

He blew out a sigh and dived under the water to clear his head and get his blood flowing away from his groin.

As soon as Gamble shut down his bike, Victoria said, "You forgot to swing through a drive-thru, G."

He patted her thigh and she swung off, allowing him to do the same. He pushed his shades on top of his head. "No, we'll have it delivered. Should give us just enough time to shower before the subs get here."

She took her purse out of the saddlebag while he went to unlock the front door. In the small foyer, he disarmed the alarm. When he turned around, Victoria was in his space. She shoved his shirt up. He loved feeling her fingers on his skin and to give her more access he tugged his shirt off.

He cupped a hand around her neck and kissed her. Hard.

She broke away with a coy grin. Her hands shoved his trunks down and she sank to her knees.

His sigh mingled with a groan as he felt her hot mouth on his dick. He didn't want her sucking him off in the middle of the living room, but he couldn't stop himself from twisting his fingers in her hair and pumping his hips. His swim trunks fell to his ankles.

"Goddamn, you feel like heaven, kitten."

"Mmm," she hummed against him, and he felt like he would shoot in seconds, which brought him to his senses.

He pulled away from her gently and stepped out of his trunks. Then he crouched, shoved his hands under her pits, and hauled her over his shoulder in a fluid motion.

"Ohmigod! How did you do that?" she squealed.

He smacked her plump ass. "Very carefully is how I did it. But we need to be on the bed, kitten."

"Why? The carpet is plenty soft. It felt brand new."

"It is new, but this way, you can suck me off while I eat you out, and we both get what we want."

He gently put her on the bed. Her heated gaze sent more blood straight to his cock. His fingers grabbed the sides of her bikini and he tugged. "Time to get you out of this suit."

Her legs bent and she raised her hips to help him. He tossed her bottoms to the floor, then moved to the other side of the bed. She sat up and took off her top.

He couldn't stop himself from saying, "You have the most beautiful breasts."

"They're fake," she said, laying back down.

He rolled on top of her, his left hand kneading her tit. Her eyes heated and he swore the hazel hue looked greener. He pinched her nipple. She moaned. More blood rushed to his cock, and he smiled. "So what? Gorgeous is gorgeous."

She turned her head away, and he watched her neck slowly turn pink as she blushed.

He shifted off of her, then situated himself with his head at the foot of the bed. "They're still just like you. Fucking stunning."

She blew out a breath, leaned up on her elbows, and stared at him.

He arched a brow, daring her to argue with him. When she kept quiet, he said, "Now climb on top of me and finish what you started, baby. Love having your mouth on me, but I'll love it even more while I eat your twat."

She chuckled as she threw a leg over him. "Aren't you missing the first step from your t-shirt? Smoke pot?"

He pulled her pussy to his lips. "That happens later tonight. Makes the fireworks that much better."

Rather than wait for her response, he flicked the tip of his tongue across her clit, and she gasped. With a smile, he sucked on her bundle of nerves, and she sank down.

He let her go. "You gonna return the favor, kitten?"

She groaned. Then he had her mouth on his aching cock. He captured her clit in his mouth again. She moaned against him and squirmed. He grabbed the globes of her ass to hold her in place. She gave a keening cry and began to ride his face.

He liked that so much he groaned. She applied more suction and his hips bucked. Her fingernails scraped down his thighs forcing them wider.

He plunged two fingers into her pussy. It took her by surprise.

"Yes, Gamble," she said on a gasp.

He let go of her with his mouth and caressed her clit with his thumb. "Get back to work, Vic."

"You are bossy," she complained.

His retort fled his mind because she took him so deep it scrambled his brain.

He closed his eyes, making a noise he'd never heard from himself. Then he heard a pop from her mouth.

"Get back to work, Gage."

His body jerked with a silent laugh. A woman who could make him laugh while he got a blowjob for the record books? No doubt about it. He'd fallen in love with her.

He got back to work, and so did she.

He came not long after. She took him deep and swallowed him down.

Then he made sure she came. She did it hard, and best of all, she did it on his tongue.

CHAPTER 13

MAN-EATER

VICTORIA

I woke up before Gamble, with a start. The light outside made me wonder if it was the next morning or late evening. It irked me when this happened after a nap, but as I become more aware I knew it was late afternoon.

Gamble's bulky arm lay across my waist. As I slowly turned to him, I saw he was still asleep.

Against all odds, he looked even more boyish as he slept. Even though we were complete opposites, I could get used to waking up with him, no matter what time of day.

That was foolishness on my part, though.

We were having fun, but I suspected when my situation was resolved, we'd go our separate ways.

"What are you thinking about?" he asked in a husky voice.

I caught his eyes dancing over my face, and I smiled. "Nothing."

"That's bullshit, but I'll let it go. I'm guessing it's late. We should get moving. What time did you tell Heidi to get to the clubhouse?"

"Six."

He kissed my jaw. "Good. We should hustle, though."

Almost an hour later, Gamble parked his bike next to my Nissan. The forecourt buzzed with people and the area behind the clubhouse was nearly full of vehicles.

After I put the helmet on the bike seat, I checked my phone. Ten minutes ago, Heidi had texted that she was fifteen minutes away.

I looked up at Gamble. "Heidi will be pulling in soon. I'm thinking I should wait for her outside."

Gamble tipped his head forward. "That her Miata?"

I looked over my shoulder, then back at Gamble and smiled. "Yep."

"No need to wait, then."

From across the yard, a male voice boomed, "Yo, Gamble! Get over here. We need another set of hands."

Gamble waved and gave a chin-lift. Then he caught my gaze. "Take her in through the front door. There will be a shitload of activity in the kitchen. And I probably gotta lend a hand dealing with the pig."

"The pig? Like a whole pig?"

His lips tipped up. "Yeah, kitten. But if that's not your thing, there's low-country boil tonight, too."

"Okay."

He gave me a peck and jogged across the yard-slash-parking area.

I moseyed over to Heidi's car as she angled out of it. "Happy Fourth of July."

It hit me that I had been wrong yesterday. Heidi hadn't needed me to go shopping with her if her ensemble was any sign. I had expected her to be completely over-the-top, but instead she'd almost gone conservative –for Heidi. She wore a tight crop-top which had a diagonal slash of blue with white stars, on the opposite side were red and white stripes. It was edgy, revealing, and provocative. She'd paired it with cut-off jeans shorts, and a thick leather belt with a humongous silver cowboy buckle shaped like the American flag. Her outfit screamed I'm-going-to-a-biker-party. Whereas I suddenly felt like my flirty red summer dress said I'm-going-to-a-garden-party.

Heidi said, "Same to you. Where's lover boy headed?"

"He's got to help someone out. Apparently we should go in through the front door."

She fell in step beside me. "Why? He doesn't strike me as being controlling. Especially since you don't go for that kind of thing."

"How do you know?"

"You're not the type."

"Neither are you," I muttered.

"Most of the time, I'm not."

I gave her a sideways glance.

"Eyes forward, Vickie. You may have the legs of a gazelle, but that also means you're easier to trip."

I faced forward, shaking my head and rolling my eyes.

"Why are we going around our ass to get to our elbow like this?" she asked.

Chuckling, I led her around the corner of the clubhouse. "Because they have a bunch of food in the kitchen and Gamble wanted us to stay out of the way."

We walked through the front door, moved in four paces and Heidi stopped me with her hand on my forearm. "You don't belong in a place like this."

I shot confused eyes her way. "What are you talking about?"

"This is not the group for you, law-woman."

I shook my head. "I'm not an officer of the law, Heidi."

Her face turned fully to me. "No, but you uphold it all the same. You're all about that woman holding her scales while blindfolded."

"These guys are about justice, too," I said. Then I added, "Just without the blindfold."

"No, honey. They're about vengeance and retribution. And my guess is they leave the blindfold in the bedroom."

From where we stood in the crowded common room, we could see the back door. It suddenly swung open, and an older woman bustled through yelling, "Joules! They need you to help turn the hog."

Heidi shot wide eyes at me. "They have a whole hog out there?"

I nodded. "That's what Gamble said, and it's what he was helping with, so I guess it's rather... big." I was trying not to think about it.

An older man strode out the door, and slammed it shut after he left.

157

Heidi shook my shoulder playfully. "You are always so squeamish! I gotta see this set-up. It's out back?"

I nodded.

She smiled. "You comin' with me?"

I grimaced. "No, thank you. My stomach's churning just thinking about it. I'm getting a drink. Don't get lost."

She scoffed. "As if!"

I watched her open the back door, then she scuttled backward because Block pushed forward carrying a humongous metal pot. Even from my vantage point, I heard Heidi say, "Sorry, old man. Had no idea you were out there."

Block curled his lip at her, and I could see he spoke, but I couldn't hear what he said. Heidi gave him a smile she reserved for catty women and... now Block. She shot me a wink and moved out the door.

Movement from one of the pool tables caught my eye and I noticed Fiona coming toward me. I smiled. "Hi, there."

"Hi, yourself. You aren't sticking with Heidi?"

I moved closer to the bar and Fiona moved with me. "I don't want to see an entire animal being cooked."

She tipped her chin up. "Yeah... I'm with you. It's hard to stomach that."

All three prospects were behind the bar. The one closest saw Fiona and nodded. "What can I get you, Fi?"

Fiona pointed a finger at me. "She's the empty-handed one, but I'll take another glass of red wine."

Gamble sidled up to me. "Victoria's having an Abita Purple Haze, same as me."

With my best sideways glare, I said, "I am?"

He grinned at me. "You are. Noticed how much you liked that yesterday. Besides, I love drinking that when I'm getting high."

Fiona leaned forward. "What do you mean, 'getting high?' You're like, on deck for dealing with the hog and shit."

Gamble shook his head, grinning huge. "Nope. Joules got himself a helper. In Heidi's words, 'Never underestimate a short chick.' I know when there are too many cooks in a kitchen."

I gaped at Gamble. "You're joking!"

The prospect put two pint glasses in front of us, then handed Fiona her wine.

He shook his head. "No. Your friend's a lot like you, babe. Feisty and full of surprises."

Fiona threw her head back and laughed. "On that note, I'm gonna find Cynic."

I sipped my beer and thought of Heidi's older brother, Blaine. My eyes widened, I put my glass down with a thud, and turned to Gamble. "I need to go find her."

He grinned. "She's fine out there."

I shook my head. "Her brother always said, 'If she isn't *in* trouble, she's *starting* trouble.' And I've realized over the last seven years, he's dead right. So, I need to see what she's up to."

His face came closer. "No, kitten. You need to come with me."

With one hand he grabbed his beer. His other hand grabbed mine and I snatched my pint glass before he led me out the front door.

We went the opposite direction from how we entered, to the far side of the forecourt, Stephanie and Kenzie were playing cornhole.

Stephanie saw me, and imitated my Uncle Mick when she yelled, "Vic-tor-ia! Come play cornhole. Kenzie's got beginner's luck. Other-wise, I think she's cheating! Or, she lied to me, which I wouldn't put past her at all!"

"Maybe later, Steph," Gamble said. "But look for her friend Heidi. I bet she could give you a run for your money."

We kept walking, and then we rounded the clubhouse.

I swallowed a sip of beer. "Where are we going?"

"You'll see."

We passed a large metal shed. The door stood open, and I could see a number of weight benches and other work-out equipment.

I glanced up at Gamble's profile. "That equipment looks much better than the stuff at the gym. I'm surprised you keep your gym membership."

He glanced down at me. "There's no air conditioning in there. Well, a window unit, but that doesn't do shit in the middle of the day during the summer."

"I see," I whispered.

We made it to an open area at the back of the property. Har, Roman, and Trinity were there along with a woman I didn't know, but who looked vaguely familiar. Gamble let go of my hand and took my beer from me, for some reason.

Har turned to us. "You got my message. Victoria, good to see you."

"Thanks, it's quite the party tonight."

Roman grinned. "Hasn't even gotten started yet."

Har nodded at the woman standing next to him. "Not sure if you've met before, but this is Bridgette Wentz. She practices family law with Gower and Gower."

That explained it. Gower and Gower sponsored some of the area Bar Association mixers. I had seen her there, but was more familiar with the criminal defense attorneys.

I smiled and extended my hand. "Victoria Carlton. Nice to meet you."

Her grip was firmer than I expected. "And you. My colleague says you've recently moved up the ranks in the PD's office."

"You could say that," I hedged.

I was defending more clients, but to me that wasn't exactly moving up the ranks.

She smiled and tipped her head at Har. "Mr. Walcott and Mr. Merino mentioned you're looking to move away from that specialty."

I suspected Har was Mr. Walcott, but I had no idea who Mr. Merino would be. Then Gamble whispered in my ear that she was talking about Block.

I nodded at her. "Yes. I'm interested in probate or corporate law, though I did a brief internship with a family law practice between semesters in law school."

"Right. The resume you sent us reflected that," she said and something in her tone kept me quiet. Then she added, "We're looking for a junior associate in family law. If you're interested, give me a call tomorrow."

My brain almost froze at her words, but then I forced myself to think about my schedule. I wasn't supposed to be in court until later in the week.

With another nod, I said, "Absolutely. Thank you."

She aimed a wry smile at me. "Thinking you have a few other people to thank instead."

I pressed my lips together, then whispered, "Right."

Her smile turned more genuine. "Don't worry about that. It's a cliché because it's true. It's not what you know, but who you know."

She turned back to Har. "Mr. Walcott, thank you for inviting me out here. I need to get home before sunset. Tell Mr. Merino I received the check."

"I'll see you to your car," Har said, and they walked away.

I felt someone staring at me and saw it was Roman. He opened his mouth to say something and then closed it. His golden-brown eyes focused on me a bit longer before he glanced at Trinity.

My hunch was the embarrassed look on my face drew him up short. I appreciated the opportunity to meet Bridgette, but I couldn't help feeling like a charity case.

"So, you've got an interview?" Trinity asked.

I shrugged. "Hard to say, but she wants me to call her. And she's looked at my resume, so it's a start."

Gamble handed me back my beer. "You don't sound too thrilled, kitten."

I looked up at him. "I told you guys you didn't need to do this."

He dipped his chin at me. "And I believe it was Cynic who said it's the least that firm can do for us."

I dipped my chin at him. "That really isn't how it works."

"It does in our world," Roman said.

I looked his way, but he'd crouched down, lining up wires and what looked like boxes. "Things are different in legal circles."

Then I realized we were standing next to the fireworks. I looked back at Roman. "Are these even legal?"

He chuckled. "I'm a pyrotechnician. They're legal when launched by a professional."

My lips twisted with skepticism. "Aren't you supposed to be some-where else tonight? Like doing the city's display?"

Gamble slid his arm around my shoulders. "Don't worry about him, Vic. He's always got us covered."

A sly smile crossed Roman's face. "If you're worried about having to report a crime, Victoria, you should be more concerned about your man there and what he's got in his pocket."

Gamble exhaled hard, but I kept eye contact with Roman. "You mean the fact he's going to smoke marijuana?" I asked.

Roman gave me a slow blink as he slowly shook his head and turned his hands up like I could be right or wrong. "I didn't say that."

"Shouldn't have said any damn thing, Ro. We're headed back inside."

I glanced at him. "Why? It's a little... people-y in there."

Trinity laughed. "That's an understatement."

Gamble chuckled. "Funny, kitten. Before I dragged you out here, you were all concerned about Heidi on her own."

I held up a finger. "You're right. We could get her and bring her back here. This is kind of nice, though some shade would be good."

Roman shook his head. "Can't launch mortars with trees around."

"Later, Ro," Gamble said, and he guided me back the way we came.

Inside, Gamble took my glass from me. At my questioning look, he said, "You aren't drinkin' warm beer on my watch. Hit the kitchen, babe. If Sandy made her nachos, get us a plate and meet me back here."

I paused on my way to the kitchen and glanced down the hall. Heidi had come out of a bedroom across the hall from Cynic's room. She leaned against the closed door with her eyes closed. Then she licked her lips like she'd had the best dessert.

"Are you serious right now?" I asked.

Her head whipped up and she strode down the hall toward me.

"What?" she asked in a voice full of innocence and light.

I laughed sardonically. "After *you* told me they're dangerous... you had—"

She scurried up to me holding her finger to her lips. Her head jerked back toward the rooms. "That was a one-off." Her eyes widened at me. "You and the way Gamble looks at you, though? That looks like forever. *That,* coupled with your job, makes him especially dangerous."

"You're seeing things. And you've changed the subject. Whose room were you in?"

Her eyes darted to the side and back to me. "You don't know?"

I gave her a look. "Let's just say I know whose room it isn't... so how 'bout you spill the beans, chica?"

She huffed out a sigh, and whispered, "Block, okay?"

I gave her some side-eye. "Isn't he a little...older?"

Outrage mingled with a confused expression. "I don't know. And it doesn't matter because it's a one-time thing." She paused then held up a finger at me. "Even if it weren't a flash in the pan, it wouldn't matter any damn way, right? Weren't you the one who told me age is just a number?"

I suppressed a smile and nodded. "I did. You're absolutely right, hon."

She nodded. "Good. Now let's go get some pulled pork."

"No way. Gamble sent me over here for nachos if they're ready, and I am *not* about to go see that poor piggie get decimated."

She waved a hand at me. "That already happened. They got heaping platters and shit out there."

I shook my head. "I'll stick to the nachos."

She grinned. "Your loss. I'm getting a plate. And just to let you know, I'm leaving before the fireworks. I gotta get into work early tomorrow."

Gamble

Gamble approached Victoria as Heidi walked out the back door. "Did I see her come from somewhere down the hall?"

Victoria gave him a regretful smile. "Yes."

"I'd ask if you let her into my room, but I've got the door locked and you don't have a key."

Her head tilted. "Really?"

"Really, babe. There's a crapload of people here today that don't normally come to our hog roasts. Some of them have probably never been here, and I'm not takin' chances with one of them goin' in my room."

She nodded. "That makes sense. I didn't think of it that way."

He handed her a beer. "Whose room did she come from?"

Her fake-pout almost made him laugh. After a beat she cleared her expression. "Block's, but I really feel like that isn't your business."

He chuckled. "In a way it isn't. But I'd find out soon enough."

She frowned. "Not if he didn't tell you."

He grinned. "Seeing as I know half the brothers are at the bar, after a perimeter check, I'd be likely to narrow it down to him and possibly one other brother. Believe me, kitten, this works just like a huge family. There are few to no secrets. Everything comes out in the end."

"Fabulous," she muttered.

"Hey," he whispered. She looked up at him. "He's a great man."

"He looked at her, and me, as though he couldn't stand us. It's just... I don't want her to get hurt."

He couldn't help but laugh. "Your girl can take care of herself, that's obvious. I think Block is the one who has to watch out."

She laughed. "Maybe so. I didn't get to the food before I noticed Heidi. Did you want a pulled-pork sandwich?"

He put a hand to the small of her back. "I don't care, Vic. I'm good with a burger, nachos, whatever."

In the kitchen, they found the fixings for nachos, but Sandy bustled in with a fresh platter of burgers.

She handed them to Gamble and speared Victoria with her eyes. "You and I haven't officially met. I'm Sandy. I keep most of these boys in line, no matter what they might think."

Victoria chuckled nervously. "I've heard nothing but good things about you."

Sandy tipped her head at the platter. "You're having a burger. They don't get any better than those."

Before Gamble could say anything, Victoria asked, "How come?"

Sandy grinned. "Because I made 'em. Grated onion, some garlic, and a few other secret spices mixed into those patties, like nothing else you've ever had. Now, buns are over there. I got cheese slices on a plate in the fridge. We gotta get you set up, girlfriend."

"Sandy. Take it easy on her, huh?" Gamble said.

Sandy's brown eyes flared at him. "I have taken it easy. This is the first time I've run into her since you got your shit together and brought her around."

Victoria wheezed out a laugh.

Gamble glared at Sandy. "You're lucky she finds you funny. It's the only thing saving you, lady."

Sandy hooted with a giggle. "You keep tellin' yourself that, Gamble."

Joules came into the kitchen carrying a platter mounded with pulled pork. "Woman. I can hear you bickering with him from outside. You're gonna scare off Victoria, you keep it up."

With a saucy grin at Joules, Sandy said, "He'll have to learn to work harder then, won't he?"

"Wow," Victoria said.

Joules had set the platter down and sauntered toward Victoria. "Don't let her wow you, Victoria. She meddles like it's an Olympic sport, so beware."

Sandy gasped. "I do not. You need to stop telling people that, ol' man."

Once Victoria had her burger ready to go, he noticed her eyeing an unopened bag of salt and vinegar potato chips. He snatched the bag up, which earned him more of Sandy's ire. Then he caught Victoria's eyes and tipped his head toward the back door.

He led her toward a secluded area, close to her parked car, where they could eat.

She put her plate on the wooden picnic table and sat down. "How did you know I wanted those chips?"

"You're easy to read."

They ate in comfortable silence. Just as Gamble was going to take their plates to a trash can, Heidi sauntered up.

"Thanks for making me your plus-one, Vic. But it's time for me to go."

Gamble scanned the crowd outside and caught Heidi's eyes. "Where's Block? You didn't kill him, did you?"

Heidi's eyes slid to Victoria and back to him. "Don't know why you'd think I killed him. He's older, but he's not that old."

"Nearly fifteen years older than me," Gamble muttered.

Surprise lit Heidi's eyes for a second, then she hid it behind a smile. "I left him dead, all right. Dead to the world sleeping, so no worries, biker man."

Victoria grabbed Heidi's hand. "Are you sure you have to leave? It's not quite dark out."

Heidi nodded. "Definitely. The Fourth is like New Year's Eve but in the summertime. Amateur drinkers who think they're excellent drivers, but aren't. Add in the tourists, and you bet I need to get home. We'll talk this week when I swing by to check out your new digs. Bye."

Gamble watched Heidi's car slowly move through the forecourt. Then he caught sight of Block standing outside. He was at the edge of the clubhouse watching her car. Even from fifty yards away, Block's jaw looked like granite.

"That doesn't look good," Victoria said.

He turned to her and saw her eyes pointed at Block. "No, but he'll get over it."

She scoffed. "*He'll* get over it? Trust me, I'll be helping my girl put her heart back together."

"Nah. She's a man-eater. That's clear enough. Strange that Block didn't see it."

"She's not a man-eater. That's crazy. And even if she is, maybe Block likes it like that? At least, that's what I get from the look on his face."

They were sprawled out on a blanket Gamble had laid on the ground. The sky lit in a spray of red and gold as the first two mortars exploded. In the dimness of the clubhouse outdoor security lights, Gamble saw Victoria's hazel eyes widen. "Oh, my stars, that's loud!"

"It's like music, kitten. Always better when it's loud."

She gave him a saucy smirk. "I'd almost think you're talking about something other than fireworks."

Gamble felt especially loose since he'd smoked a joint half an hour ago.

A lazy smile curled his lips. "Don't worry, it applies to sex, too."

Her head resting on his outstretched arm turned away and she laughed hard enough she curled her legs up.

Another firework went off. The explosion made the ground shake and she rolled toward him. "Are you sure we're safe here? I'm thinking we're way too close."

She was way too close, all right. Too close to his cock, which had taken notice of her husky voice and her tits pressing against his side.

"It's fine, Vickie," he said, and kissed her quick.

She stared at him for a beat. "You're trying to distract me, aren't you?"

He bit back his grin. "Nope. Calming you down. I want you to stay focused because *this* is the best part. Fireworks are never better than the Fourth of July."

Shades of green glittered above them. He wanted to look up, but he loved how it reflected off Victoria's awestruck face.

She caught his eyes on her. "Why are they never better than tonight?"

He lifted his opposite shoulder. "That's what Gramps always said."

"He did?"

"Yeah. Though, Brittney always said that was to keep us from begging to go to Disney World."

She chuckled. "I can see where that would save some money."

"Yeah," he whispered.

Then he leaned forward and kissed her again. Except this time, he did it long and lingering. They didn't stop until three mortars exploded in quick succession and Victoria went stiff.

He pulled away and gave her a squeeze. "We can move—"

She shook her head. "No. No. I'm being paranoid. You told no lies. This far and away beats what the city puts on."

When it became clear the finale was over, Victoria pulled away, but he stopped her progress. She looked at him in question.

"You sure you can't take tomorrow off?"

She smiled. "I wish I could. My sister's coming in the day after to-morrow. That's going to be a circus. On top of that, I'm calling Bridgette Wentz tomorrow. If she or her partners want to interview me, I'm gonna need my time off in order to juggle my schedule for that."

He pulled her on top of him. "Why's your sister comin' to town going to be a circus?"

She put one hand on his sternum and her other hand on top, and then rested her chin there. "Mom blames me for Miranda going to med school."

"Come again? Most parents would be thrilled to have a doctor in the family. The tuition would be a bitch, but..."

"Yeah, well, Mom wanted us to get education degrees. Always telling us to get into school administration. Become a principal. Never listening to anything Miranda or I had to say about what we wanted to do with our lives."

"That blows," he whispered.

"She's been living vicariously through Miranda for a *very* long time. When she tried to do that with me, I fought it. Guess I have too much of Dad in me or I spent too much time with Uncle Mick, but I told her I was my own person."

He jerked with a suppressed chuckle. "Or you're just argumentative."

She widened her eyes at him. "Maybe. But, right after that, Miranda changed her major. Mom blames me still. Every time Miranda comes to town it all comes up again. And her tone... God, I don't know if she even hears it herself. She's so bitter; we're both disappointments to her. Even though by other people's standards we've accomplished a lot."

"Shit," he whispered. "Definitely not looking forward to meeting her."

Victoria's eyebrows jumped and she continued. "The worst part of it is that Miranda's in the middle. I can't... it's just fucked up." She pulled away, rolling to her back. "I'm sorry. That wasn't very festive Fourth of July talk."

He rolled to his side and stared down at her. "Sweetheart, you don't have anything to apologize for. But... if I didn't ask this before, I'll ask it now, where is your dad in all this? Why in the hell doesn't he put a stop to it?"

She sighed. "I don't know. But let's go inside."

CHAPTER 14

LOVE CAN MAKE YOU STUPID

VICTORIA

"Victoria?" my boss, Judith, asked.

I looked up at her. "Yes, ma'am?"

"I reviewed the police report on your apartment break-in."

I nodded, unsure where this was headed.

"The report says you think relatives of a former client are responsible. You know I should have been informed. Any reason you didn't tell me?"

"It was an oversight, Judith. It won't happen again."

She gave a short head shake. "No, it won't, because you're taking a leave of absence."

"What?" I gasped.

"I understand you're dealing with extreme circumstances and undue stress. For your sake, it would be best that you take some time off. You'll get a call from human resources when you're expected to return."

I picked up a file to explain what I'd been working on, but she shook her head. "Don't worry about it. Your paralegal will get us up to speed."

That seemed extreme, but I wasn't going to argue.

In my car, I sent my sister a text asking if she had a ride from the airport or not. Since it wasn't even ten yet, here, and she was in California, I didn't expect a response anytime soon.

169

Even though Judith had placed me on a leave of absence, the shock hadn't worn off yet. I felt like I'd been fired. Rather than go home, I motored to a Starbucks close to Uncle Mick's pizzeria and went inside.

I found an empty armchair without anyone else close by, a rare thing for me. While I sipped my coffee, my fingers itched to text Heidi. Problem was she didn't need another reason to cut out of work, and sometimes I felt like I laid too much on her anyway.

"Vickie?" a deep voice asked, pulling me from my thoughts.

My coffee threatened to go down the wrong pipe as I stared up into Uncle Mick's eyes. I swallowed and grinned. "Hey, Uncle Mick."

He dropped into the chair adjacent to mine, a lock of his dark hair falling on his forehead. "What are you doin' here, Vickie?"

I took a deep breath. "Thinking."

He shook a finger at me. "That isn't a lie, but you're hiding something. I got some time before I gotta hit the kitchen. Talk to me, sweetie."

As I told him about my troubles, I felt the annoyance rolling off him. I wrapped up my story as fast as I could because Uncle Mick got loud when he was angry. Or louder.

To my surprise, he leaned forward and spoke in a low voice. "It doesn't sound like you're fired, Vickie. But it also doesn't sound promising."

"Yeah."

He sat back suddenly. "Welp, it's a good thing your sister'll be in town this week. Get you away from that biker."

"What? Dad likes him!"

He turned his head to make his side eye more effective. "Well, that don't mean much. Henry likes everybody. My jury is still out."

"Still?"

He nodded.

I realized quite a bit of time had gone by. "Did they forget your order?"

He shook his head. "Haven't placed it yet. I'll do that once I know you're okay."

I shook my head. "I'm fine." Gamble came to mind, and his question from last night tumbled out of my mouth. "Uncle Mick, why doesn't Dad do more about Mom's negativity?"

He laughed, but it held no humor. "That is a question for the ages. But as my grandmother said, love can make you stupid."

I gaped at him. "I had no idea you didn't like—"

He frowned. "Didn't say I don't like your mother. I don't like what she does to you girls. Told Henry that, but that's his battle to fight."

I sighed. Then I felt Uncle Mick's hard stare on me. "Why do you ask now, sweetie?"

"Mom... discouraged me from calling Miranda and letting her know about my attack."

"The hell?"

I nodded. "As much as I want to assert myself, I get where Mom's coming from, Miranda's in her last residency and so close to graduating. Plus, it isn't exactly over-the-phone information."

He put a hand on my forearm. "Sweetheart. It don't make a difference if it's telephone worthy. She should know if you're in pain or in trouble."

"You sound like Gamble."

He made a harrumph sound. "Maybe I like him after all."

I nodded. "You should, he's likeable. But, don't let me keep you. It's almost eleven."

We stood and Uncle Mick gave me a bear hug. "Don't let your mother bring you down, darlin'. And tell your sister to come see me."

I grinned up at him. "She'll want green olives too, you know. Better stock up."

He chuckled. "Don't remind me."

By the time I was ready to leave the coffee shop, it was eleven-thirty. Rather than head straight to my car, I found a table outside, since nobody was out there. Then I called Ms. Wentz.

After we exchanged pleasantries, she said, "This is unlikely to work for you, but the partners are willing to meet with you today at two, if you can break away."

My head reared back, and I was grateful she couldn't see my reaction. "That won't be a problem. I'll be there."

I hustled to my car and drove home. Since I wasn't scheduled for court today, I had worn business casual clothes. That wasn't how I wanted to show up in front of the Gower and Gower partners.

In the driveway, I hit the brakes hard as the garage door rolled up because Gamble stood next to his bike with his gun drawn. He tucked it behind his back when he recognized my car, but still my heart was pounding.

Guess I didn't like guns after all.

When did that happen?

He moved to the far side of the garage, and I pulled inside.

"Are you home for a nooner?" he asked as he rounded my car.

I shook my head. Then I explained about work and my upcoming meeting.

He gave me a swift hug.

"The leave of absence sucks, but maybe it happened this way for a reason."

I nodded. "Yeah. I keep telling myself of that."

"Gonna eat lunch or are you too nervous?"

"There's no choice on that. I'll botch everything up if I don't eat."

He grinned. "I'll make you a sandwich while you get ready."

"Weren't you heading out when I pulled up?"

"Was headed back to the clubhouse, but eating with you is a better option."

I went into the bedroom to put on some makeup and change clothes. When I walked into the kitchen, Gamble had plated up a grilled cheese sandwich for me.

He sat down next to me with his sandwich. "You gonna tell me why you don't like it?"

"Pardon?"

He grinned. "My gun. Noticed your expression in the car, babe. I know that wasn't what you expected, but you looked terrified. I thought guns didn't bother you, but it's clear there's something you don't like."

I shook my head. "It isn't that I don't like the gun. I didn't like pulling up to the garage and you had the gun in hand. Did you really expect someone else to open the garage door?"

His eyes widened. "Didn't expect you to come home from work, Victoria. My guard's up these days. Even though you probably didn't expect me to be here either, why didn't you call to let me know you were swinging by?"

I sighed. "You're right. I should have called. It slipped my mind since I didn't expect an interview so quick."

He nodded while giving me a closed lip smile. "Right. Neither one of us is in the wrong here. But, I need to know if you got problems with guns. I have more than one, though my others are at the clubhouse."

After a moment, I said, "I guess I have no issue with them as long as I don't have to use one. Before going to law school, I didn't give it much thought, but there's something about being confronted with the evidence of that sort of violence."

His head shook once. "That sounds like you got a problem with guns."

I shrugged. "I don't really. It's just presenting photos of gunshot wounds forces me to compartmentalize my judgment—"

"Victoria—"

I held up a finger. "I know that doesn't tie back to your gun specifically, but it kind of does. Since I've had to shove my thoughts about guns to the side for the sake of cases, I know I can get over being in the house with a gun."

He kept quiet and I stared into his blue eyes. Unbidden, I remembered the night he tried to mansplain my job to me and how Fiona shouldn't be sitting around waiting to be questioned. When Fiona told him I had nothing to do with the case and she and I had just struck up a conversation, he looked contrite. We'd locked eyes then and I had admired how I could see his emotions shifting behind those blue irises. Now he wore a similar expression, and I couldn't guess what he'd say next.

"Sweetheart, I don't want you to 'get over' me owning guns."

I waved my finger around to indicate the whole house. "But this is temporary. Once this is done, you'll—"

"What do you think we're doing, Victoria?"

"We're dealing with me getting raped, and you stepped in because my apartment was vandalized—"

"Seriously?"

My eyes went to the side, and I realized things between us were so much more than that. "Okay, well, we've given into our chemistry."

He nodded. "Yeah. Some bikers nail any woman who comes their way, but I normally wait until I know I have 'chemistry' with someone."

My jaw clenched for a moment. "That attitude really isn't necessary."

"It wouldn't be if I didn't think you were being oblivious. You're smart as hell, I know that, so I don't know how you're missing this."

"I am smart, but neither one of us has said anything outright."

He turned his head and stared at the fridge for a moment before he skewered me with those eyes. "Last Monday night at your uncle's restaurant, why do you think he stared at me so long? Hell, why do you think I let him do that?"

At the time, I wanted to think it was a strange manly pissing contest, but I knew better then, and I definitely knew better now. "You want his approval."

His eyes widened. "And why would I want that?"

I took a deep breath. "Dial it back, Gage. If you don't know what mansplaining is, you're encroaching on it again."

He blew out a breath. "Well, fuck, kitten. Then you explain to me how I can open your eyes? Because a fuck-ton more is happening here than me protecting you. I love you and I thought you had caught that."

My heart soared, but my temper went to the stratosphere along with it. "Since this is the first time you've *said* that, you'll have to forgive me for thinking you might drop me when my pain-in-the-ass shit is over!"

"When did I make you think I would drop you?"

Thinking back, he hadn't, so I kept quiet.

"Victoria," he prompted.

"You didn't, but I... this has been so intense. You're serious, though? You love me?"

His chin dipped and he stared at me. "Wouldn't have said it if I didn't."

My hands shot out to cup his cheeks and I pressed my lips to his. I heard his chair scrape the floor before his hands grabbed my waist and hauled me up against his body. My legs wrapped around his hips then my back hit the wall and he pressed against me as he deepened the kiss.

After a moment, I remembered my interview and I broke the kiss. "I love you, too, if you didn't catch it."

His heated cobalt eyes danced over my face. "I caught it all right."

"But we can't ruin my suit. I don't have an iron, and I can't—"

He kissed me quiet, then set me on my feet.

When he broke the kiss, he rested his forehead against mine. "I'm buying the house from Fiona."

I blinked. "You are?"

He stepped back from me, and his hands stroked down my sides, smoothing out my blouse. "Yeah. You said if you didn't have student loans, then broke off from that. I spent some time here a couple months back, and thought it would be a great starter house to own."

I nodded.

"Shit happens for bizarre reasons, Victoria. Now, like I said, I don't want you to 'get over' me owning a gun. But we'll talk about that more tonight."

"All right, honey."

One of his brows jumped as his lips tipped up. "All right. I gotta get out of here before I make both of us late."

"What are you running late for?"

"Club business."

I nodded. "Then you aren't following me to the interview?"

"Shit," he whispered. After a beat, he said, "Seeing as it's the middle of the day, you should be fine. Depending on when church is over, either Mensa or I will be there when you leave."

Gamble

Gamble walked into church surprised to see only Cynic and Block in the room. "Where is everyone?"

Block glanced at his phone. "You're ten minutes early, G."

"Is your text to Fiona serious?" Cynic asked.

He lifted his chin. "If she wants to sell, I got a decent down payment saved."

Both men looked impressed, which made him feel proud. Then bitterness washed over him, because without them, he'd have no reason to feel pride. His father wouldn't give a damn that he had a down payment for a house. No, that wasn't true. At the first indication Gamble had money, his dad would demand his cut. Wouldn't bother to call it a loan.

That had been happening since he was ten, when Dad's mom would send a ten-dollar bill in his or Britt's birthday cards. He'd take it and say he deserved half for putting a roof over their heads. He promised two fives made a ten, which was true. Except neither Gamble nor Brit ever saw their five in change.

He closed his eyes and swallowed hard against the memory.

"What brought Gamble in here so damn early?" Brute asked.

Gamble opened his eyes and shook his head. "Nothing, Veep. Thought I was right on time, but found out otherwise."

Half an hour later, Har said, "That's all the business we have, unless someone else has something."

"Wait, what about the Abeyetas?" Gamble asked.

Har stared at him, but Brute asked, "What about them?"

Gamble forced himself to stay calm. "They're out on bail. They fucked Victoria over again—"

"We've done what we can for her," Har said.

He glowered at his president. Then he whispered, "Come again?"

"You haven't claimed her."

Block nodded. "She's not your woman, just a—"

"Shut the fuck up," Gamble bit out.

"You need a fine?" Cynic asked.

"She is mine. But if this chapter's done, then I'll deal with it."

Har glared at him, but kept quiet.

176

Brute looked from Har to him and back to Har. "Didn't you order him to stand down on this shit?"

"That was before they got out."

Roman's fist hit the table. "You better take a brother with you, whatever the fuck you got planned."

Gamble's eyes slid to Roman. "Like you had a plan with Ink?"

Roman's lips pressed into a thin line. "We talked about that shit, man. This is different. The Abeyetas... you need a plan."

He nodded. "You're right."

Tiny said, "Then we're done here, since we aren't gonna have Gamble's back?"

"That isn't what Har said," Cynic bit out.

Tiny shrugged. "Isn't it though?"

Gamble shook his head. Tiny liked stirring the pot, so he didn't know if Tiny cared or if he just wanted to cause more trouble.

"She reported the break-in, she's moved into Fiona's old house. We do something to Luis or Ernesto, the cops are gonna come here first," Block said.

Brute said, "No different than when they dropped her here."

Gamble clenched his teeth. For the first time he felt like his brothers were letting him down. Yet, he knew that was a knee-jerk reaction and he tried to ignore it.

"So, no changes, or should he read between the lines?" Roman asked.

Har's chin dipped a fraction. Then Gamble's gaze slid to Roman, who arched his brows at him.

"Gamble, are you claiming an old lady?" Joules asked.

He didn't have to think about it. "Yes."

Block's head reared back. "That fast?"

"Hasn't been 'that fast,' but yeah. I'm sure," Gamble said with a glare.

Har banged the gavel. "We're finished, until next week."

"Hope we ain't got to bail anybody out," Brute muttered.

"Yo! Wait up, Gamble," Roman yelled after him.

He turned around, halfway to his bike. "What?"

"You goin' after them tonight?"

He crossed his arms. "No."

"You're not just saying that to keep me out of your business?"

Movement from the back of the clubhouse caught his eye and he noticed Mensa and Tiny ambling out. He didn't need three brothers getting up in his business.

His eyes met Roman's. "No, I'm not doin' shit tonight."

He walked toward his bike, but Roman fell in step beside him. "Then what's the hurry?"

"You know damn well Tiny's on his way over here, and I don't need him stirrin' shit up. I'm already hanging on by a fuckin' thread, Ro."

"We're a brotherhood, man. You're hurting, and I saw that look on your face."

He shook his head. "I'm not hurt."

Roman's eyes widened. "Maybe not, but if it were me in your shoes, I'd feel betrayed."

"No. That's extreme. Har's doin' what he has to for the club. That's how it's always been. Club first."

"And that's bullshit," Tiny said, coming in front of them.

"No, it isn't," Gamble said.

Tiny shot him a flat look. "Yeah? You think shit wouldn't be all kinds of different if it were Stephanie? Think Brute wouldn't be tearing the city down brick by brick if it were Kenzie? Neither of them would give two shits about the fuckin' club at that point."

"You're wrong," Roman said.

"The hell I am. They'd care about not getting caught. That's about it."

Mensa sidled up to them. "Speaking of not getting caught, what are you gonna do, G? How are you going to fly under the radar?"

He tore a hand through his hair. "I don't fuckin' know, man." He glanced at Roman. "No plan means I'm not doin' anything tonight. Brute comparing this to June reminded me that I need to let the law do its thing. Much as I hate that shit. I'll give it a week."

Tiny growled. "I don't like that idea. Strike while shit's hot, I say."

Mensa shook his head. "Better to be safe than sorry." He pointed a finger at Gamble. "But don't do anything without someone at your back."

He clenched his teeth. "I know, Mensa. Heard you motherfuckers loud and clear."

Mensa held his hands up. "Jesus. Don't bite my head off. Get your ass a candy bar or something."

Gamble chuckled. "Let me get on my bike, maybe I will."

"Forget what Mensa said, you need to get laid. That always takes the edge off," Tiny said.

"Sex is your answer for everything, Tiny," Gamble said.

Tiny shrugged. "Sex is never wrong. As long as it's consensual, of course."

"He's got you there," Mensa said.

"Let Gamble get on his bike," Roman muttered.

He gave them all a chin-lift and got out of there.

CHAPTER 15

AGAIN

VICTORIA

My stomach growled as I left the offices of Gower and Gower. It never failed: being nervous left me hungry no matter how much I ate beforehand. The empty pit of my stomach reminded me I needed to hit the grocery store before going home, but that had to wait until after swinging by my condo. I had forwarded my mail to Fiona's address earlier that day, but nearly a week's worth of mail should be in my box. The Gower and Gower offices weren't that far from the condo, so it made sense to get it today.

When I pulled into the parking lot, my cell rang with Miranda's ringtone.

I smiled and answered, "Hey, sis!"

"Hi, yourself. Mom wants to know why you haven't responded to her texts."

My brows furrowed. "Um, seriously?"

"Believe me, I'd rather talk to you about this man she doesn't approve of instead, but she's—"

"Yeah, I get it. She's hounding you. Hang on, let me see if I have something from her. I swear I didn't see any notifications."

I swiped at my cell screen, and there was a text icon, but other notifications had rolled in after it.

With a head shake, I put my cell to my ear. "Okay, well, I see she wants me to call her. I'll do that now, so she'll get off your back."

Miranda made a non-committal sound. "Whatever, she needs to get her panties untwisted. Did you miss her message because you were in court?"

My lips tipped up. "No. I was in an interview. My boss put me on—"

I cut myself off because that would require telling Miranda about being raped. Even if Uncle Mick said Miranda would want to know over the phone, I still wanted to tell her in person.

"Your boss did what?"

"Nothing, when do you fly in? Am I picking you up?"

"My guess is that's what Mom wants to talk to you about. But, you're hiding something from me."

I shook my head. "I'm really not. So, you're here for a week right?"

"No," she sighed. "Flying out Sunday. Some stuff's come up at the hospital, and well, I won't bore you with it, but I have to cut my time short to get back to work on Monday."

That was disappointing, but I smiled to hide it from my voice. "Well, that's plenty of time for you to make your rocky road brownies."

"Tori! That's you. *All* you."

Now a genuine smile curled my lips as I recalled making those brownies with her when we were teenagers. Since we didn't have a set recipe, we'd made a huge mess, which was half the fun. After that first batch, only I had luck recreating them again. "Fine. Text me with your flight deets, and we'll get you taken care of."

"By we, does that mean you and your new man? Or you and Mom?"

I smirked. "How do you know about that?"

"Uncle Mick. What can I say? He keeps in touch."

I barked with laughter. "Yeah, right! He meddles is more like it!"

She chuckled. "Seriously. I want to meet him. Is he really a biker?"

"Yeah," I whispered.

She paused. "Oh, hell. That tone —even in a whisper— you like him."

"No. I love him."

"L-love him? Really?"

"Yeah."

"Uncle Mick wasn't lying."

"When did you talk to him?"

"Last night."

"I'm surprised Gamble and I would be a topic of conversation."

She chuckled. "Uncle Mick is the biggest gossip I know, and he *loves* watching people fall in love. You know that! It's why he insists on being so fancy at night. Anyway, bring Gamble when you pick me up."

"He rides a bike, Miranda. And I'm not so sure he'll fit in my Sentra. Plus if I bring him, you'd have to sit in the backseat."

She chuckled. "If he's anything like Uncle Mick described, *you'll* have to sit in the back seat because he'll insist on driving."

I felt my lip curl a little because she was probably right. With a shake of my head, I said, "Whatever. I doubt he's going to be able to break away from work, but you're going to meet him, don't you worry. Hell, you could stay in the guest room—"

Again, I had to cut myself short.

"He has a guest room?"

It wasn't *exactly* a lie, so I said, "Yes. And if Mom gets to be too much, you could stay there."

"I'll consider it, but you need to call Mom. I love you, and I'll see you soon."

"Love you, too!"

I ended our call and dialed Mom while I still had a smile on my face.

"It's high time you called me, Victoria."

"Hello, Mom. I was in an interview when you called earlier."

Her tone was just shy of condescending. "You mean an interrogation, don't you?"

I took a deep breath. The easy thing to do would be to lie, but I didn't have it in me. "No. I had a job interview. Miranda said you needed to talk to me. Are you picking her up tomorrow? Or do you want me to handle it?"

"I would appreciate it if you picked up Miranda, but don't tell her about your father and me separating."

I clenched my teeth for a moment. Then it struck me that if Uncle Mick kept in touch as well as Miranda indicated, then she might already know something's up. "No problem, Mom. That's not mine to tell."

"Good. And don't tell her about your problems from last month either."

My jaw dropped. I couldn't believe my ears. "Have you lost your mind?"

"No, Victoria. And you can stop with the —"

"I can stop with the what? Attitude? The drama? Forget that! I learned all that from *you*. And as two men I love pointed out to me, if ever there were a time when I need my sister –hell, need my *family*– it's after being brutally raped! Miranda deserves to know because I'd be pissed as hell if she kept something like this from me for too long."

"This should not be a stressful trip for her."

"Then maybe you shouldn't tell her you're leaving Dad. But I will let her know about my attack because that isn't going to be stressful for her. She'll be more than happy to help me, be a shoulder for me to lean on, but I'm not keeping her in the dark any longer, Mom."

There was a lengthy silence. Then Mom said, "I should have known your father and Mick would—"

"It wasn't Dad," I put in. Immediately I realized I should've kept my trap shut.

"It wasn't... oh, was it your biker who said you need your sister?"

Between the way she enunciated the word 'biker' and her using the word 'need', I itched to hang up. "No, Mom. He couldn't believe I'd kept it from her. Purposefully. Because of you, no less. He has an older sister, and he knows I needed my sister to help me out."

"Well, you've gone this long. You're a very strong young woman, Victoria."

"Good God, do you hear yourself?"

I heard her sharp inhale. "Not everything has to be unloaded, Victoria."

My words slipped from my lips. "Maybe if you'd unloaded years ago, you and Dad would still be together instead of separating because you can't see past your own self-centeredness."

Mom gasped. "Victoria Hazel! Do not speak to me that way."

"So, will Dad be around... or are you going to lie to Miranda about that?"

"Young lady, show some respect."

"Mom. I'm picking up my sister from the airport tomorrow. If you come down on her like a ton of bricks or put her in the middle the way you normally do, she won't be around this visit. I've got a room she can stay in, and she knows it."

"We'll just see about that."

I rolled my eyes. "Okay. Talk to you later."

"That's all you have to say?"

"Love you, Mom."

"I love you, Victoria."

I ended the call, got out of my car, and went to my mailbox. There was plenty of junk mail wadded up in the small box. I tucked it under my arm and had just locked the box when a heavy body shoved me up against the wall of mailboxes.

I felt someone's hot breath against my ear. "Drop the fuckin' charges, bitch." As the man spoke, I smelled beer on his breath.

I croaked out, "I don't know what you're talking about."

He pulled me back only to push me up against the metal boxes again. "Bullshit. You don't know who broke into your condo. Drop the fuckin' charges."

I wanted to ask, 'or what,' but someone else answered that.

A lower pitched voice said, "If you don't, you'll be dead. One less dumb bitch to fuckin' shut up."

My body went tense as the man at my back shoved me again. "Yeah."

It took a while before I realized they'd left.

With care, I backed away from the mailbox console. I felt where the boxes had pressed into my cheek.

Then an older woman said, "Are you okay, dear? My daughter tells me I get worked up about my mail, but you seem quite shaken."

Rather than look at this woman, I shook my head while lowering it. "No, not shaken. I'm fine. Thanks for asking."

As I walked away, I stumbled and dropped the mail. I stooped over, grabbed the bills, and scurried back to my car. Thank heavens for my key fob, I was able to unlock the doors while my hands shook like leaves. Once I was in the car, I locked the doors and took some deep breaths.

While I couldn't see Ernesto or Luis, I didn't assume they'd left. I started my car and drove back to the bungalow.

For some stupid reason I couldn't bring myself to get out of the car after I turned it off. I hit the garage door clicker so the car wouldn't be visible from the street and rested my forehead on the steering wheel.

No sooner had the door slammed closed than it rolled upward again. My head whipped up. "What the fuck?"

Then Gamble walked his bike inside the garage.

In the rear-view mirror, I caught sight of myself. There was a pink line on my face from a mailbox door. Otherwise, I didn't look any different. I took too long examining my face because Gamble whipped my door open.

"You just get in?"

I looked up at him with a grin. "Yeah. That's pretty coincidental, huh?"

His posture went rigid. "What's wrong, Victoria?"

I shook my head. "Nothing. How was your meeting?"

He took my hand and helped me out of the car. "Fine. More important question is how was your interview?"

"Good. Better than I expected. They said they're still considering another candidate, so," I shrugged, "hopefully I'll hear more next week."

His left eye narrowed on me just before his finger traced the line on my cheek. "What's this?"

I closed my eyes. "It's nothing."

When I opened my eyes, Gamble's were wide and full of outrage. "It's not nothing, and we have to be honest with each other, Vickie."

The sun beat down on the garage at this time of day and with the door closed it was getting hot fast.

"Can we go inside, please? Get out of this awful heat."

He swung a hand out for me to precede him.

I disabled the alarm and he stalked into the kitchen. I hung my purse on a chair as he leaned against the counter with his arms crossed.

He brought a hand up to stroke his chin. "What happened to your face, kitten?"

I sat down. "After the interview I went to get my mail from the past week."

He sighed. "Should have told me you were going to do that."

I hung my head and stared at my lap. "Yeah. I didn't see them, but I believe Luis and Ernesto cornered me at the mailboxes."

The air wasn't tense, it was downright electric with his fury. "What do you mean they cornered you?"

I told him what they did and what they said. Then I said, "That's where the line on my face came from."

His entire body seemed frozen, except his thumb stroking his bearded chin. I focused on his chest to see if he was breathing heavy, but it didn't look that way. Then he turned his face and I saw his jaw tighten.

He blew out a lengthy breath. "They shoved you into a bunch of fuckin' mailboxes?"

"Yeah," I whispered.

He turned around and pressed his fists on the counter. "You call anyone? You gonna do what they said?"

Since he had his back to me, I couldn't get a read on him. His voice was so calm, I knew it was deceptive —even if he didn't mean it to be.

"No, I didn't call anyone, though one of my neighbors saw me afterward. Asked if I was okay, but I don't think she saw what happened or noticed my face. She just knew I was shaken up."

He whirled around at that.

"You were shaken up... and you didn't call anyone about that?"

He was driving at something, but I didn't appreciate the accusation in his tone.

"Gamble. I just wanted to get out of there. I didn't know where they'd gone, but I figured they still had eyes on me."

"Yeah," he breathed. "And that's why you needed to call *me*."

My hands went to my hips. "I'm not in the wrong here. I did what I had to do to get home and—"

"They could have taken you again! This was what? An hour ago?"

I glanced at the microwave. "Yeah, probably."

"God help me, this will be the last time something like this happens to you, but any time some asshole fucks with you, your first call needs to be *me*, Victoria."

"It wasn't my fault!"

"I know that! But now I don't know where those assholes are. If you'd called me, I'd have been there. My brothers and I could've found them, because you're right. They probably did stick around to watch you."

"I doubt it."

"Not what you said earlier. You figured they had eyes on you, and you were probably right."

He opened his mouth, paused, and closed his eyes like he was arguing with himself. Finally, he looked at me. "Are you calling the cops about this?"

"I don't know."

"Then don't call the cops. I'm taking care of this shit."

His voice held an edge I'd never heard. "Wait. What are you saying?"

"Not repeating myself, kitten. This shit's gone unanswered for too fuckin' long."

I stared at him, but his long legs took him past me in short order. "Where are you going?"

"Out."

"Gamble!"

He stopped at the door. His eyes bore into me. "I love you. I'll be back."

The sound of the garage door opening spurred me into action. I opened the door to see Gamble astride his bike. He powered up his Harley, flicked a finger at me and walked his bike out of the garage.

"Where are you going?" I yelled.

"Don't worry about it," he yelled back.

I wanted to follow him, but as I stepped further into the garage he shook his head. "Go inside, Vic!"

"You stay—" I stopped short because Gamble had his bike outside the garage, and he'd engaged the door to close.

I hustled back to grab my purse intent to follow him, but my phone was ringing. The display showed Miranda was calling. I sent it to voicemail.

At my car, I realized Gamble had too much of a head start on me. We may have shared two rides total, but I knew the speed limit was something he only observed when he had to, which meant he was long gone.

I felt helpless stuck at Fiona's bungalow, but I had to do something. As I headed back inside, it hit me. I could call Fiona. If anyone would know what to do, it would be her.

"Fiona Brinkley," she answered.

"Fiona, it's Victoria."

"Hey, are you okay? You sound freaked."

"Yeah, I am. Gamble just left here, and I think he's going to do something he shouldn't."

"Okay," she breathed out, then I heard sounds like doors closing and there was less background noise. "Is this club business? And if so, are we talking about violence or something else?"

"He got really angry after I told him about being shoved up against the mail console at my old condo. And he said this shit's gone on too long or something like that. He acts calm, but my gut says he's flying off the handle. I'm not sure what to do, but I know I shouldn't call the cops and you were the first person to come to mind."

I heard a door open again before she said, "You need to call me, don't ever hesitate. And you did the right thing. No matter what Gamble might say later."

Dread settled deep in my belly. "I wouldn't be so sure, Fiona. If he's gone after Luis and Ernesto on his own," I shook my head, then whispered, "I've never seen Gamble in a fight, but those guys are awful."

"Have faith in your man, Vickie. But you're right. There's power in numbers. I need to call Cynic so some of the brothers can help him out."

"Okay," I whispered.

"Okay. And I'm going to come by the house in fifteen minutes, cool?"

"Definitely."

Gamble

Gamble strode straight to his room at the clubhouse. The place was quiet, but at five o'clock after a holiday weekend, he wasn't surprised. Inside his room, he tore his t-shirt over his head and put on his armored t-shirt. It wouldn't help if he got shot in the shoulder, but it was better than nothing.

He called Roman, but it went to voicemail. Back in the hallway, he knocked on Cynic's door.

Mensa stopped at the mouth of the hall and said, "'Nic's at the bar. Something came up. You need something?"

He blew out a breath and walked toward Mensa. "The fucking Abeyetas cornered Vic at her mailbox."

"They found where y'all are staying?"

He shook his head. "She had a pile of mail at her old place."

"Shit. Is she okay?"

He sighed. "She says she is, but there's a mark on her cheek from where they pressed her up against the boxes. She isn't reporting that shit, and I'm done waiting."

"Do you know where they are?"

"I know where they normally hang."

Mensa dug into his pocket. "I'm comin' with you."

"Do you need to get a gun?"

"Already on me."

"Let's go."

Twenty minutes later, they pulled up outside the neighborhood bar off Iberville Drive where Gamble knew the Abeyetas hung out. As he and Mensa swung off their bikes, Cynic roared up on his chopper.

Gamble shot Mensa a glare. "You tell him about this shit?"

Mensa's brows lowered ominously. "No. Got no idea how he knew we'd be here."

Cynic strode to them and crossed his arms. "Am I late for the party?"

"There is no fuckin' party," Gamble bit out.

"You need your brothers –plural– to have your back, G. Mensa's good and shit, but you said you'd let someone know."

"You aren't my keeper. How the fuck'd you find out anyway?"

"Don't matter."

His head turned a fraction. "That's bullshit. Victoria doesn't have your number, so how the fuck did you find out?"

Cynic stroked his beard. "She has Fiona's number, and don't you get pissed at her. She's worried as fuck about you. And we don't have time for this shit. Sun hasn't set yet, and we stand out like sore thumbs. Let's find these fuckers and get out of here."

The clientele in the bar were predominantly black and Hispanic, which meant Gamble, Mensa, and Cynic garnered everyone's notice.

Gamble led them to three empty seats at the bar. An older black woman stood behind the bar. Her hair was cropped short, her brown eyes were razor-sharp, and her full lips were formed into a pout. She had an angular figure. She was so thin.

As she moved toward them, she arched a brow for a moment. "You bikers need to turn your asses around."

Cynic placed an order for all three of them while Gamble scanned the rest of the room.

"I don't see them," Mensa muttered.

"Were you even looking?" Gamble asked.

"I'm always looking, G, you know that."

A burly black man lumbered toward them. If it was who he thought it was, Gamble had heard about the leader of the Miscreants –a local street gang. He'd earned his street name, "Inch" before even joining the gang. Compliments of his father, he had a scar running down his face. In retaliation, he'd attacked his father and beaten him to within an inch of his life– or so the story went.

"You assholes need to get the fuck outta here," he said to Cynic.

"Luis or Ernesto Abeyeta been in here tonight?" Gamble asked.

Inch's eyes never left Cynic. "Got nothin' to say to him... or you for that matter. Sooner you leave the better."

The bartender set three glasses of liquor in front of them.

"Luis and Ernesto raped my woman. They threatened her again this afternoon. I got no problem with you or anyone else in here. I just want to find them."

Gamble's focus had been on Inch, and he hadn't realized the bartender was within ear shot until she let out a disgusted groan.

He heard her say, "I told you those two were—"

Inch's eyes slid to her. "Enough, Nia." He glanced back at Cynic. "You bastards got nerve walkin' in here."

Gamble looked at Nia, but turned back to Inch when the man reached forward grabbing Gamble's drink. "She knows they're trouble?"

"Every man's trouble around here," Nia muttered and prowled to the other end of the bar.

"Anybody with sense knows they're trouble, but they ain't here tonight and haven't been in over two months. Now, get the fuck out of here or do I have to kick you motherfuckers out?"

Mensa shoved his drink toward Inch. "Let's go, G."

Cynic nodded and put a fifty on the bar. "Thanks for the info, Inch."

Gamble hesitated. Something told him Inch knew more about Luis and Ernesto than he was letting on, but he knew he'd gotten as much out of him as he could. Still, it rubbed him the wrong way that Inch would hold out like that.

"Let's go, G," Cynic clipped out.

"They don't deserve your protection," Gamble muttered.

Inch laughed. "Those paint fumes went to your head. I don't protect any-damn-body."

He felt Cynic and Mensa's eyes on him, so Gamble strode around Inch and left.

On his bike, Mensa said, "Shit. I'm low on gas. You head back without me."

Gamble shook his head. "Not a chance, Mensa. There's a convenience store up the road."

Cynic stared at Gamble for a moment. "You're good, right? No more bullshit tonight?"

Gamble clenched his teeth. "I'm not good. But I got no idea where they would be... so, I'm headed home."

Cynic pointed a finger at him. "Your woman did the right thing calling Fi. Hell, I didn't think she had that in her."

He gave Cynic a chin-lift, but Victoria would still get a piece of his mind. While it was good to have Cynic with him tonight, she never should have involved another brother's old lady.

Gamble and Mensa watched as Cynic pulled out of the parking lot. Then they rode in the opposite direction to a nearby gas station.

They pulled up to the pumps only to find the card readers weren't working.

Gamble called out to Mensa, "You sure you can't make it closer to the clubhouse?"

Mensa shook his head. "No, man. Sorry."

After pre-paying for their gas, they walked out of the convenience store. Ten feet from the store, they were grabbed from behind.

"You're on the wrong side of town, biker," a man said in Gamble's ear.

From the corner of his eye, he saw Luis had Mensa in a headlock, which made it likely Ernesto stood behind Gamble holding him by the arms.

What were the odds they'd get blindsided by the Abeyetas?

Gamble broke the hold on his right arm and swung his body out to partially face his attacker. Ernesto's brown eyes glittered with malice. A whir of motion came toward his face. Gamble ducked the punch while pulling his gun from his waistband.

With a vicious jerk of his left arm, he broke completely free of the hold.

He moved in close to Ernesto, pressing the gun up against his rib cage. "Ought to kill you now, but you deserve a slow death, motherfucker."

Any other neighborhood and the cops would be on the scene already, but they wouldn't get any help here from the police. Not from the clerk. And *especially* not from the few bystanders, since they were already gone.

"You don't have any fuckin' balls," Ernesto spat at him. "Couldn't do shit for your sister and you couldn't save the lawyer either."

Driven by anger, he shoved Ernesto backward until he heard a gunshot. The distraction made him pause. Ernesto landed a punch to Gamble's eye.

His head swung to the left. He saw Mensa and Luis struggling for the gun. The blow to Gamble's face allowed Ernesto to step away. Instinct kicked in and Gamble shot him in the chest.

His ears ringing, Gamble heard a man yelling. Then he heard two more shots as pain exploded in his lower leg and his chest.

Pain he knew well from ten years ago. His last thought before blacking out was that he'd been shot.

Again.

CHAPTER 16

DANGEROUS

VICTORIA

B y the time Fiona knocked on the door, I suspected I'd done the wrong thing. Gamble was a grown man, and I should trust him to take care of himself.

Still.

I'd never seen him so angry, and yet he was calm, which made me think he was more likely to fly off the handle.

With a smile I didn't feel, I opened the door to her. "Hi, come on in."

Her lips tipped up. "No need to fake it for me, Vickie. It's okay to be worried about him."

I followed her to the couch, but stopped myself from sitting down. "You want something to drink? I might have a bottle of wine in the fridge."

She chuckled. "As good as that sounds, I'm thinking we need to stay sober for right now."

My eyes widened. "Really?"

She patted a spot on the couch. "Sit down, sweetie. I got a hold of Cynic before coming here. He had a hunch on where Gamble would be. If we're lucky, he'll have headed him off from any danger."

I gave her a closed-lip smile. "Then why do I feel so full of dread?"

She grabbed my hand. "Because you care about him."

We fell silent until my stomach growled. Fiona arched her brows, but I shook my head. "I couldn't bear to eat anything right now."

She shrugged a shoulder and pulled out her cell phone. "I'm gonna order a pizza anyway. It'll keep and you can have some later."

Gamble and I had been staying in the bungalow for close to a week, but we hadn't gone to my place to get my flat screen. It was one of the few things not vandalized in my apartment. This meant I couldn't turn on the television to occupy me and Fiona. Instead, I pulled up a music streaming app on my phone.

Since I'd last asked it to play music based on Gamble's favorite group, Slightly Stoopid, we were listening to mellow music when the doorbell rang. Even though I was expecting it, my body still jerked at the sound.

"Calm down, Victoria," Fiona said, and went to the door.

After she closed the door, I realized the sun was setting.

I got Fiona a paper plate for her pizza. "How do you deal with it?"

She looked at me over the top of the pizza box. "What do you mean?"

"How do you handle the fact Cynic might be helping Gamble commit a crime?"

She grinned. "Honey, did it occur to you that it might be the other way around?"

"He's helping Cynic? No. He was deceptively angry when he left. I know he could kill them in cold blood and not give a damn."

Fiona nodded. "Right. Well, I guess I'm accustomed to it because my father used to be the chapter president."

My head reared back. "Really?"

She nodded. "There's a lot more to it than that. But you need to understand, the brothers go to great lengths to make sure nothing blows back on the club, and damn sure not on their women."

My lips twisted with skepticism.

"I see you don't believe me. It's going to take some adjustment for you, especially with your legal background, but have faith in your man, Victoria."

"Right," I whispered.

She shoved a small box at me. "Have a breadstick at least. It'll give you something else to do. Besides, you're so damn skinny, you can afford a few carbs."

I nibbled on a breadstick, wishing I could go outside for a run. Swallowing my food, it felt like a lead weight in my belly.

"It's freaking miserable being this helpless."

Fiona nodded sympathetically. "It is, but men who join the Riot have to take care of things on their terms."

I dipped my chin. "Really? Because so far, it's been done more on my terms. The legal system and all that."

Her head wobbled side to side. "Yeah, and my hunch is that Gamble would point out that didn't go very well for you, did it?"

"I suppose, but—"

"No buts, Victoria. That's a big reason so many of those men are part of the chapter. They don't commit crimes everyday —or at least, not anymore— but they hardly ever trust the government to do right by them."

Had I been fresh out of law school, I'd have argued that point. But having worked on so many cases, I knew Fiona was right.

Someone knocked on the door. Moving into the foyer, I checked the windows alongside the door. Heidi stood there in the waning sunlight giving me big eyes.

I opened the door. "What are you doing here?"

She bustled inside. "I told you I was coming by this week. Someone's got to inspect your new digs."

I locked the door behind her as Fiona came out of the kitchen. "You think I'd rent a slum to her, Heidi?"

"Wait, this is your place?"

Fiona nodded and went over to the sofa.

Heidi followed. "That's cool."

"You gonna tell us about you and Block?" Fiona asked.

Her question so took me by surprise that I fell onto the couch next to Heidi.

Heidi glared at me. "Geez! Did you tell her?"

"No! I don't know how she knew."

Fiona chuckled. "You two need to recognize something: nothing gets by unnoticed at the clubhouse. Especially where officers are concerned. You didn't hear this from me, but Block never follows a woman out of his room. He's the king of one-and-done. So, Heidi, what'd you do to him?"

A sly grin curled Heidi's lips. "Nothing another woman hasn't done to him before, I'm sure. Your man was seeing things that night."

I barked out a laugh. "Nope. I saw how Block watched your car roll out of the forecourt. He didn't look happy."

Curiosity lit up Heidi's eyes for a moment, then she shuttered her expression. "You're imagining things."

Fiona shook her head. "You protest too much, and believe me, Cynic said something very similar. Block was in a foul-ass mood the rest of the night."

Heidi gave me an expectant look. "Did you run into him again that night?"

I pressed my lips together. "Can't say that I did."

Fiona said in *sotto-voce*, "She was too busy making out on a blanket under the fireworks."

"Fiona!"

Heidi laughed.

Then Fiona's phone chirped. She pulled it out of her purse. "That's Cynic. He caught up with Gamble and Mensa at a sketchy bar. They're leaving now."

"Okay," I whispered.

Heidi's eyes were questioning. I shook my head.

"It still doesn't make me feel better for some stupid reason."

"Hey, what happened to your cheek? It's like... did you cut yourself there or something?" Heidi asked, gently stroking my face.

"Or something," I muttered.

Fiona scoffed. "Victoria, you need to be honest with your friends when shit hits the fan."

Heidi's expression turned stern. "What's she talking about?"

I hesitated too long, and Fiona said, "She got cornered at her mailbox by those bastards who raped her."

Heidi's eyes widened. "I thought lover boy had people following you all the time!"

My chin dipped and I gave her a regretful smile. "Yeah, except this afternoon I had an interview at Gower and Gower which fell during church for the brothers... but Gamble thought I'd be okay."

Fiona tossed a hand out toward me. "Did Gamble know you were going to drop by for your mail?"

I shook my head. "No."

Fiona's eyes widened. "You shouldn't have done that."

Heidi shot a disgusted look at Fiona. "This isn't her fault."

Fiona shook her head. "I didn't say it was, I'm just saying you can't make assumptions when things like this are going on."

Heidi looked at my cheek for another beat. Then her eyes caught mine and she smiled half-heartedly. "Yay about Gower and Gower though, right? How did you snag their attention?"

"Lover boy," I admitted.

"Well," Heidi said, her voice haughty as could be. "I guess he's all right after all."

Fiona laughed. "Why do you have a chip on your shoulder about him?"

Heidi settled back into the couch. "I don't have anything against Gamble, I just think it's dangerous for Vickie to get involved with him. Unless she's looking to settle down, that is."

I turned to Heidi. "He told me he loves me."

She jabbed a finger toward me. "I told you he was dangerous!"

"Love is dangerous?" Fiona asked, disbelief lacing her tone.

Heidi nodded. "For her with him, you betcha."

"Oh boy," Fiona muttered.

Heidi and I stared at her. "What's that mean?" I asked.

Fiona gave a short head shake. "I don't know, but something tells me I should warn Block about you, Heidi."

Heidi threw a hand out at her. "Nah! He told me he's been around the block a time or two —and he didn't even excuse his pun— I'm sure he's more than fine."

Fiona checked her phone again and her eyes widened. "Jeez. It's been almost an hour since Cynic texted. Can't believe I lost track of time. I gotta run. I'm sure Gamble will be here soon, sweetie."

That unsettled feeling intensified. Biloxi wasn't that big, and even sketchy bars weren't an hour away. If it had been an hour, Gamble should have already come home.

Fiona's phone rang and she shot us a flat look. "That's Cynic now." She tapped her phone. "Hi, there."

She paused, then, "Yeah. And I'm still with Victoria, her friend Heidi showed up, and I lost track of time."

Another pause.

She looked at me and Heidi. "Yeah, I get that, honey, but if you're home from that side of town, why the hell isn't Gamble here? It's even closer to the clubhouse or the bungalow."

She paused, but her lips turned down just enough I knew she was concerned. "Doesn't take long to gas up a bike. Even if both of them needed fuel."

My hand moved of its own accord to grab Heidi's. She gave me a squeeze, but neither of us stopped watching Fiona.

"All right. Got it. Love you too."

Fiona ended her call and stood. She approached us and waved her hands for us to make room for her.

She sat down between us and grabbed both my hands. "Cynic's calling Mensa and Gamble now. He agreed they should've been back, but they might have swung by the clubhouse."

I nodded. "But you're worried too? Or is my vibe just filling the room?"

She shook her head. "No, you're right to be worried, sweetie. I believe in listening to your gut."

The three of us sat together on the sofa for a while listening to the streaming app. I knew his favorite band was playing again. No matter how I tried to ignore the words to "Anywhere I Go," the more I focused on them.

The song threatened to rip my heart out as I realized how much it described me and Gamble. He was the person I needed no matter where I went or what I did, and I would dream of him.

No, I'd never felt anything like this before.

While it felt like over an hour had elapsed, I knew it was more like twenty minutes. I didn't have the best grip on time, but my every instinct said Gamble was in danger.

Fiona's phone rang as the song changed. "Hey, Steph—" Then a business-like expression crossed Fiona's face. "Right. We'll be there."

Heidi leaned forward and made eye contact with me. She whispered, "It'll be all right."

Fiona tucked her phone into her purse. "Okay, both of you get in my car. I'm driving."

"I like you and everything, but I'm not getting in your car with you if I don't know where we're going," Heidi said.

Fiona gave her a look. "I'm taking Victoria with me. You can follow or ride with us, but we're headed to Merit Health. The quicker the better. Gamble's been shot and Mensa was stabbed."

Har, Tiny, and Roman were huddled together when Fiona and I walked into the waiting room.

They broke and Har strode to us. "Fiona. Victoria. He's in surgery. That's all they'll tell us."

"What about Mensa?" Fiona asked.

Roman joined us. "He's being discharged into custody."

That caught me by surprise. "Why into custody?"

Har looked over his shoulder at the nurse's station where an officer stood watching us. Har caught my eyes. "Ernesto was shot. Died at the scene. Mensa and Gamble both got shots off, so until they know who killed him, police are arresting them and Luis."

My mind froze at the idea of Gamble surviving this only to be arrested and face jail time.

I didn't even realize Heidi was next to me until she asked, "What about surveillance footage? No way your men just attacked two people out in the open. They had to have been defending themselves."

Har's eyes danced over Heidi's face before he weakly grinned at her. "Block is looking into that."

Had I not been watching, I'd have missed Heidi's neck turning pink at hearing Block's name.

She shook her head. "Well, good. 'Cause this is bullshit."

I looked to my right when I heard high heels clacking on the linoleum floor. Monica Wright, a criminal defense attorney for Gower and Gower had her eyes on the nurse's station. Then she saw Har and stopped short.

As she approached, she caught sight of me, and her lips pursed. "Are you representing Mr. Abeyeta?"

I shook my head. "I'm not here in a professional capacity."

She gave me a slow nod. "Good. Otherwise, I'd wonder why Mr. Walcott and Mr. Sanchez were talking to you."

Roman shot her a grin. "We know about our right to remain silent, Mrs. Wright."

She returned his grin. "I'm sure. However, it's always better to trust but verify. If you need me, I'll be speaking with that officer."

As she left us, I moved to an empty chair and plopped down.

Gamble was in surgery, fighting for his life because he wanted my problems to stop. I'd found the man I loved, and I could lose him because of revenge.

I hated that I'd ever represented one of the Abeyetas. My stomach churned at how fucked up the entire situation happened to be.

"He's gonna be all right," Heidi said, leaning her shoulder on mine.

"Pray to God that's true, Heidi. I don't think I can handle falling in love this fast only to lose it just as fucking quick. Especially since it feels like it's all my fault."

Fiona sat in the chair on my other side and grabbed my hand. "Don't you dare put that on yourself. None of this is your fault. And you can't beat yourself up like this. Things happen like they're supposed to, no matter how fucked up it seems at the time. Got it?"

The tough-love tone in her voice kept me from arguing, and I nodded.

Roman squatted in front of me, grabbing my free hand. "She's right, Vic. Gamble was getting antsy. Hell, he's been antsy since they dropped you at our door and it never went away." He looked back at the police officer, who was still talking to Mrs. Wright. When he continued, he lowered his voice. "It rubbed him raw that we hadn't done anything to them sooner. If I hadn't missed his call this afternoon..."

I squeezed his hand. "Don't dwell on that."

He widened his eyes at me. "I won't. But only if you take your own advice. Can you do that?"

My head tilted. "It isn't that simple."

He edged closer. "It's just that simple. We can all play that game, but it gets you nowhere. So don't do it. You gotta be strong for him."

I nodded.

He gave my hand a squeeze, then stood.

Tiny lumbered over to us. "You ladies want coffee? No idea when that surgery will be done, so I'm getting a prospect to bring us Starbuck's."

The mention of Starbuck's made me think of my sister and I groaned.

"What's wrong?" Heidi asked.

"Miranda comes in tomorrow. I'm supposed to pick her up. I'm not gonna be able to—"

"I got it," Heidi said. "As long as she isn't traveling with a huge suitcase, it's no problem."

I glared at her. "She gets in during the middle of the day, Heidi. I don't want you getting into more hot water at work because of me."

"I'll get her," Fiona said. "The practice is closed all week. It's no biggie. Especially since Cynic will be tied up with club business tomorrow, I'm sure."

"I owe you so much, Fiona. I'll give you—"

"Hush," Fiona insisted.

A petite, African-American nurse wearing a purple surgical cap that matched her purple scrubs strode into the waiting area. "Garrison family?"

I stood up. "That's me."

Monica Wright was still at the nurse's station, and I felt her focus on me, but I only had eyes for the nurse.

"Are you next-of-kin?"

The lie tumbled out of my mouth. "I'm his sister."

She lifted her chin slightly. "Come with me, he's out of surgery. The doctor wants to speak with you."

I held Gamble's hand while standing up because the nurse said I wouldn't have much time with him before they moved him to the intensive care unit. Tears were threatening, but I forced myself to fight them off.

He looked so pale, I worried he'd need a blood transfusion. They told me the bullets had been removed, and after that my brain shut down. Two bullets had hit him. My eyes scanned his body. A blanket covered most of him, but he'd been shot in the calf, so one leg was bandaged where they'd stitched him up. That leg was outside the blankets so nurses could keep an eye on the dressing. Thanks to his muscular calves, the bullet hadn't made it to the bone though the nurse said muscle damage was just as bad.

Looking at his hand in mine, I forced myself to ignore his other hand since it was cuffed to the bed railing. There was nothing I could do for him with that, but I prayed Monica Wright would get things resolved. She was damn good at her job. I'd once heard my boss say if it weren't for Mr. Gower, Monica would be the best defense attorney in Biloxi.

I shook my head to get rid of my thoughts.

As I leaned over to kiss Gamble's cheek, I whispered, "I love you. You better get through this, Gage. You're not allowed to go anywhere on me. Not now –actually– not *ever*, if I have anything to say about it."

His eyes fluttered open. "Kitten," he whispered.

I shushed him. "Go back to sleep, honey. I love you and I'm not going anywhere."

He stared at me for a moment, but I had a feeling the drugs were still working in his system. His eyes closed and the nurse poked her head around the curtain. "Was he awake?"

I nodded. "For a second. He said my name, but I told him to save his energy."

She nodded. "Good. We're going to move him now."

I nodded and went back to the waiting area.

Heidi rushed up to me as I entered the room. "Is he... did he wake up?"

"For like a second," I said.

My eyes were fixed on Har. He had his phone to his ear, and I caught snippets of what he was saying.

When he saw me, I had a feeling he wanted to talk to me. Then he said, "Right, Brittney, she just came out, so I'll let you talk to her if you want."

I felt the blood drain from my face. Heidi rubbed my arm. "It's okay, his sister sounds like she's pretty cool."

I glanced at her. "How would you know?"

"He had her on speaker earlier. Just talk to her," she muttered.

Har handed me the phone. "It's Brittney."

With a nod, I put the phone to my ear. "Hello."

"Hey, Victoria, right?"

"Yeah. Are you, um, on your way down here?"

She sighed. "I would be... but, let's just say my partner is more over-bearing than my brother."

My lips tipped up. "I find that hard to believe."

I could hear the smile in her voice. "He's headed to the FBI soon, and finds it deplorable that my little brother is part of a motorcycle gang. Believe me, he's his own brand of bossy."

A weak grin crossed my face. "Say no more. They're moving him to intensive care right now. He woke up for like a fleeting second."

"That's good, right?"

I nodded. "I think so, or at least the nurse said it was. I'm just happy they got both bullets out. Now we have to pray he doesn't develop any blood clots or get an infection."

Brittney let out a quiet breath. "All right. Tell Har to give you my number. You can keep me posted. And, I wish we'd have met under different circumstances, but it's still good to get to talk to you. Gage has never talked to me about a woman before, so you must really be something to him."

"Thanks, and I agree. Meeting you because of this is pretty surreal. But, I love your brother and I told him he can't go anywhere on me. I mean, that's just rude, right?"

She chuckled. "Well, he's never shied away from being rude, so I wouldn't tell him that."

"Right. I'll keep you posted, Brittney."

I handed Har's phone back to him.

Heidi wrapped me up in a hug. "I told you she sounded cool."

I pulled away from her hold. "You should go home. I'm serious, I don't want to be the reason you get fired or some bullshit."

Heidi shook her head, her gold hoop earrings swaying violently. "You worry more than anyone I know, Vickie! But I'll call you in the morning."

"You need to head home too, lady," Har said.

I shook my head. "No way. I told him I wasn't going anywhere, and I meant it."

He frowned at me, then gestured to an empty seating area. "Have a seat, Victoria. Tiny brought you a latte, it might still be warm."

CHAPTER 17

MUSCLES

GAMBLE

G amble opened his eyes expecting to see Victoria, but instead he saw Har's green eyes fixed on him.

He parted his lips to speak, but Har held up a hand. "Save it man. Glad you're still with us. Gave your woman and the rest of us quite a scare."

His mouth felt like a desert. He turned his head and saw a small pitcher.

Har lifted his chin and poured Gamble a cup of ice chips. He held the cup out. Just lifting his arms was a supreme effort.

"Shit," Har whispered. "I don't nurse people, G, so you better keep this shit to yourself."

The ice chip felt and tasted like nectar of the gods. He would never take water for granted ever again.

"Mensa," he croaked.

"He's fine. Got stabbed, and shot, but it was a flesh wound. You weren't so lucky since Luis shot you in the back."

Gamble gave a weak nod. "Ernesto?"

"Dead. Cops wanted to arrest you, but the convenience store had cameras that actually worked. Footage showed it was self-defense. Or at least our lawyer convinced the district attorney of that."

Relief rolled through him like a calming wave. He knew that wasn't a good reaction, but knowing one of the men who hurt Victoria wasn't out there any more...that was better than any form of traditional justice.

"Vickie?"

"She's right outside. I'll get her in a minute."

He sighed.

"Feels like we owe Victoria for your life."

Gamble's brows lowered.

Har nodded. "Fiona went to her place, lost track of time. It was only because 'Nic got home, called Fiona to find out where she was. She told Victoria he was home, and your woman knew shit was wrong since you weren't home. Cynic called Roman before hauling ass back to that 'hood."

"What?" he whispered.

Har's lips pressed into a flat line. "Roman hadn't shown up when he did, you probably would have bled out. Possibly Mensa too."

He sighed again.

"Anyway, your bikes weren't impounded, which is a miracle. Roman had the prospects get them back to the compound." Har's eyes turned serious. "Not that there's gonna be a next time, but if there is, wear a full fuckin' vest. That t-shirt should have had armor in the back but didn't. Why the fuck you bought it, I'll never know."

"Only cowards shoot people in the back."

Har shrugged. "Doesn't matter now. They cut that useless piece of shit off you."

As his mind cleared of the cobwebs, he realized Har didn't show up to talk about Gamble's clothes. "What's really going on?"

Har blew out a breath. "You're young, G. You, Mensa, Finn, at some point you'll be in an officer position."

"No," he whispered. The thought didn't appeal to him, and it never would.

Har nodded. "*Yes*. But I'm dropping the ball if I don't make sure guys like you and Mensa grasp the importance of brotherhood."

"We get the brotherhood."

Har's lips pressed together into a strange grimace. "You don't, but you will." He stood, and gave Gamble's shoulder a squeeze. "I'll send your ol' lady in."

"She's not—"

He gave him a hard stare. "She's not, but she will be. Did you forget you claimed her in church? She proved her salt when you were attacked... and she proved it more this past week while you've been in-and-out of it."

"A week?" he breathed.

"Yeah."

"Fuck," he muttered as Har walked out the door.

Victoria hurried into his room and while her dark hair, hazel eyes, and lithe frame was a sight for sore eyes, he swore she'd lost ten pounds. Weight she didn't need to lose.

She propped a hip on the edge of his bed, slid a hand through the hair at the side of his head and planted her mouth on his. "I love you. Thank God you're awake," she breathed against his lips.

Her long hair had fallen over her shoulder. He loved feeling it tickle his arm.

When she pulled away, he tried to speak, his voice cracking, "Love you too, kitten."

She got him an ice cube. Her nursing him was far better than Har doing it.

Her hazel eyes examined him for a long while. He could see she was deliberating something.

He said, "What is it?"

She gave him a closed-lip smile. "I shouldn't tell you this, but you have Uncle Mick's full approval. I'm not saying getting shot was what did it, but... it didn't hurt –figuratively, obviously. And, my sister says that if you didn't want to meet her, you should have just said so. Getting shot was taking it a tad too far." Her eyes slid to the side like it pained her to say that, then she made eye contact again. "And those are all the freaking jokes I can tolerate about you being shot in the back."

He reached out for her hand. "Sorry I missed her."

She grinned. "Heidi says if you and your brothers don't like drama, then it was better for you to be here. You missed what she calls the mac-daddy of all dramas."

"What?"

Her hazel eyes widened as she nodded. "So, Miranda found out our parents were separating, which you know, that's dramatic. But Dad slipped and mentioned my rape." She shoved a lock of hair behind her ear. "That's when she called me... but I was here."

"So, I saved you from that?"

She shook her head. "The nurses —and Tiny, of all people— insisted I go home. Heidi took me."

"Okay."

"Miranda showed up at the bungalow in an Uber. Mom was blowing up my phone. It was crazy."

"Turn your phone off," he muttered.

Her rueful laugh filled the small room. "Yeah. Heidi took Mom's call, and well, their relationship is done. Which upset Heidi, because she really dug Mom and she needs a good woman in her life."

"Sounds like she's the only one who digs her."

Victoria frowned. "She's not bad. She just needs... help."

"Not sure this sounds like 'mac-daddy drama.'"

She shook her head. "Mom showed up to take Miranda back home. Dad had followed her. They —my whole damn family— were yelling in Fiona's driveway. It was so embarrassing. A neighbor called the cops. It was...*a lot*."

He frowned. "Should have been there for you."

She smiled. "Someone also called Fiona, and Cynic showed up. As he said at the time, 'shit works out.' And he's right. Being confronted by a patrol car really opened Mom's eyes."

"Still," he whispered.

A doctor knocked on the door and walked into the room. "Mr. Garrison, your sister's been worried sick. She's very devoted."

After a beat, Gamble realized he was talking about Victoria when she ducked her head, suppressing a grin.

Gamble nodded at the doctor. "That's why I love her."

Victoria stared at him, her eyes wide as saucers. He smirked.

"You're going to need physical therapy since that bullet wound on your lower leg will impact your gait. However, you should make a full recovery. Presuming your condition doesn't change or deteriorate in the next twenty-four hours, we're discharging you tomorrow."

"Good," Gamble said.

Victoria

"Where are you going?" Gamble asked, his voice groggy.

I tied my high-top sneakers and stood up. "It's Sunday. Gotta open the gym and coach some basketball."

"Comin' with you," Gamble said in a husky voice.

I glared at him. "Honey, you've been out of the hospital for two weeks and you're on crutches for at least another six. Luis is facing two counts of attempted murder, plus the charges from my rape since the DNA evidence finally came back. There's no more danger, Triple G."

He shook his head. "Nope. Don't trust that. Besides, gotta show Muscles that I'm serious about you."

I squinted. "'Muscles?' You mean Royce? You're crazy."

He sat up. "Not crazy. A little possessive, yes."

"Speaking of possessions, do you expect me to wear a cut that says I'm your... property?"

Although I loved the Riot MC family and I loved what they stood for, something about being property of Gamble *and* advertising it just rubbed me the wrong way.

His hand ran through his hair, which wasn't as spiky since it needed a cut. "Not enough time to get into that, kitten. I need to piss and get dressed."

He hobbled into the bathroom.

I went to the kitchen and started a pot of coffee. While I waited, my thoughts drifted to Gamble's extended family. Roman had brought Trinity to the hospital while Gamble was out of it, to offer moral support. She didn't wear a cut with Roman's name on it. Though I knew Roman had driven Trinity's car. I didn't know if it was something she only wore when on his bike, if Roman hadn't insisted she wear one, or if it was because she was a businesswoman and every time I'd seen her, she was dressed to impress.

The sound of Gamble's crutches coming down the hall pulled me from my thoughts.

I set a cup of coffee on the table for him. "You really need your rest, honey. Being shot is bad enough, but that leg wound was a whopper."

He sipped his java. "I'm comin', Vic. They want me movin' more, anyway."

My first impression of him back in June was right. He was as stubborn as me.

Probably more so.

"What's gimpy doin' here? Did he come for the snacks?" Heidi asked.

I chuckled. "We don't do snacks except for the last session."

Heidi nodded, her thick bamboo-style hoop earrings swaying. "Oh, right, that's next week." She widened her eyes at Gamble. "You're early, lover boy."

I let Heidi and Royce into the building, then held the door for Gamble to go through on his crutches.

Royce eyed Gamble. "You go after them for her?"

Gamble nodded.

"Rumors true?" Royce asked.

Gamble shook his head. "Haven't heard the rumors."

Royce crossed his arms on his chest. "They say—"

I jumped into the conversation because I suspected what the rumors were. "I am still obligated to report a felony, Royce."

"Could be his angle, kitten," Gamble muttered.

"For crying out loud," I said.

Royce pursed his lips and stared Gamble down. "Never thought she'd fall for a man like you. Take care of her."

I scurried to the equipment room.

As I unlocked the door, Heidi grabbed my shoulders from behind. "I *told* you so."

"Gloating is *so* unbecoming. Isn't that what you always say?"

"No, but you're close. So, point taken, girlfriend."

Heidi grabbed the portable scoreboard.

I snagged the bag of basketballs. "Is there a chair around here? I really don't want Gamble to sit in the bleachers. You gonna help me convince him to keep his leg elevated?"

"Florence Nightingale, I am not, Vickie."

I grinned at her. "Maybe I'll see if Block will swing by."

She pointed a finger at me. "Stop it. I'll do my best to encourage Gamble to cooperate, but that's really your job."

Gamble grabbed my right hand, then reclined the passenger seat while I drove us home.

"Are you okay?" I asked.

"I'm good."

"Good at lying," I said.

"Kitten, it's been two weeks since I got out of the hospital. I'm getting better."

I nodded at the windshield. "Yeah, but that doesn't mean you needed to stand around for an hour with Brute while Aubrey had her practice."

He didn't say anything to that. At a traffic light, I glanced at him. He had a big, beautiful smile on his face. The joy in his expression almost made me think he was stoned, but I knew better.

"What are you smiling about?"

His eyes stayed closed as he said, "I'm fucked, but I like it."

"Pardon?"

He opened his eyes. "It's always gonna be like this, isn't it?"

The light changed, I faced forward, and we motored onward. "Is what going to be like this?"

"Us. The bickering, the fussing... and even your girl Heidi fussing over me. That's how it's going to be, isn't it?"

I pressed my lips together. "I don't know," I murmured.

His seat came forward. "You know, and it's true."

We were in the driveway. I tried to wrest my hand free, but Gamble hit the clicker with his free hand. I pulled the car forward and he hit the clicker again. He let my hand go so I could park and turn off the engine.

Gamble shifted and cupped my cheeks. "You love me, right?"

My chin dipped. "More than I knew I could love anyone."

His eyes lit up. "Right. And I'm yours in a way I never knew I could belong to anybody."

"Okay," I said hesitantly. "What brought this on?"

"You're mine the same way right? You belong to me?"

I nodded... still hesitant.

"That's what the property patch is about, kitten. At least for me. I see a woman with a brother's patch on her back, it doesn't just tell me she's off-limits. It tells me that brother found a woman he cares enough about to make her his. And crazy as you might find it, that makes me happy for that man."

I nodded and his hands fell away. "But some of your brothers haven't put cuts on their women. I haven't seen Kenzie wearing anything like that or Trinity."

Gamble laughed. "Kenzie was wearing one at the Fourth of July party, but you probably didn't notice because of Stephanie accusing her of cheating at cornhole."

"Okay, fine. And Trinity?"

A lopsided grin crossed his face. "You might say Trinity made Roman hers, but really, you'd have to ask Roman about that. I don't know why he hasn't given her a cut, and God knows Sandy has to be nagging the hell out of Roman about it."

"That's not saying much. I think she enjoys nagging your brothers."

"Yeah. But, we recognize women have rights. Set your feminism aside. If I give you a property cut, it's an honor, Victoria."

My lips twisted to the side.

He grabbed my left hand. "If I put a ring on your finger, you'd wear it, right?"

I nodded, but my expression stayed skeptical. "That's different, you know."

His brows rose in question. "Is it, though? It's accepted mainstream culture, is what it is."

My head bobbed as I rolled his words over in my mind. "Probably."

"The property patch is part of our culture."

My expression cleared and I nodded. "Okay. You've made your point. Can we go inside? This car is turning into a sauna."

Thirty minutes later, I turned off the shower. With Gamble on crutches, I knew where he was almost all the time. Yet, my mind played tricks on me sometimes because I thought I heard him even when he was on the couch.

I opened the curtain only to find him standing there, grinning, and shirtless.

"What are you doing?" I asked, grabbing my towel.

He held out his favorite t-shirt that I had claimed. "Wanted you to wear this. I already did the first one, but I need you to sit on my face so I can smile a lot afterward."

Heat rushed through my body. "That sounds great, but I'm not sitting on your face. I don't want to hurt you."

He dropped the shirt on the counter and shuffled over to me. "Baby, it won't be any effort for me if you do all the work. But I gotta have a taste of you. I'm hungry. You wouldn't deny a starving man, would you?"

I chuckled. "You're not hungry, you're horny."

"I'm both. And you're supposed to take care of me," he said, bringing his lips to mine.

Standing in the tub gave me just enough height that we were nose to nose, and I didn't have to tilt my head when he kissed me. I still had the bath towel in hand. I raised it to my shoulder, but Gamble took it from me, dropping it to the floor.

"Goddammit," he whispered. "If I weren't hurt, I'd carry you out of here."

I kissed his cheek just above the line of his beard. "You'll have other chances to carry me."

He left the bathroom, and I admired his muscular back.

"What's the hold-up? Move your fine tush, kitten. You don't have a limp like I do."

Stepping out of the tub, I picked up the towel from the floor and hung it up. "You're lucky I dig you being bossy!"

He chuckled and I heard his jeans hit the floor. "You'll dig my mouth on your clit even more."

By the time I entered the bedroom, Gamble lay on the bed with two pillows stacked behind his head. It struck me, an upside to his injury was that I might have a little more control in bed since he hadn't been cleared for strenuous activities. I would be doing 'all the work,' so I was determined to get more than oral.

As soon as I was within arm's reach, he grabbed my ass and squeezed. "Get up here, baby. You don't know how hungry I am."

I straddled his waist and he growled. That made me grin. "I heard about that. Poor baby."

He exhaled hard. "You're too low, Victoria. And you're facing the wrong way unless you can contort your body and I don't know about it."

Slowly, I traced my fingers up his torso taking my time around his Riot patch and the letters of 'Learn.' My lips peppered kisses along the way. His fingers drove into my hair, and he guided my lips to his.

He kissed me far harder than I expected. I smelled the distinctly sweet scent of marijuana while his kiss tasted like beer.

When he broke away, he whispered, "Come feed me."

"You are tenacious," I said, moving to turn around, but his grip tightened.

"Changed my mind. I want you watching while I make you come. Then I can grab your tits or your ass while you squirm on top of me."

Wetness rushed to my pussy at the thought. I couldn't wait to feel all of that, and I scrambled up on my knees just the way Gamble wanted me.

His bearded lips twisted into a devilish smirk. Then he gently licked me. I sighed at the sensation. He did it again which was nice, but by the fourth lick I realized he was being *too* gentle.

"Gamble, I thought you were hungry. What is this slow and sweet business?"

He applied a little more force, then said, "You were a bad girl, kitten. Teasing me like that. Gotta tease you right back."

I gazed down my body and into his blue eyes. "I didn't *tease* you."

His hands squeezed the globes of my ass. "But you did."

My fingers ran through his hair. He smiled and I felt his beard grazing my thighs. His tongue darted out and finally he licked at me with purpose. My hips bucked and reflexively I settled more of my weight on him.

"Mmm," he hummed.

I lifted a little so I wouldn't hurt him, but he pulled me farther down. One of his hands came around and gripped my breast. I gazed down at him, feeling the strength of our relationship. It wasn't just sexual. In fact, sex between us served to solidify our bond. Keeping eye contact with him enhanced that even further.

His pointed tongue flicked at my clit, and I threw my head back on a moan. His fingers wrapped around my neck, and I tipped my chin down, our eyes locking. The skin surrounding his eyes crinkled, his coarse beard tickled my thighs, and I knew he was smiling.

"God, I love you," I breathed.

He broke away. "I bet you do."

I shook my head. Realizing he'd loosened his grip on me, I quickly moved. His cock was as stiff as ever and I sank down on him, bare.

I caught his heated eyes on me. "You're excellent at eating me out, but I'm serious. Everything between us is...the fucking best."

"Victoria, get a—"

217

"I'm on the pill, honey. You're clean. I'm clean. And for once, I get to make love to you."

To my dismay, he sat up wrapping his arms around me. "Fine. But, I'm helping you."

I tilted my head. "No strenuous activity means I have to do all the work, Gage."

He smirked. "There's a reason I lift every fuckin' day, kitten. I got serious upper body strength and I'm going to help you. Now, make love to me like you mean it."

I rose up with a grin. "Like I'd do it any other way."

CHAPTER 18

OPPOSITES

GAMBLE

"Double checking here, kitten. You're cool with ditching condoms from here out?" Gamble asked after he came out of the bathroom.

Victoria wriggled into her panties. "Yes. I take it that rocked your world."

He tugged on his boxer briefs. "You do that any way."

As she slipped his t-shirt over her head, he knew she couldn't be any sexier.

His cell rang with Mensa's ring tone. "This can't be good," he said, leaning forward to grab the phone.

"Yo," he answered.

"You need to get down here, brother," Mensa said.

"Why the fuck would I do that?"

"Older man's here who looks a helluva lot like your woman. Says he knows you and wants to find out how he can join the club. Motherfucker rolled in driving a fuckin' Scion."

He swallowed down his laughter, then he caught Victoria's gaze. "Your dad drive a Scion?"

Her brows pulled down over her eyes as she nodded. "Why do you ask?"

To Mensa he said, "We'll be there soon."

"What is going on, Gamble?" Victoria asked.

He grabbed the crutches and maneuvered across the room to grab jeans and a t-shirt. "Seems your dad is at the clubhouse."

"What?" she shrieked.

He chuckled. "Yeah. Wants to join the Riot. Mensa thinks I need to swing by."

"You're darn tootin' *we* need to swing by. My father can't join a biker gang at his age!"

Gamble leveled a stern look at her. "Not a fuckin' gang, Vic."

She opened her mouth, closed it, and turned her head to the side as though she realized her mistake. When she looked at him again, she said, "I know that, but for him it's—"

"For him.. for any man, it's a club. Period. We're not a gang. It's important you understand that, Victoria."

"I do! But my father is not cut out to be part of your club. Not unless you're having a party... and even then, I'm not so sure."

She'd touched a nerve with her words, and while he wanted to let it go, he couldn't get his anger to subside. He was proud to be part of the Riot. Hell, she should be proud that he was part of the Riot, which meant her father joining them should make her proud, too.

"You can come to our parties, but not your dad? Not any of your family? Are you ashamed, Vic?"

Her mouth dropped open and he swore she paled. "No! I'm not ashamed at all. I overreacted and I'm sorry I called it a gang. I apologize for that. However, can you take a step back and see this from my perspective? He's my father, who just left my mother or vice versa, but now he thinks he needs to join your club? He doesn't even own a bike! I doubt he's ever ridden."

He took in a deep breath, though it didn't do much to calm him. After a moment, he saw it from her perspective. People did crazy things when shit got real, and trying to join an MC when he didn't even ride a bike... yeah, that took the cake.

Once he had a t-shirt on, he hobbled over to the bed to put on his jeans. If Luis weren't in jail, he'd go out of his way to hurt that motherfucker again. Being on crutches drove him up the wall, even though he knew he had it far better than many others who got shot in the leg.

"Are you going to say anything?" Victoria demanded.

He glanced at her and grinned. "Apology accepted. We need to get to the clubhouse. You're right. He doesn't need to prospect for the Riot. The sooner we get there, the better. Wouldn't put it past Tiny to try and recruit him for shits and giggles."

Mensa cut off Gamble and Victoria when they approached the back door. "You're a lucky fucker. If Tiny were here, we'd have a new prospect."

Victoria put her hands on her hips. "I'm confused. How did he know where your clubhouse is? I didn't think just anybody could show up here unless y'all are having certain types of parties."

Mensa shook his head. "Someone either brought him here or gave him directions. I thought it was you, but maybe your girl in the Miata?"

Gamble sighed. "Doesn't really matter now. Thanks for the update, man. You get out of the way, we'll get him on his way."

Mensa's eyes widened. "Doubtful. He's had three shots. One with the prospects, one with Joules, and one on his own."

Victoria gasped. "How long has he been here?"

Mensa grimaced. "Three hours... probably?"

"And you waited to call me?" Gamble asked.

"Brother, I rolled in here forty-five minutes ago."

Gamble waved his crutch toward Mensa. "Move it and we'll deal with it, brother."

Sitting at the bar, Henry set his beer down and looked at Gamble. "I'm pretty sure I want to join the Riot MC. How do I make that happen?"

"What?" Victoria asked with a laugh.

Henry looked about the place. "No, really. I could live like this. Especially if Erin cleans me out, which she said she's gonna do."

The prospect behind the bar stopped drying pint glasses and caught Henry's attention. "Sir, there's nothing happening here right now. But, four or five hours from now, this won't be your scene."

Gamble nodded when Henry looked back at him. "He's right. And you'd still have to prospect first. Not sure you'd be down with that."

"I can take some hazing."

"Dad! You and Mom are going to work things out," Victoria insisted.

Pain and outrage filled Henry's eyes as he looked at Victoria. "You told me more than once that she played favorites and I brushed it off. That never should have happened, Vickie. How the hell I could be so blind, I don't know. But I *really* don't know how she could treat either of you girls like that. She never did that when you girls were little. I just—"

Victoria put a hand on Henry's forearm resting on the bar. "Dad. You can't beat yourself up like that. It's over. Miranda and I made our own decisions." She paused. "In a weird way, it might have helped make us who we are."

"But it hurt you, too, and I have to wonder how much better off both of you would be if she'd been more supportive, encouraging, and positive."

Victoria shook her head. "We'll never know. Back to the real issue here, you aren't joining the Riot Motorcycle Club."

"Watch your tone, young lady."

Victoria's head tilted. "Dad, you don't even own a bike. Do you know how to ride?"

"I'll learn," he said, holding his pint glass up to the prospect.

"Do not give him another," Victoria said.

The prospect looked at Gamble. "Do you want me to listen to her?"

Victoria looked between them and stared at Gamble. "What's he talking about?"

"Only brothers can give a prospect an order, though sometimes the old ladies can. But you're not my old lady. Yet."

"My daughter can join your club, but she's giving me a hard time about it?" Henry asked.

"Dad! That's not the point. You don't need another beer."

Henry's eyes widened. "I'm already soused. Another beer won't hurt."

Gamble gave the prospect a nod. Victoria shot him a glare and he bit back a smile. Before he could say anything, three hard, rapid knocks came from the front door.

Cop-knocks, if ever he heard them.

From the other end of the bar, Joules muttered, "What the fuck?"

Gamble limped toward the door as Mensa did the same. "Mensa, let me. The crutches might make them go easy."

Mensa scoffed. "Bullshit. We'll both open the fuckin' door."

When his brother opened the door, Gamble almost fell over. Brittney and Taylor were there, his sister grinning like a schoolgirl at a boy-band concert. She wore a white and black patterned summer dress that went down to her ankles, and her light brown hair nearly touched her hips, it was so long.

"Hey, little bro!" she shouted.

"Goddamn! Come give me a hug. You should've called. We'd have picked you up."

Brittney moved inside the clubhouse and wrapped her arms around Gamble's neck. "Not from New Orleans, you wouldn't have."

"We fuckin' would," he said into her neck.

Brittney rocked back and forth, and he returned the gesture.

He heard Victoria speaking, and let go of his sister. Taylor smiled at Victoria, but it looked a little strained.

"Taylor. Good to see you again," Gamble said, holding out his hand.

Taylor took his hand and patted his bicep. "Yeah. Sorry to hear about your leg."

Brittney's eyes widened at Victoria, and she held her arms out for a hug. "Oh, my God. You're nearly as tall as him. I love it! It's so good to meet you in person, Victoria."

"You too, Brittney," Victoria said, giving his sister a hug.

Gamble asked Taylor, "What brings you down here? She said you're moving to Quantico, this is well out of the way, man."

Taylor's lips set into a firm line. "You got a place we can talk? Private-ly?"

Gamble jerked his head toward the back door. "Let's hit the patio. You two want a beer or anything?"

"Damn sure wouldn't hurt for this conversation," Taylor muttered.

Twenty minutes later, he sat across from his sister and Taylor. Victoria had slipped her arm around his waist, and he tucked her close to his side.

"Two days ago, Seattle PD apprehended a man who'd been following Brittney."

"What?" Victoria asked.

Gamble looked at Brittney. "You didn't tell me you were being followed."

Taylor lifted his stubbled chin. "I didn't want her to."

Gamble shifted his glare to Taylor.

"Why not?" Victoria asked.

"Less he knew about it, the better. And given what sent him to the hospital, it was for his own good. And yours, too."

Gamble didn't believe that, but there was no arguing with Taylor when it came to law and order.

Victoria looked between Gamble and Taylor. "So, was this just random?"

Taylor's dark eyes shifted to her. "Not random. Three and a half weeks ago, Luis Abeyeta paid him to find Brittney. He'd reported back to Luis that he'd found her. Supposedly, Luis wanted him to assault Brittney, but this bastard wouldn't carry it out since he was waiting on another payment from Luis. Brittney noticed the man tailing her, the same day he was shot." Taylor jerked his head toward Gamble. "Problem was, the bastard figured out he'd been spotted. Took way too damn long to apprehend him."

Taylor stared at Victoria for a moment. "You know they threatened Brittney on the note when they dropped you here."

Victoria paled. "Yeah. I'd pushed that out of my mind. The note, I mean."

Gamble squeezed her shoulders. "You got enough shit to work through, kitten."

Brittney wheezed out a laugh.

224

He frowned at her. "What?"

Her wan smile made him brace. "You probably don't remember this, but Dad used to call Mom that."

"Bullshit," he bit out.

She shook her head. "No. I was in third grade, which means you would've been five years old."

He refused to believe he did *anything* like his father.

"I'd remember that shit, Brittney."

They lapsed into silence.

Victoria broke it. "Did you travel all this way to tell us about an arrest? You could've called. Not that I'm not thrilled to meet you both."

Brittney fidgeted like she was suddenly uncomfortable.

Taylor tapped the smartwatch on his wrist and nodded. "Yeah. We're going to have to leave soon."

Gamble grabbed Brittney's hand across the picnic table. "What aren't you telling me?"

She took a deep breath. "We're meeting Mom and Dad at McElroy's tonight. You can come if you want. But, I'll understand if that's not—"

"Never," Gamble snarled.

Victoria leaned away but put a hand on his chest. "Maybe you should consider—"

"No. Not happening, Vic."

He saw her eyes slide to Brittney. "There went my nickname, I guess."

Gamble shook his head. "Victoria, those assholes didn't just encourage me not to join the Riot. They begged me for money, if it weren't for Block and Cynic being so damned intimidating, they'd probably still hit me up every chance they got. I am *not* exposing you to that bullshit."

Her hazel eyes were tender on him, then something flickered there. Somehow he knew he wasn't going to like what she had to say. "It's been years, honey. They could have changed for—"

"They haven't," Brittney said.

He whipped his eyes to her. "What?"

Brittney shrugged a shoulder. "We called to tell them we were flying down, they hit me up for money."

"You didn't tell me that, babe," Taylor said, with his teeth clenched.

She smiled at him and at Gamble. "No, but they do that to me, I *know* they'll do it to you." She glanced at Victoria. "Hell, they'll take one look at you, hear you're a lawyer, and assume you got money to set on fire."

Victoria snickered. "I'm not even making fifty grand a year, and my student loans are huge."

Brittney nodded. "They don't know that, and it wouldn't matter to them even if they did."

"Right," Victoria whispered. Then she asked, "Did they stop going to Gambler's Anonymous meetings?"

Brittney's lips pressed together for a long moment. "I don't know. From what Mom said, Dad still buys scratch-offs with what little 'spending money' he can scrape together. But she assures me that's all it is."

Taylor sighed, shaking his head. "They better not ask you for money tonight."

Victoria looked at Brittney. "Don't you think he should at least talk to them? We only get one family."

"Vickie," Gamble started, but Brittney squeezed his hand to shut him up.

"I don't, actually. I know where you're coming from, but no. They did us both wrong growing up. But they really did Gage wrong. I should've taken him with me, but I couldn't. I was eighteen and barely taking care of myself. Compared to him, I keep in touch with them, but it isn't much. I haven't seen them in...over ten years."

"Okay," Victoria said.

"I talk to them on the phone twice a year, tops. And it's always *me* who reaches out. Never them. That's pretty fucked up. He lives in town, they still live here, and they only want to talk to him if he's got money."

"But if they've stopped the heavy gambling, why would they need money from either of you?"

"They still got debt, which means they need money." Taylor said.

Gamble shook his head. "Know this isn't the plan, but you two should stick around here for dinner instead. Fuck them."

Victoria's eyes widened. "That attitude is exactly why I think you should tag along. Leave me to take Dad home, but that deep-rooted negativity isn't good, honey."

226

His sister laughed. "I never in a million years thought you'd fall for a woman who was so completely your opposite."

Victoria stiffened. "I'm not his opposite."

Brittney raised an eyebrow. "Do you smoke weed, carry a concealed firearm, and have a jaded outlook on the world at large?"

Victoria opened her mouth, then closed it, her lips twisting into a sardonic grin. "He's not that jaded."

Brittney threw her head back with laughter. She got herself under control and pointed a finger at Victoria. "He's completely jaded. But, yeah, you two are such opposites. I love it." Then his sister looked at him. "And I love that you didn't run from it, because I know you wanted to even if you won't admit it."

He stroked his beard and stared at her. "Don't you have somewhere to be?"

Taylor chuckled. "We do, though I'm more inclined to take your offer. Saw someone with a big-ass pot out front. Guessing that food will be better than wherever we're headed."

Brittney nudged Taylor's shoulder with hers. "Stop it. You'll get your seafood while we're here."

Victoria

"I know we just met, but I gotta know. Are you sure about him?" Taylor asked me.

Gamble and Brittney had headed for the car a few moments ago because the crutches slowed Gamble down. Even though I couldn't hear her, I knew Brittney was giving him a hard time. Not to mention every so often she playfully slugged him in the bicep as only an older sister can. The love between them practically visible.

I kept my eyes on them, but replied, "He's a very good man."

"He's a criminal."

Grinning, I turned to Taylor. "He has no convictions."

Taylor stared at me for a long moment. Inside an interrogation room, that dark-eyed stare, coupled with his angular facial features and prominent five-o'clock shadow would unnerve anyone. Certainly, if they were attracted to men like him.

Finally, he said, "You aren't exactly a straight arrow."

I smiled. "Nobody is, really. Everyone bends for something. The question is whether or not they break. Gamble is a man I would break for, because he's loyal like nobody I've ever met, and he loves me with a ferocity I've never known."

He sighed. "Sounds like his sister."

"Then I'd say that makes you a very lucky man, Taylor," I said, standing to follow Gamble and Brittney.

He fell in step beside me. "You're right. And their parents did at least one thing right to teach those two how to be loyal and love that deeply."

My hands twisted up in a questioning gesture. "I wouldn't be so sure it was their parents. My hunch is it was their grandparents. But we're both lucky to be with them."

"On that we agree."

We caught up with Gamble and Brittney. I gave Brittney a light hug. "Are you two staying in town? It would be great to do breakfast or something."

A wan smile curled Brittney's lips. "No. After dinner with my parents, we're driving to Pensacola."

Taylor added, "My brother lives there and we're meeting my niece for the first time."

As we watched Brittney and Taylor drive away, Gamble wrapped an arm around my shoulders. "You seem sad, kitten."

My lips tipped up at the nickname. "Not sad. Just... I don't know. I'd like to get to know your sister, but that isn't to be, this trip."

He squeezed me. "You sure Taylor didn't say anything to bring this on?"

"Not exactly, but it's hard to miss he has a chip on his shoulder about your affiliation with the Riot."

He chuckled. "Affiliation. Only you would call it that."

We worked our way back toward the clubhouse. "Speaking of affiliations, are you or your brothers really going to encourage Dad to join the Riot?"

He sighed. "Having a bike is a requirement, Victoria. But, if your dad buys a bike and finds a brother to sponsor him as a prospect, I can't stop that."

I exhaled slowly. There was no need to rehash our earlier argument, but the idea of Dad making such a drastic change boggled my mind.

"You got nothing to say?" Gamble asked.

I shook my head. "Not really. It's kind of like you said, I can't stop him. But, I know divorces can be lengthy ordeals. And if Mom tries to fleece him, then that will drag out the process."

"Would you represent him?"

I laughed. "No. Conflict of interest, and even if it wasn't, I don't want to be exposed to that ugliness from both of them."

Monday morning, Gamble and I slept in until after ten. We wandered down the hall to the kitchen, only to find Dad sitting at the small kitchen table with a cup of coffee.

"Don't you have work today?" I asked.

"'Good morning' is what you mean, Victoria Hazel, but I called in sick. Come to think of it, don't *you* have work today?"

I growled a little at myself for walking into that. "I've got the day off too," I semi-lied.

He might have been hungover or simply caught up in his own thoughts, but Dad bought my fib.

With a cup of coffee, I sat down across from him. "Do you need me to drive you home?"

Dad scowled. "I'm sober as a judge."

"You certainly have the disposition of one," I muttered as Dad's phone rang.

He glanced at the screen. "Third time she's called me."

My eyes widened. "I'd take it if I were you. Not cool to make her worry."

Dad answered, then his eyes widened. "Just because I didn't come home doesn't mean I cheated on you, Erin."

That went straight to uncomfortable. I downed the rest of my coffee and shoved my chair back, but Dad pointed a finger at me.

"You want proof, I'll put Vickie on the line. She knows where I've been since yesterday afternoon."

There was a lengthy pause, then Dad said, "She was here, that's what matters. And I couldn't have come home because I tied one on last night worse than our wedding night, and you still haven't forgiven me for that."

Nope. No. *Now* it was uncomfortable. I went to the sink to rinse my coffee cup and give Dad some modicum of privacy.

Strong arms wrapped around my waist before Gamble nuzzled my neck. "You eat breakfast yet?"

I shook my head. "Nope."

"What's up with your dad?"

I tried to turn, but he held me tight. "Mom called. Sounds like a crazy conversation."

"Did she accuse him of cheating?"

My head whipped to the side. "How did you know?"

He smirked but it looked a wee bit melancholy. "Let's just say, I heard my mom accuse my dad of that when he'd stay out all night."

"He stayed out all night?"

"Nothing tore him away from a table if he was hot. And he never understood that table could go cold just as fuckin' fast."

I felt his grip loosen and I turned to him. "That sounds so awful, honey. I'm sor—"

His face came so close our noses brushed. "Stop, kitten. It was bad at the time, but in strange ways those experiences have all prepared me for things I never saw coming. Like my woman dealing with parents who suddenly don't trust each other."

My hands resting on his pecs slid up to his shoulders where I gave him a squeeze. "I love that you see it that way, but you shouldn't have had to endure any of that. Especially since you were probably under fifteen when it happened, right?"

He shrugged, but the look on his face told me he knew exactly how old he was the first time his mom accused his dad of stepping out.

I smiled. "You know, I'm on to you, Garrison."

Surprise washed over his face. "What's with this 'Garrison' bullshit?"

"Just driving home my point. You're trying to protect me again, and while I love that about you, I can handle the truth."

A mischievous light hit his eyes before he asked, "Is that your phone ringing?"

My eyes narrowed. "Are you serious right now?"

"Yes. Your phone's ringing."

From over his shoulder, Dad looked at us. "I'd get that if I were you, pumpkin."

I scurried toward the sound of my phone ringing. In the nick of time, I answered the call.

"Ms. Carlton, this is Mr. Gower. Do you have a moment?"

My eyes widened while my heart swelled. "Of course."

"Good. I have a proposal for you."

EPILOGUE

WHOLE HOG

Gamble

As Gamble and Mensa walked inside Bayou Moon Pizza, Mick bellowed out popular lines from the song, "The Gambler." He rolled his eyes and shook his head, but smiled despite himself.

Mensa chuckled. "That shit always makes me laugh. I wonder if Joules can carry a tune?"

"Shut the fuck up, Mensa," Gamble grumbled.

"Glad to see you're off the crutches. What'll it be, biker?" Mick asked.

"He's been off the crutches since September, man," Mensa said.

Gamble said, "We'll have a large pepperoni and a pitcher of beer, two glasses."

After handing Gamble the receipt, Mick said, "You hear about the prison riot last night?"

Gamble shook his head.

Mick's eyes shone with outrage. "Don't you watch the news?"

He grinned. "Nope."

"Well, it seems Luis and Ramone Abeyeta were wounded."

"They were mentioned by name on the news?"

Mick nodded. "They were both rushed to the hospital. Ramone died in transit, and Luis didn't make it through the night."

Gamble whispered, "That leaves Juan without his brothers."

"What's that?" Mick asked.

Gamble shook his head. "Nothing. Thanks for letting me know. I'll pass that on to Victoria."

A satisfied grin spread across Mick's face. "Both those fuckers who messed with my girl are gone. It's a good day."

Gamble nodded.

Mensa grinned as he took the glasses and the pitcher of beer. "That means Victoria won't have to take the stand against Luis. That's *really* fuckin' good news."

Luis had pled guilty to shooting Gamble and was serving time. Victoria's rape trial had been scheduled for later in December. Gamble hated the idea of her testifying and reliving that awful night, but she was determined to get justice. Her not having to testify made for a definite silver lining.

"Yeah," Gamble said. He couldn't help but think that left Juan. It wasn't the revenge he wanted for his sister. Yet he felt things were even, now.

At their table, Mensa poured two beers. "Why do you seem dissatisfied that Luis and Ramone are dead?"

Gamble frowned. "Be better if it had been all three of them."

Mensa sipped his beer. "You're a demanding fucker."

He chuckled. "Brittney deserves to breathe easy just like Victoria."

Mensa contemplated that. "Yeah, but it seems like she made peace with that a long time ago."

Gamble took a deep breath to keep his temper in check. "She still has to live halfway across the country because of it."

Mensa's eyes narrowed a touch. "Does she? She's shacked up with that cop. I know you don't want to hear this, brother, but she stayed up in Seattle for a lot of reasons. The rape instigated it, but she lived her life and now she is breathing easy."

Gamble took a large swig of his beer. He knew Mensa was right, but he didn't have to like it.

A sly smile curled Mensa's lips. "Gamble. Juan's family is gone now. Brittney might not be in town, but she's living free and moved on. That's the best fuckin' revenge there is."

"You're right."

Mick walked over with their pizza. "I shoulda made you come to the counter like everybody else, but it's Christmas time, so here's your pie."

"Thank you, sir," Mensa said.

Mick nodded, then fixed his eyes on Gamble's. "Rumor has it, you're popping the question soon."

Gamble turned his head to the side and blew out an exasperated breath.

Mensa roared with laughter.

"What's so funny?" Mick asked.

Gamble turned back to Mick. "Was gonna do it tonight, but now I'm rethinking that."

"What the hell for?" Mensa demanded.

"I'm not giving her a ring on the same day she finds out—"

Mick shook a finger at him. "Good news comes in twos and threes, Gamble. Pop the question tonight...hell, do it here. I'll call Henry, and he and Erin can be here when you do it."

That was the last thing Gamble expected him to say, and it wasn't the plan he had in mind.

Mensa laughed again. "You should see your face, G."

Mick laughed. "He's right. You really should. You're like a deer in the headlights, and constipated to boot! But seriously, Vickie would love it if you did it here."

"Not sure I want her mother involved in this... or at least, not tonight."

Mick pointed at him. "That's the exact reason to do it here. Erin's working through her issues, but this would force her to be happy for Vickie."

Gamble shook his head slowly. He'd finally met Erin Carlton in late July. She had come to see Victoria. It had been civil, but it had also been supremely tense. He knew she didn't approve of him. That didn't matter to him until he saw how uncomfortable it made Victoria.

He looked at Mick. "I respect what you're suggesting, but it isn't my responsibility to make that woman happy."

Mick dipped his chin. "You're right. But if I know my Vickie, she's gonna want to go whole hog. Big-ass dress, huge reception, and—"

"No, she won't." Gamble insisted.

"Bub, you don't know my girl. She's had stars in her eyes about getting married since she was five."

Gamble's slow sigh made Mick smile.

Mensa said, "That's true of all little girls, but I'm pretty sure Gamble's right. Things have changed for Victoria."

Mick shook his head, keeping his eyes on Gamble. "You don't want Erin trying to steal Vickie's thunder. That's all I'm saying. And you pop the question here, *I'll* make sure she understands that, even if Henry doesn't."

Gamble nodded. "I'll consider it, and let you know. But, don't rent a tux. Friends of ours just came back from eloping in Vegas. Vickie told me she thought that was the best idea ever."

Mick grinned, his eyes gleaming. "Of course she did. That's going whole hog. You make a reservation. I'll hide that ring in her champagne."

"Appreciate it, but her ring isn't coming out of a champagne glass."

Victoria

Four years later...

"You can't ride any more," Sandy decreed as she gazed at Gamble's shoulder.

His eyes cut to her, and she clamped her mouth shut.

In a low tone, he said, "I'll still be able to ride."

Sandy glanced my way. "You're gonna stay home, right?"

My eyes widened and I chuckled. "How could I? Three kiddos with doctor bills! One of us has to have stellar benefits."

Gamble, who held one of our sons, turned toward me. "You want to stay home with them, we'll make that work."

I shook my head. "I'm taking my maternity leave and we'll see where we are after that. Besides, joining Gower and Gower four years ago was the best career move I ever made."

From across the hospital room, Tiny said to Uncle Mick, "They need to name them Keith, Ronnie, and Mick."

Uncle Mick stood a foot from him, frowning. "They can't do that. It has to be Mick, Keith, and Charlie. Every rock band needs their drummer."

"We aren't naming my sons after the Stones," Gamble groused at them both.

Kenzie and Aubrey were sitting on a small couch watching Uncle Mick and Tiny walk around holding the other two babies I'd delivered three days ago. By some miracle, I carried them longer than my doctor expected, and they had only needed to be in the NICU for two days.

Aubrey's light blue eyes whipped to me. "Wait... sons? I thought you were having a girl, too?"

I smiled. "We did." My eyes cut to Tiny, who held our daughter in his huge arms. "Mikayla's smitten with Tiny; she only calms down around him. Or maybe he's a baby-whisperer, I don't know."

Kenzie chuckled. "Are you going to call her Mick for short?"

Uncle Mick sidled up to Tiny. "It will be confusing, but we'll make it work, won't we, Mick?"

Tiny glowered at him. "Don't wake up button."

"Button?" Aubrey asked.

Tiny grinned at her. "Yep. This little beauty is as cute as a button."

Kenzie stood. "If you'd let me hold her, we could verify that."

Tiny's brown eyes caught mine. "Are you cool with this?"

Gamble shot Tiny a look. "Of course, we're cool with that. Our babies need all the love and attention the world has to give."

When Tiny finished handing over Mikayla, Uncle Mick sidled up to him again. "You can hold one of the boys. They're just as cute."

Tiny shook his head adamantly. "Nope. No can do."

"What's wrong with holding one of my sons?" I asked.

Tiny's expression turned serious. "Won't hold or watch your boys. I'm a bad influence."

I bit back laughter. "You're joking, right? Do you know how crazy that is? They wouldn't know what you're saying even if you told them how to execute the perfect crime."

Tiny wagged a finger at me. "Not taking any chances."

I waved my hand toward me. Luckily Tiny caught my drift and came closer to my hospital bed. "You're *not* a bad influence on baby boys. Men my father's age, perhaps, but seriously, you're not a bad influence *at all*."

Tiny's lips twisted into a smirk. "A lot you don't know about me, Victoria."

I shrugged since that was likely true. "When are you settling down?"

He blew out a breath while shaking his head. "We'll see, darlin'. But don't go holdin' your breath. You got three more mouths to feed. Gonna get out of your hair and hit the road."

After the door closed behind Tiny, it opened again, and Heidi bustled inside. "Aren't you getting discharged today?"

With a slow nod, I said, "I am. Are you here for moral support? I doubt your car has room for a car seat."

Heidi gave me a flat look. "I know lover boy is going to drive you all home in the behemoth SUV he put you in when you got knocked up. Doesn't mean I don't want some snuggles with my littles."

"Coach Heidi! Come see Mikayla. She has her eyes open," Aubrey whisper-yelled from the couch.

"Can't miss that, now can I?" she said and sat next to Aubrey.

Gamble sauntered over to me. "I think he's getting hungry. Have you decided what we're naming the boys?"

I bit back my smile as I took my son from him. The idea of naming our children after The Rolling Stones appealed to me in a way, but Gamble clearly didn't want to do that.

"Are you sure you don't want a Gage Junior running around?"

He rolled his eyes. "Not a chance. Grown women find my name appealing, but growing up with it sucked."

We should have been fully prepared for this, but neither of us could decide on boy names. I glanced around the room. My mind wandered toward Gamble's family, but the last four years proved the Riot MC was his family. I recalled that it was Cynic and Block who recruited him years ago.

"What's Cynic's real name? Or Block's?"

His lips tipped up. "Cynic's name is Ryan, which isn't a bad idea. Block's real name is Robin, but he goes by Rob with civilians."

"Ryan Henry has a nice ring to it."

"Gonna name one of them after Bird, huh?" he asked, referring to Dad's nickname with the Riot brothers. He hadn't joined the club. Regardless, over the last four years, he hung around enough to earn a nickname. Though I was never clear as to why they called him Bird. My best guess had been the fact a shorter version of his name would be 'Hen,' but Gamble said it wasn't that.

I stared down at my baby boy —one of them. It was still difficult to wrap my mind around having three babies all at once. His bright eyes stared up at me and his face started to scrunch. I adjusted so I could breastfeed him.

Once I had him situated, I glanced at Gamble. "No, making his middle name the same as Dad's first name isn't the same as naming him after him."

Gamble nodded as he watched us closely. "What about Michael?"

"That could work. Was that your grandfather's name?"

Gamble's head swayed side-to-side for a moment. "It was his middle name, but it's Har's first name."

I nodded. "Mom will like that. Her dad's name was Michael."

His eyebrows arched. Dad and Mom hadn't divorced. At least not yet. Their relationship was strenuous at best. The upside to all the drama four years ago was that Mom finally went into therapy. Now, she and Dad were going to marriage counseling. I hoped it would work out, but I knew it would take more time.

Gamble pulled me from my thoughts when he asked, "What about Michael Victor?"

My brows knit together. "Because my name is Victoria? I don't think so."

His head tilted. "Michael Carl? It isn't as stuffy-sounding as Michael Carlton Garrison."

I chuckled, which caused my son to unlatch and let out a disgruntled wail. Carefully, I shifted him to my other breast. Then I said, "You're determined to name one of them after me, even though you don't want the same for yourself. That's all right, I guess, but it doesn't sound very biker-ish."

Gamble leaned down and snapped the hospital gown at my shoulder. "Are you joking? M.C. Garrison definitely sounds like the son of a biker."

I groaned. "How about Michael as a middle name? It's going to be too confusing with Mikayla and a Michael."

Gamble blew out a breath. "You're right. Shit."

I smiled and shook my head. This was exactly why we didn't have our ducks in a row. We'd get to this point and draw blanks. We didn't want to name all three with the same initials, and we wanted to have as little confusion as possible.

"This shit's killin' me," he muttered.

My eyes widened at him. "That's it."

"What?"

"Killian Michael, Ryan Henry, and Mikayla Grace."

A slow smile lit his face. "Love it, kitten. I'll go fill out the forms."

As Gamble and I made our way to the SUV, with the triplets, we were stopped by an older couple. It didn't take me long to realize the woman had Gamble's striking blue eyes.

With a timid smile, she said, "Hi, baby boy. Can't believe you're a daddy now."

I glanced up at Gamble, and from the set of his jaw, he was holding back his anger.

His dad eyed us, and I knew something was up. He caught Gamble's eyes. "People give you all kinds of shit when you have a baby, some even give you money just because you had a kid." He shook his head. "Three babies... I'm guessing you're flush with cash, Gage."

Gamble raised his fist, and I grabbed his wrist. "Don't, G."

His dad aimed a sly grin at me. "Pretty and gentle."

I stepped toward him. "I'm far from gentle. You *had* the chance to meet your grandsons and granddaughter, but you squandered it to ask us for cash. What kind of person does that? Not someone my husband will waste his time with that's for sure."

Gamble's mother arched a brow over her icy blue eyes. As I stared into her eyes, I realized Gamble's were a deeper shade of blue and that he probably got them from someone else in the family tree. Her lip curled before she spoke. "Now who do you think you are to talk to my husband that way?"

"I know I'm the woman who cares more about your son than the two of you ever could. Get out of our way. You need cash, go work for it. Might teach you a sense of value beyond the casinos and lotto tickets."

I maneuvered the stroller past them, unsure if Gamble was keeping up with me.

We loaded our babies into the backseat in silence.

"I made sure they left, Victoria," he whispered as he fastened Mikayla's carseat strap.

When we were both seated in the SUV, I turned to Gamble. "I'm sorry. I shouldn't have shown my ass like that with—"

His hand cupped the back of my head, and he cut me off with the hardest kiss he'd ever given me. When he pulled away, his eyes glittered at me. "Don't apologize for that, kitten. It's their own damn fault they're missing out on the beauty of our life and the lives we brought into the world."

Those words made my heart soar as tears sprang to my eyes. I blinked them back. "You are my world, honey."

He grinned, then whispered, "You were right. You love me more than those two ever did, I'm the luckiest man in the world because of it."

Thank you for reading Gamble's Risk. *The Riot continues with* Block's Road. *Turn the page for a peek.*

Be sure to sign up for my newsletter for the latest information about upcoming titles. Cynic's sister, Lisa has a book coming this fall and you won't want to miss it!

BLOCK'S ROAD SNEAK PEEK

PLANS

Heidi

In the thick of rush hour traffic, a biker followed me. That wasn't unusual. Between the tourists, the Air Force men and women who needed cheap wheels, and other people who dug two-wheeled transportation...it could be anybody. But something told me I knew this biker.

Maybe it was the way he held his stocky frame on the Harley. Maybe it was the way he wore his sunglasses under that half-helmet. Maybe it was the set of those damned lips as he stared at the back of my Miata.

If it was who I thought it was, I had to lose him.

I'd had him once, but it was nothing.

No, that was a lie. It was definitely something. If nothing else it was the best quickie I'd ever had. Probably ever *would* have, for that matter. How the hell we packed so much sex into thirty short minutes, I'd never know. We hit nearly all the high points of any bedroom romp. Even if I did say so myself, it was the best blow job I'd given in my life. Which was saying something, since I'd been honing my skills since fourteen. But he hadn't let me finish. No, he tossed me onto his bed and showed

243

me some of his wicked tricks. It was more fun than I'd had in ages. Just thinking about it made me squirm in my seat.

But that was life for you. Get your hands on one of the greatest experiences ever, and you couldn't recreate it. I knew that from many a trip to Orlando. There was nothing like the first time on a roller coaster. Sure, the second and third times were great, but they were missing that certain thrill you *only* got the first time.

Nothing beat the first time. Ever.

So, yeah, I had to lose this bike and the biker on it.

The traffic light turned green, and I put my little sports car to the test. I cut off a truck in the left lane, surged forward and took the ramp to the I-110. It had been a rough day and I wanted nothing more than to get a glass of wine and take a bath, but losing him was first priority.

Since I didn't have anything at home for dinner, a trip through a drive-thru was second priority. Twenty minutes later, I swallowed the last bite of my burger.

I pulled into the tiny parking lot for my condo building with a curse. "You've got to be joking."

Block stood leaning against his bike, which he'd parked in a small grassy area surrounding a humongous oak tree in the middle of the parking lot. A tree that just happened to be next to my space.

How the hell did he know where I lived?

He had no reason to be here.

I opened my door and rounded my car.

"You can't be here."

He stared at me. With those weatherized mirrored shades, I couldn't even see his light blue eyes.

His silence unnerved me. Knowing him, he probably knew that.

I waved my hand between us. "We worked for two reasons only, Block. The first is that we can't stand each other, and Mother Nature being a master of irony, that makes the sex off the charts. The second because it was a *one*-off. And subsequently we both *got* off. That's it. So, I'll say it again, you can't be here."

I turned on my heel and headed for the door to the inner stairwell.

"You're wrong," he muttered.

I stopped and looked at him over my shoulder.

He continued, "I never said I couldn't stand you."

As I turned around, I scoffed. "Some messages are non-verbal. Believe me, it came across loud and clear."

His lips pressed together, and a muscle ticked along his jaw. I had a hard time not pointing out that his reaction only proved my point.

"You forgot the third reason we're so fucking good."

When he kept silent, I tossed out a hand in a gesture for him proceed.

"It might have been the Fourth of July. But we didn't start fireworks, we started a full-on fire. You want to put that fire out just as bad as I do."

I chuckled. "No. Actually, I don't."

"Come here," he demanded.

I stood just a few feet from him. There was no need to move. "Why?"

"I have a message for you."

"And I'm standing right here."

"For this you need to come closer."

I don't know why I gave in, but I walked to him. His lush lips curled upward. Then everything happened fast.

I knew he was in his forties, but I didn't think we were in the nineteen-forties. He wrapped an arm around my waist, curled his body around mine forcing me backward over that arm and he laid a kiss on me like it was the end of World War Two and we were in New York. My nipples pebbled, my heart raced, my fingers curled into the back of his leather cut, and I hung on for dear life.

Jesus. In two months, I'd forgotten how great a kisser Block was.

Know what I hadn't forgotten in two months? How well-endowed Block was. His erection pressed against my thigh, and I had the urge to drop and give him twenty. Licks, that is.

A horn honked and we broke apart.

He righted me, but I was still dazed. Luckily, I came out of the daze in time to catch the bag he threw at me.

Through the white cellophane I saw a box of condoms.

"This is presumptuous of you. One and done, Block. That's how it has to be."

He moved so his front was pressed to my side. His lips went to my cheek next to my ear. "No, Heidi. One *full* night. Then, *maybe* we'll call it done. I haven't done half the shit I want to do to you, and I know you've never had it as good as I can give it."

Talk about cocky.

Unfortunately, cocky men were my Kryptonite.

I resisted the cocky biker. Staring at his kelly-green Harley, I lied, "I have plans tonight."

His teeth closed around my earlobe. His tongue swiped side to side along the outside edge giving me a shiver from head to toe and many places in between. He dragged it between his teeth causing a wave of heat to chase the shiver.

"You don't anymore. Unless you're talking about the crate of wine you got delivered today. If that's the case, I took it inside earlier. Took the liberty of putting the bottles of white in the freezer in case that's your preference and the sweet reds are in the fridge chillin'. The two cabernets will be fine at room temperature."

Woodenly, I turned to him. My jaw dropped and I felt blood infuse my face. "You were... you went inside my...*What!*"

His thick index finger went under my chin and closed my mouth.

He had the gall to smile. "You leave a key under your mat, what do you expect, Heidz? Getting past that door behind you is a fuckin' piece of cake. Even if my credit card can't do the trick, your neighbors are very accommodating."

"Don't call me 'Heidz,'" I bit out.

"Don't lie to me, woman, and I won't."

"Now who's lying?"

"Still you. Let's go. Time to start the fuckin' weekend right."

###

Available in March 2023

ACKNOWLEDGMENTS

A thousand-and-one thank you's to my readers. I would be nowhere without you. I can only hope you love Gamble and Victoria as much as I do!

Thank you to the members of my reader group. As always, your ready input on teasers, graphics and so much more is appreciated much more than I can say!

This book would be nothing without Barbara J. Bailey. Thank you for catching my blunders and oversights. You are the best!

Thank you to Enticing Journeys and the many bloggers who do what you do so well. I appreciate your efforts more than you know.

Love and gratitude to Golden Czermak and Brandon Schlaegel. To say I had a difficult time figuring out the final image for this book is an understatement. Yet, this cover captures my vision of Gamble so thoroughly, I simply *can't* thank you enough.

To the Romance Unraveled group — thanks for your honest responses to blurbs and cover options for this novel. I appreciate it so much.

'Thank you' and 'gratitude' are inadequate words for my mother. I love you so much, and I don't care that I'm breaking the "rules" when I send you my books at the same time I send them to my editor. I wouldn't have it any other way, and I'm extremely grateful to have the opportunity to do that with all of my books. I'm glad you loved Gamble and Victoria's story... with any luck, you'll love the next two stories just as much! Thank you for so many things... not the least of which are telling me what 'writer's block' meant when it came up in *The Facts of Life* on that fateful sick day I stayed home from school at a very young age. And also for being so adamant that I pursue advertising while I was in college. Crazy as it is both of those things were pivotal in my writing career.

To Cookie & Jellybean... everyday I'm grateful that you both support me in this endeavor better known as indie publishing! You two are the *very* best for putting up with my crazy ways and even crazier ideas... actually, no, you two are simply *the* best period. I love you both to the moon and back!

Thank you to the many other friends and family members who are supportive of my books. I appreciate it so much because I'm making a go of my life-long dream, and that doesn't come easy – so thank you from the bottom of my heart.

OTHER BOOKS BY KAREN RENEE

Please visit your favorite eBook retailer to discover other books by
Karen Renee:

The Riot MC Series

Unforeseen Riot

Inciting a Riot

Into the Riot

Calming the Riot

Foolish Riot

Respectable Riot

Starting the Riot

The Riot MC Box Set Series

The Riot MC Box Set #1 (Books 0.5, 1, 2, & 3)

KAREN RENEE

The Beta Series

Beta Test

The O-Town Series

Relentless Habit

Wild Forces

Abrupt Changes

O-Town Series Complete Box Set

Riot MC Biloxi Chapter Series

Harm's Way

Brute's Strength

Roman's War

Cynic's Stance
Gamble's Risk

Block's Road

ABOUT KAREN RENEE

Karen Renee is the author of the Riot MC, Beta, and O-Town series of books. She once crunched Nielsen ratings data but these days she brings her imagination to life by writing books. She has wanted to be a writer since she was very young, but it's taken the last twenty plus years for her to amass enough courage and overall life experience to bring that dream to life. Some of those life experiences came from the wonderful world of advertising, banking, and local television media research. She is a proud wife and mother, and a Jacksonville native. When she's not at the soccer field or cooking, you can find her at her local library, the grocery store, in her car jamming out to some tunes, or hibernating while she writes and/or reads books.

CONNECT WITH KAREN RENEE

I really appreciate you reading my book! Sign up for my newsletter and get a FREE novelette *Friendsgiving Riot* (Susan & Turk's story). Click here to sign up.

If you liked *Gamble's Risk*, I would greatly appreciate it if you left a review.
    You can follow me on any or all of the following places:

Facebook

Reader Group

Twitter

BookBub

TikTok

Instagram

GoodReads

GAMBLE'S RISK

Pintrest

Website

Made in the USA
Coppell, TX
16 November 2022

86499937R00150